"How can you make such a demand of me?

"Yes, I married you, but I did so only to save my father from prison. Did you think I would go willingly to bed with you, a person who tore me from my family, who used such evil means to coerce me into this devil's bargain?"

The silence that ensued was so long, Rebecca thought perhaps she'd frightened him away. Or made him so angry he couldn't speak. Her eyes strained for a shadow, her ears for the sound of him pacing or breathing.

"It seems," he said, his voice so low Rebecca had to tilt her head to hear him, "that Mr. Winters used extreme measures to get you to agree to this union. I was not aware, I can assure you. I ask only that..." Rebecca thought she heard him utter a low curse. "Yes, I can understand how this happened. I imagined a girl like you would jump at the chance to become a duchess."

"I was never given a choice, Your Grace, though I am certain I would have declined had Mr. Winters come to me with such a proposal. Do you not realize how awful it is to be married to a man one has never seen? Who hides in the darkness even on his wedding night? Whatever it is that is wrong with you, it is better to know than to allow my imagination to run amok."

More Historical Romance from Jane Goodger

Marry Christmas
A Christmas Scandal
A Christmas Waltz
When a Duke Says I Do
The Mad Lord's Daughter
When a Lord Needs a Lady
The Spinster Bride
Behind a Lady's Smile
How to Please a Lady
Lady Lost
The Bad Luck Bride
The Earl Most Likely
Diamond in the Rough

The Reluctant Duchess

Jane Goodger

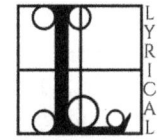

LYRICAL PRESS
Kensington Publishing Corp.
www.kensingtonbooks.com

LYRICAL PRESS BOOKS are published by

Kensington Publishing Corp.
119 West 40th Street
New York, NY 10018

All Kensington titles, imprints, and distributed lines are available at special quantity discounts for bulk purchases for sales promotion, premiums, fund-raising, educational, or institutional use.

Special book excerpts or customized printings can also be created to fit specific needs. For details, write or phone the office of the Kensington Sales Manager: Kensington Publishing Corp., 119 West 40th Street, New York, NY 10018. Attn. Sales Department. Phone: 1-800-221-2647.

Lyrical Press and Lyrical Press logo Reg. US Pat. & TM Off.

First Electronic Edition: July 2019
ISBN-13: 978-1-5161-0944-9 (ebook)
ISBN-10: 1-5161-0944-9 (ebook)

First Print Edition: July 2019
ISBN-13: 978-1-5161-0945-6
ISBN-10: 1-5161-0945-7

Printed in the United States of America

Prologue

Oliver Sterling, eleventh duke of Kendal, trailed his index finger along the fine curve of the young woman's jaw, eyes intent on his progress. She was the loveliest creature he had ever seen. And the most vibrant and colorful. Everything he was not.

"Who is she?" he asked, straightening from the painting and turning to look at his guardian.

Philip Winters, the man who had raised him, hesitated a brief moment before giving a dismissive shrug. "I have no idea, Your Grace." A tight smile. "But I can find out. Shall I have her delivered?"

Oliver swallowed down his disgust at the offer, even as his body reacted to the idea of lying with a woman as lovely as the one in the painting. He'd been spending long minutes over the last two days studying her, though he could not say why. His library was filled with beautiful objects, portraits of beautiful women. This one, though, he could not stop thinking about.

She wore a red velvet gown with white lace peeking from the sleeves and neckline. Demure and yet strangely erotic. Perhaps it was that bare toe peeking from the hem of her gown. As she gazed out at an impossibly blue-green sea, she smiled slightly, as if she was thinking of a secret. Or a lover. Oliver wondered if the artist had taken any license, for it was unlikely such perfection existed. Her hair, a deep auburn, cascaded down her back, alive with movement. But it was her profile, that sharp, perfect jawline, the delicate curve of her lips that drew his eyes, even in the dim light of his library.

Winters would often travel to London and return with such paintings so Oliver would get to see the parts of England he could never view on his own. This one was titled "St. Ives Girl" and had been painted along the southern shore, far from Oliver's home in Horncliffe. His poor eyesight was only one of the reasons he could not travel. The larger reason, of course, was his freakish appearance. He couldn't stomach the stares, the women who pulled their children away in fear, the men who quickly crossed themselves at the sight of him. His own servants looked away when he entered a room.

As isolated as he was, he was still aware of the rumors. Even in this modern year of 1879, the villagers looked at him with suspicion and fear. The Ghost Duke, they called him. They knew, of course, because servants were wont to talk, that his mother had taken one look at him and demanded he be removed from the house. When his father refused, she'd left. Five years later, they heard she was dead. A year after that, his father died at the breakfast table, a memory Oliver wished he could erase from his mind.

It was his father who suggested Winters care for him—no one else would and Winters had little option, given his ambiguous position in the household. He was an obscure relative with no family and had been living in a limbo between servant and family member since he'd come to Horncliffe Manor thirty-five years earlier, before Oliver had even been born. Oliver had come to rely on him for nearly everything.

"Have you ever been there, to St. Ives?" Oliver asked.

"I have not, Your Grace."

I should like to go. He nearly said it aloud, but stopped himself short, knowing Winters would purse his lips in sympathy.

Turning back to the painting, Oliver bent low so he could better see the details. By God, there was something about her that pulled at him. He was twenty-eight, and though he was not a virgin thanks to Winters' infrequent gifts of willing women, he couldn't help but wonder what it would be like to have a woman such as the one in the painting to give him comfort at night. To ease the madness of his loneliness.

Straightening once more, he glanced back at Winters, who stood as he so often did, silent, still. "Find her."

Winters' lips twitched slightly upward. "Yes, Your Grace. It may take some persuading if she's not the accommodating sort, but I am certain I will succeed."

"I don't believe you understand me, Winters. I want her as my bride. Marry her by proxy. Do whatever you must. But bring her here before the first snow falls."

Chapter 1

Rebecca couldn't remember the last time her father had summoned her to his study. Firstly, the man was rarely in his study, leaving the running of the household to her and her mother. Secondly, he was not often in St. Ives, preferring to spend his time in London, which, he said, held far more entertainments.

Everyone in the Caine household knew that "entertainments" was simply another word for gambling.

Her father had returned home just last night to much fanfare. Despite the fact his habits had the family teetering on the brink of ruin much of the time, each of her three sisters adored their father. Even Rebecca's weary mother seemed happier when her husband was home. After all, Thomas Caine was not a man who chased skirts, he was simply a man who loved to wager. Like her sisters, Rebecca adored her father, choosing to ignore the tightening in her stomach whenever he'd announce it was time to return to the city. Yet despite his seeming happiness at seeing his four daughters, Rebecca thought she detected something slightly off in his manner when he'd returned this time. He'd acted too happy, as if he were hiding something, and that never boded well for the Caines and their unstable bank account.

Still, the Caines had been in this situation before and always managed to come out of it. In the past year, Rebecca had begun selling bits of her crocheted items in a local shop and even (and rather scandalously, according to her friend Eliza), posed for artists who often came to St. Ives to paint. The money she earned was enough to pay for the household daily expenses, at least for a time. Rebecca wasn't unduly worried about her father's summons until she stepped into his study and realized he'd

Jane Goodger

been joined by a stranger. Rebecca dipped a quick curtsy, noting the man's impeccable dress, and shot a questioning look at her father. The stranger's dark gray suit was tailored to perfection, and though he was not a tall man, he seemed to exude power, the sort that was not always welcome in a household that often lived on the brink of ruin.

"Mr. Winters, this is my daughter, Rebecca," her father said, his voice sounding oddly strained.

Looking quickly from the stranger to her father, Rebecca felt her stomach drop even further when her father would not meet her eyes. This study had always been a haven, a place where she would spend hours when she was a girl, hovering about her father, playing with the dolls he would bring from London. In the afternoons, the sun would shine through the tall windows and dust would sparkle in the air, making it easy to imagine fairies lived hidden in the room. Now, though, on this gray, misty day, the room seemed muted, almost ominous, and Rebecca suppressed a shiver.

"A pleasure to meet you, Miss Caine," Mr. Winter said with fluid grace. The man stared at her, his eyes sweeping her form in a manner that was just shy of insulting. His eyes, a dark brown, held little emotion, however, and little interest despite that assessing look. He was pale, his brown hair parted on the side and ruthlessly combed over and across his forehead. His was the sort of face that looked slightly pudgy even though he was quite thin, a deceivingly calm and friendly countenance that held menace behind his bland smile. Why Rebecca thought so, she could not have said.

"Papa?" He sat behind his desk, one that Rebecca noted was littered with papers, seemingly stacked haphazardly. Rebecca always kept the desk meticulously organized, and she swallowed down a small bit of irritation that her father had created such chaos in the short few hours of his being home.

"Oh, dear, I'm not certain I know how to say this." He took a deep and shaking breath. "I owe Mr. Winters a great deal of money, Rebecca. More than I could ever repay in this lifetime. That is, not without selling everything we own, the house and lands included. Your mother and sisters…" His voice trailed off and Rebecca could feel the other man's eyes on her, though she refused to look in his direction.

"I have come to your father with a proposal," Mr. Winters said smoothly. Rebecca tensed. "No." It was an instinctive response.

Mr. Winters let out a low chuckle. "No? Is the answer no, Mr. Caine?" His tone was so mocking, Rebecca felt her anger grow.

"Rebecca, as the eldest child, you have a certain responsibility to your sisters—"

"What of your responsibility to all of us?" she cried, not caring that he flinched.

"Now, now," Mr. Winters said, stepping forward. "Let us not fall into hysterics. My proposal is this. Marry the Duke of Kendal and the debt will be forgiven."

If Mr. Winters had proposed that she marry the man on the moon, she would have not been as surprised, and she bit back a bit of laughter. "The *Duke* of..."

"...Kendal," Winters supplied. "Of Horncliffe. It's a bit north of here."

"It's very nearly in Scotland," Rebecca returned, and she could tell he was surprised that she knew even that much. "I've not heard of this duke." Her friends and she often pored over the London gossip column *The Tattler* and she could not recall ever seeing a mention of the Duke of Kendal. And how ridiculous for a squire's daughter to marry a duke. Rebecca felt as if she were experiencing a strange yet horrifyingly realistic dream.

"The Kendal title is one of the oldest and most respected in all of England," Winters said, his tone holding just a hint of derision. For the first time, Rebecca recognized distaste on the man's face; he did not approve of this transaction any more than she did.

"How did His Grace choose me? I'm no one. My father is but a squire and I'm quite certain I have not had the occasion to meet him or even be in the same room." She pressed her fingers against her temples in an effort to gain control of her emotions. "I do not understand any of this."

"His Grace saw a painting of you," Winters said.

Rebecca's cheeks immediately heated, even though she knew all of the portraits done of her were tasteful; her father had no idea she'd sat for more than one visiting artist.

"Painting? What's this?"

"To earn pin money, Papa. Mama approved."

"His Grace was quite taken with you," Winters said. His words were innocuous enough, but something in his tone told Rebecca he found the idea of her posing for an artist objectionable.

"My answer is still no," she said, but her voice trembled. "How can I possibly accept a marriage proposal from a man I have never met, who has never met me. And perhaps it has escaped your notice, but I am far from the rank that any duke would consider even as a paid companion."

"It has not escaped me in the least," Winters said, his tone and expression frigid.

"Rebecca," her father said sadly. "You must. And you will be a duchess. Imagine what that will do for our family, for your sisters. If you do not..."

"If I do not, everything will be gone," she said, finishing her father's sentence when it became obvious he could not. "We shall be impoverished. You will end up in debtors' prison."

The tears welling up in her father's eyes did what his words could not. How could a girl who adored her father ignore the real pain she saw? But how could she agree to marry a man she had never met, knew nothing about? He could be old or cruel or mad or any number of horrid things. What defect must he have if this was the only way he could obtain a bride? He was a duke, after all. Even an old and decrepit duke could manage to marry aristocracy. Any girl in the kingdom would jump at the chance to be a duchess. Except her.

She turned to Mr. Winters. "Is he mad?"

"No."

"Old?"

"He is twenty and eight."

"Cruel?"

"He is all that is kind," Winters said, his tone mocking.

Rebecca furrowed her brow, confused by his answers until it occurred to her that the duke might be an invalid or deformed in some way. It didn't help that she'd just finished reading about poor Quasimodo in *The Hunchback of Notre Dame*. "Is he deformed?"

"No," Winters said with only the slightest hesitation, but his eyes remained direct and Rebecca could detect no prevarication.

"I don't understand why the duke is not here himself. Does he not think meeting his bride is important?"

Winters pressed his thin lips together, a hint of annoyance in his dark eyes. "It matters not why he cannot attend the ceremony, only that he wishes for it to occur. It is my duty to make certain his wishes are fulfilled."

"He will not attend his own wedding ceremony?" Rebecca asked, her trepidation only growing.

"You will marry by proxy." He gave a mocking bow. "I am His Grace's proxy."

Suppressing a shiver, she looked to her father and said, "If I do this thing, you must promise never to gamble again, Papa. Ever. Promise me."

"I promise," he said with no hesitation.

Rebecca shook her head. "I don't believe you. What next, Papa? Shall Carol be married off to someone else to settle your debts? You must *promise me*. Think what you have wrought. Think what you have done to me."

Her father buried his head in his hands and wept, saying over and over, "I promise," and Rebecca swallowed down the tears that threatened. It was Mr. Winters who stopped her tears. His cold, emotionless gaze held only one thing: satisfaction.

"It's utterly the most romantic thing I have ever heard!"

Rebecca looked at her friend Eliza with complete disbelief. "Romantic? I think it's bloody odd," she said, swearing only because she knew it annoyed her friend. She and Eliza were the only two of their small group of friends to remain unmarried. Her "wedding" was the next day and her mind was still whirling with what had happened just that morning. The two women were lying crosswise on Eliza's massive four-poster bed, nearly drowning in the thick comforter that covered it. Eliza blew a dark brown curl from her head and rested her chin on one hand, her blue eyes dancing with excitement. Rebecca supposed from Eliza's perspective, it was all exciting. Imagine a duke seeing her portrait and becoming so entranced, he would demand her hand in marriage. It was the stuff of fairy tales, not real life. And though Rebecca adored fairy tales in theory, being part of one was not nearly as enjoyable as reading one.

"Hmm. A bit odd, yes. And I did tell you posing for those artists was unseemly. But a duke, Rebecca. Honestly, I'm so jealous I could scream. To think all my untitled friends have married titles, and my one high born friend married a commoner. What does that leave for me? A farmer? A fisherman?"

Rebecca giggled. "A prince of course. He rules a tiny county on the continent and will be shipwrecked in St. Ives and you, of course, will sound the alarm and save him and his men and he will fall madly in love with you. And then you shall be a princess."

"Do you truly think that could happen?" Eliza asked dreamily.

Rebecca gave her friend a level look. "No. And neither do you." When Eliza opened her mouth to protest, Rebecca firmly repeated, "Neither do you."

Of the four of them, only Eliza had truly wanted to marry a title; the rest were content with an ordinary man. Rebecca had always thought Eliza perfectly adorable, with her bright blue eyes, curling brown hair, and smattering of freckles across her nose that no amount of cream could fade. It was a mystery to her why she had not yet attracted a husband, especially given her father was the son of a viscount. Yet none of her friends had ever dreamed of marrying quite so high above their station, particularly Rebecca. Of all her friends, her family was one of the lowest on the social ladder, which did make this match a bit miraculous.

"What if something is terribly wrong with him? Why have we heard nothing of him? And why does he need to resort to marrying a commoner whom he spied in a painting? That's not in the least romantic."

"At least we know he's not blind," Eliza said, then covered her head when Rebecca threatened to beat her with a pillow. "Did his man of business say anything about him?"

"He only answered direct questions." Rebecca picked at a bit of loose thread on the comforter until Eliza slapped her hand away. "Sorry." She laid her forehead on her arms and stared at the soft muslin, wishing she could stay in this soft, muted world. "It's only that it's a bit frightening, isn't it," she said, her voice slightly muffled.

She felt Eliza gently shake her shoulder. "Are you truly frightened? I've never known you to be afraid of anything."

Rebecca lifted her head and smiled wistfully. "It's so far away," she said, and her throat closed up as tears threatened. "I always pictured myself marrying someone local, living here, and visiting my mum every day. I thought my children would grow up in St. Ives and play along the shore. It snows in Horncliffe. Even the name of the place." She pulled a face. "Who would name a place horn cliff? Who?"

Eliza pressed her lips together in an attempt not to smile. "I believe it must be someone's name."

Turning around so that she was looking up at the bed's canopy, Rebecca let out a frustrated groan. "Horn cliff. Sounds like the devil himself lives there."

That was when Eliza let out a gasp.

"What's wrong?"

"Wait here." She ran to her writing desk and pulled open a drawer. "You know how I collect newspaper clippings that inspire my stories."

"Of course."

"I remember saving something about Horncliffe. It was years ago, so I might be wrong," she said, rifling through her papers. "Aha!" She stood, her eyes scanning over the article quickly. "Oh, Rebecca."

Rebecca sat up immediately, for Eliza sounded as if she had just discovered something terrible.

"The Ghost Duke. No one has seen him for years, but the locals blame him for all sorts of things, from sheep dying mysteriously to missing women and children. Oh, this is terrible."

Rebecca laughed. "A duke who murders sheep?"

Eliza joined in her laughter. "I suppose it is silly. Still, if the locals are that superstitious about the duke, it is unfortunate." She looked up from the clipping before going on. "And it says no one has seen him in years and 'those who gaze upon his terrible visage instantly turn to stone.' Why, I wonder? Did not his man say he was not deformed? Perhaps he is..."

"You are not easing my nerves, Eliza," Rebecca said darkly.

"Sorry," Eliza said, giving her friend a quick hug. "Still, it is odd, is it not? Ghost Duke." She grinned. "Perhaps he is a ghost and that man is his living minion who must do as he says."

"Stop," Rebecca said, breaking into giggles before sobering and nearly giving in to the tears that had threatened since she'd realized she had no choice but to marry a stranger.

"Are you very angry with your father?"

Rebecca sighed. "It is difficult to remain angry with him, for he is genuinely sorry. Mum pretends to be vexed, but I do believe she is secretly thrilled that I am to be a duchess. I'm saving all my anger for the duke."

"I should think your parents would demand to meet him before agreeing to this," her friend said loyally.

"What good would that do? I will not allow my father to go to debtors' prison or for the family to descend into poverty, no matter what he is like."

"A sacrificial lamb," Eliza said, but her tone was one of dreamy romance.

"Will you stop it?" Rebecca said, laughing. "There is positively nothing romantic about any of this."

Eliza laughed with her; then her expression abruptly changed to a frown. "I understand how the duke would fall in love with your picture, but how is it that your father ended up indebted to him so desperately that he was forced to agree to the marriage?"

Raising one eyebrow, Rebecca gave her friend a look of disbelief. "My father was made a target. It would not take much investigation to learn of his penchant for gambling."

"Do you mean to say this man manipulated your father into losing?"

"I can think of no other explanation."

"That's not a very good way to start a marriage," Eliza said, her fantasy of romance crumbling around her.

"No, it is not. But what choice do I have?"

Chapter 2

Rebecca was exhausted beyond bearing. For three days, she had been traveling, ever north, by train and coach, with Mr. Winters her constant, silent companion. She was a duchess, married to a man she had never met, a thought that frayed her nerves raw. It was still difficult for her to believe all that had happened in little more than a week.

Leaving St. Ives, her mother, her younger sisters, even her father, had been one of the most difficult things she had ever done. All her sisters had cried, Carol the most, and her mother couldn't stop her own eyes from filling. Horncliffe was so very far from St. Ives, even with the new train rails. She might never see St. Ives again, never breathe in the soft sea air, never dip her toe into the impossibly blue water. She'd looked out the window for long minutes as the coach pulled away from their rambling house, until it was hidden by the trees, until St. Ives was no longer in sight. God, it hurt, more than anything in her life before had. Her throat ached so much, she could not have spoken a word even if Mr. Winters had asked her a question. It was all she could do not to sob or open the door and escape. But she didn't. She stared out the window, her heart breaking, her eyes dry.

After days of travel, they sat in a jostling coach that probably needed new springs. It was cold, far colder than Rebecca had ever been. Her breath came out in small plumes, her hands and feet felt as if they were frozen, and her cheeks were numb. Dark, gray clouds hung low in the sky, and more than one person had looked up and commented that the clouds portended snow, even though it was only October. For miles now, Rebecca had done nothing but stare out the window at a landscape that was completely foreign to her. Great forests surrounded them as the coach climbed up one hill and down another, swaying back and forth on the uneven road. It had been hours since she had seen a village or any sign that another human was alive. Truly, she hadn't known such a place existed in England.

And all the while, all these miles, Mr. Winters looked at her. Even now, she could feel his dark eyes on her, emotionless, expressionless, as if she were nothing more than part of the very seat upon which her sore behind rested. It was quite maddening and, if she were perfectly honest, made her blood run cold. He'd done nothing untoward on this trip, had been exceedingly polite, in an exaggerated way, as if she wasn't worthy of his good behavior. Rebecca sensed something beneath the surface, something, if not evil, then malevolent. Then again, it could simply be her frayed nerves and this untenable situation that were leaving her nerves raw. Finally, she could stand it no more.

"Why do you stare?" she asked, glaring at him. His eyes narrowed slightly, as if she amused him.

"Was I?"

"You were."

"I suppose I was."

"Why?" She didn't want him to know how frightened she was and was glad that her voice sounded strong.

"I am trying to understand His Grace's fascination with you. You are a commoner, something we knew when we saw that painting. No lady would pose for such a portrait. You are far beneath His Grace and I believe I hold you in the utmost contempt." He said this nonchalantly and gave a small shrug, a bland smile. "To be frank, Miss Caine, your very existence repulses me. Is that the sort of information you were looking for?"

Rebecca swallowed and suppressed a shiver. "You may address me as Your Grace, Mr. Winters," she managed to say, though her heart beat quickly. Now that she had said it aloud, it sounded silly to her. She was no more a duchess now than she had been before the proxy wedding.

He stared at her for a long moment before bursting into laughter. "I do apologize, Your Grace." He chuckled a bit more, wiping his eyes as if her words had brought him to mirthful tears.

What a horrible man, Rebecca thought, feeling her situation settle around her even more. This man was obviously important to the duke and she could honestly say he was the most disagreeable person she had ever met. Her throat closed but she swallowed down the pain, refusing to allow him to see the tears that had been threatening since the moment she'd hugged her mother good-bye and climbed aboard the train that had brought her away from her beloved St. Ives.

And then a wonderful thought occurred to her. She was a duchess, whether she felt like one or not. He was…well, she wasn't certain what he was, but he could be made to leave. Perhaps she could convince the duke that Mr. Winters had to go. Her mood brightened considerably.

"You are an employee of His Grace?" she asked, and for the first time saw his composure slip the tiniest bit.

"I am not." His tone was cold and that malevolence Rebecca detected was nearly tangible. Sharp disappointment filled her. It would be far easier to get rid of the man if he was an employee rather than some trusted friend or worse, a relative. Rebecca gave a quick prayer that Mr. Winters was not the duke's friend, for what sort of man would consider him such? People tended to forgive relatives' behavior that would not be tolerated from an employee or even a friend. From the way he looked at her now, Rebecca feared she had made a miscalculation. Wouldn't it be better to befriend the man rather than to create an enemy no matter how disagreeable he was? She had little experience dealing with animosity as it had rarely been directed at her.

"I apologize, Mr. Winters." She forced a smile. "You never did explain your position or your relationship to my husband." His eyes flickered when she called His Grace "my husband," as if her referring to him thus caused him discomfort. The Caines, while not part of the aristocracy, were a respected family; her father was a squire and landowner and it was not entirely uncommon for her ilk to marry a title. Not a duke, perhaps, but in St. Ives, common girls seemed to be marrying titled gentlemen left and right.

"My mother was His Grace's father's great aunt's daughter."

Rebecca tried to determine what that made Mr. Winters, but she quickly gave up. "A distant relative, then."

Mr. Winters remained silent.

Clearing her throat, Rebecca said, "And you are His Grace's…"

"Keeper."

A chill ran down Rebecca's spine at that word. What did that mean? Another forced smile and she turned back to the window, trying to stop the urge to flee the carriage. But she couldn't help thinking: What sort of man required a keeper?

Oliver eyed the tiny Chippendale chair he held in his hands critically, turning it slowly beneath his magnifier, trying to find a flaw. He frowned at the cushion, its corners unrefined; sewing was not his forte. The delicate sweep of the arms, the well-proportioned ball and claw feet, everything was as it should be. But the cushion… It would have to do. He placed the chair in the second floor sitting room with its twin, rubbing his tired eyes. This sort of work, as passionate as he was about it, was exhausting and often led to a headache. The chairs faced one another, a table set for two between them, and he smiled at the result.

The room looked like any room one might find in England, only waiting for its owners to come inside and have a bit of tea. At least it looked like pictures he'd seen in illustrated periodicals. Every detail, from the finely honed parquet floor to the intricately carved mantel above the hearth, was perfection. It was, though Oliver would never characterize it as such, a work of art. And it was only one room in a dozen he had constructed in his miniature house, most of which were still awaiting decoration.

One of his creations, his highly ambitious Buckingham Palace, was displayed at the Royal Academy. He'd never been to see it, but Mr. Winters had a photograph taken showing it tucked in one corner. He had a letter from Queen Victoria herself thanking him. It was his least favorite project.

Oliver instead preferred smaller projects, homey buildings where he imagined families lived, bustling about noisily, gathering together at the end of a day for a hearty meal. He'd read about such families; the concept seemed a bit strange to him, having no siblings, no memory of his mother, and only vague recollections of his father. He remembered reading *Oliver Twist* as a boy; the name of the book attracted him initially, but it was the fictional Oliver's longing for his mother, for a home, that struck a chord with him. Even as a boy, however, he knew he would not have a happy ending as the orphan in the book had. No one would rescue him. No one could change how he'd been born.

A noise outside drew his attention and he stilled. His bride was expected home that day.

Since the day Mr. Winters had left two months ago on his mission to bring the girl in the painting home to him, his mood had gone from excitement to utter horror at what he had done. What sort of man would bring a girl from her home to this Godforsaken place to be the bride of an aberration? She would loathe him and when she got a look at him...

It didn't bear thinking about; it truly didn't. But it was there, his realization that he couldn't hide from his wife forever, that at some point, she would see him. He only prayed that he could delay such a meeting until at least she didn't loathe him. That thought was terrible enough to cause his stomach to clench. In his wildest dreams, he imagined making his wife love him, so that by the time she saw him, she would overlook his appearance. He wanted a wife, children, something, anything, to assuage the heavy loneliness that sometimes made him feel as if he might go mad.

Those women Winters had brought to him, who smelled of cheap perfume, whose breaths were sour and whose voices were tinged with fear, did nothing to stop the ache. Of course, when he was inside them, when he found his release, none of that mattered—at least for a few moments. As soon as he was done, they scurried out of bed, grabbed their clothes, and hastily dressed. He never saw the same woman twice, and they never saw him, for he kept the room in pitch blackness except for one, ill-conceived slip. Even now, years later, his gut clenched at the thought of the girl's reaction when she saw him.

Footsteps sounded on the tower stairs and he rose from his seat and stepped in front of his work table.

A knock, then through the door, "Your Grace, Mr. Winters has arrived with Her Grace." It was Mr. Starke, his butler, staring at the floor. Satan, his black cat, followed the butler in and hopped onto his customary place atop a cushioned chair in the corner. Normally, the presence of the feline calmed him but not this day.

"Yes, Mr. Starke. Thank you." Once his butler turned to leave, he clenched his fists, trying to stop the mad beating of his heart. "I'll be down momentarily." After the butler's footsteps faded away, Oliver let out a curse. Weeks he'd had to prepare for this day, and he still didn't know what he should do. She would be frightened or curious. Should he speak to her? Should he explain why he would not allow her to see him? Certainly, she would expect after such a long journey to meet her husband. Oliver swallowed hard, his breath coming in gasps, realizing he was not ready to meet his bride. Not yet. And so, he did nothing.

Chapter 3

"I am not to meet His Grace?" Rebecca stood in the center of Horncliffe's grand foyer looking around the dimly lit area in dismay.

Without answering her, Mr. Winters disappeared the moment they arrived, walking down a long, dark hall without a backward glance, leaving her alone and unsure what to do. Finally, an older man arrived and introduced himself as Mr. Starke, the butler. He seemed surprised to find her still standing at the entrance.

"Your Grace, welcome to Horncliffe," he said, with a small bow. He was a wiry fellow, with a ring of hair around his otherwise bald pate, and spectacles perched on his nose. "Where is Mr. Winters?"

"He disappeared down that hallway without a word," she said as a drop from the heavy mist outside fell from her hat and found its way down her back, causing her to shiver at the icy feel. It was cold, not fear, that made her shiver, she told herself silently

Horncliffe was the stuff one created in one's mind whilst reading a story of hauntings or murder. Perhaps it was because it was so very bleak and cold that day, but when Rebecca had looked up to see her new home, terror had gripped her heart. The house loomed above her like some stone giant, imposing and uninviting. No lights shone from the windows, even though it was nearly dark outside, and the windows themselves were covered with heavy curtains. It was all angles and odd rooflines, and to make matters worse, the front door was guarded by two hideous gargoyles, whose snarling mouths looked ready to devour her. Who would adorn their house with such creatures?

Mr. Starke pressed his lips together upon the news that Mr. Winters had left her there. "I do apologize, Your Grace. I can have one of the maids bring you to your rooms." He looked down at her trunk, which contained all her worldly possessions. "You have no maid, madam?"

Rebecca nearly let out a giggle. The four Caine girls had shared a single maid. Rebecca, more often than not, had acted as lady's maid to her younger sisters, helping them to dress and fixing their hair. A wave of melancholy struck her as she thought of her sisters, who were all fiercely jealous of her adventure. She'd let them think she was happy about it, looking forward to being a duchess, when in fact, she'd spent her remaining days at home trying not to weep. What good would it have done anyone for them to know how very frightened she was. Nothing she had seen thus far had assuaged her fear; if anything, that small ball of terror that she'd tried to press down seemed to be getting bigger each minute.

"I have three younger sisters, Mr. Starke. They had far more need of a maid than I. We passed a sizable village on the way here; I'm sure I can find someone there who can act as a lady's maid if there is no one on the staff who is properly trained."

That suggestion seemed, oddly, to startle him. "Oh, no, Your Grace. No one from the village would—" He stopped abruptly. "I am certain someone on the staff can fill the role until we find someone. If you will excuse me, madam, I will find a maid to show you to your room and assist with your unpacking." He flicked a finger toward a footman, who stepped forward and hefted her trunk onto his shoulder.

"If you would follow me, Your Grace, I can show you to a sitting room with a nice, warm fire while you wait for your maid."

"A warm fire sounds wonderful, Mr. Starke." She followed the older man, still wearing her gloves, coat, and a soft, woolen muffler around her throat. It seemed somehow colder in this house than it had in the carriage. Certainly, it was darker.

All of the wall sconces were unlit, and with dusk coming on, it seemed strange to Rebecca that no one was lighting them. "You are connected to a gasworks?" she asked. Even St. Ives, as remote as it was, had had gas in most homes for decades.

"Yes, madam. His Grace prefers darkness."

His Grace prefers darkness? What sort of person preferred the dark to light? "Is His Grace in residence? Mr. Winters did not say." A point that irritated. He must know she was anxious to meet her husband.

"His Grace is always in residence," Mr. Starke said. "He is likely in the tower. It is where he spends most days."

This news did nothing to ease the trepidation that was growing with each step she took down the long hall. The windows were all covered by thick velvet curtains that stretched from the ceiling to the floor. Only a sliver of light entered the hall and Rebecca realized that even with the sun shining outside, it would still be rather dim here. The floors were marble, and her steps seemed overloud in the utter silence. She came from a home with three younger sisters, two cats, and a dog; the Caine house had rarely been quiet. There were times Rebecca thought she'd scream if she couldn't find some quiet, but now she longed to hear one of her sisters laugh. Her throat tightened as it had done more times than she could count since leaving home, and she fervently wished that whoever was helping her with her clothes would be quick about it so she could cry in peace and without an audience.

It seemed that they walked for several minutes before Mr. Starke opened a set of double doors, revealing a pretty little room with a fire blazing in the hearth. The walls were covered with a blue floral paper and the trim and mantle were a clean white—and miraculously, two sconces on either side of the mantle were lit, giving the room a homey glow. Rebecca smiled, nearly weak with relief that something in this house seemed normal.

"I will return momentarily, Your Grace," Mr. Starke said, giving her a small bow.

How strange to be called "your grace," to have someone bow and show her deference that was wholly undeserved. Then again, she had made a great sacrifice to become a duchess, so perhaps it was deserved.

Her wait was brief, for she hadn't finished looking about the room thoroughly before Mr. Starke returned with a young maid in tow. "Your Grace, this is Darlene." The maid, who appeared to be younger than Rebecca, dipped a curtsy, but kept her eyes on the wooden floor beneath her feet. She held a small, lit lamp in one hand, obviously prepared for navigating the dark halls.

"You may look at Her Grace," Mr. Starke said softly, and Darlene darted a swift look to the butler as if determining whether he meant what he said. She looked up, quickly, before her eyes were once again glued to the floor in front of her. Mr. Starke let out a small sigh. "You may show Her Grace to her rooms," he said, before turning to Rebecca. "I am needed downstairs, Your Grace, but if you need anything, please do not hesitate to ring for me. I am bell two. The housekeeper, Mrs. Cutter, is bell one. Unfortunately, Mrs. Cutter could not be here today. Her youngest daughter is giving birth."

"Oh, how wonderful. I shall forgive her," Rebecca said with a smile but she noticed Darlene frowned as if she didn't realize her new mistress was jesting. Was she not supposed to have said such a thing? Or was the duke a tyrant, who inspired fear among his staff? The Caines had always had servants in their house, but perhaps they were not as formal as the aristocracy.

Once Mr. Starke left, Darlene darted another look at her. "If you will follow me, Your Grace," she said, then hurried out of the room, forcing Rebecca to lift her skirts and run after her. They climbed a set of stairs that curved upward to a landing decorated by a large stained glass window that was dark; night had fallen. She wondered, cynically, why that window wasn't covered as so many others were. Had they run out of dark, heavy velvet?

At the top of the stairs, Darlene turned left, then descended a small set of stairs before turning right and finally stopping to open a door. "Your rooms, Your Grace," she said, stepping back so that Rebecca might precede her inside. The lamp's small light did little to illuminate the room and instead allowed Rebecca only to see Darlene's pale, downturned face.

Her rooms, like the rest of the house, were dark and the grate held no fire. "If you could have one of the footmen start a fire, I would be grateful," Rebecca said as she walked into the room, lit only by the lamp Darlene held. Without better light, it was difficult to determine how large the room was or whether there were other rooms connected to the bedroom. The room held a chill that seemed far beyond what it should. "We can light the lamps ourselves."

"Oh, no, Your Grace. You mustn't."

Rebecca stopped and turned; the fear in Darlene's eyes was very real. "Why mustn't I," she asked softly, cautiously.

"He'll want it dark." She walked to one side of the room and Rebecca followed, not wanting to be left alone without light. "Pull the third bell afterward and a footman will make a fire for you."

Afterward.

Heat filled her cheeks. "I see." She didn't see, though, not at all. The duke would come to her in the dark and… Would he demand his husbandly rights before even meeting her, before they had even had a conversation? What sort of man would do such a thing? It was unbearable to contemplate, and she was tempted to flee, then and there, the urge nearly overwhelming her. "Is he that awful?"

Darlene stared at her, her brown eyes wide. "I don't know but I've heard he's fearful to look at. That we'll turn to stone if we do. It happened once before."

Rebecca thought she heard a sound, a man's soft laugh, and she whirled around to see nothing but a wall. "Did you hear that?"

Darlene's eyes darted around nervously. "What, mum? I didn't hear a thing."

Rebecca shook her head. "It must be my nerves." She gave Darlene an apologetic smile. "How long have you been in the duke's employ?"

"Two years, mum."

Two *years*? "And in all that time, you've never seen him?"

"I don't want to turn to stone," she said in a small voice. "No one has seen him but Mr. Winters. No one here—no one here living, that is—has ever looked at him. Never."

"That's impossible." The maid's fear was real, and even though Rebecca had little patience for such superstition, she could not deny Darlene believed what she said. "Or should I say, how is that possible? How does he take his meals? Does he never go outside? Never leave his rooms?"

"He spends his days in the tower. We don't know what he does up there. Hours he spends. No one wants to look at him…"

"…because you'll turn to stone. Was it Mr. Winters who perpetuated this story?" Darlene gave her a blank look. "How did you hear about the story?"

"John, the footman, Yer Grace. But everyone knows about Molly and what happened to her. She's in the garden still. And then there's the girls…" Darlene snapped her mouth shut and darted her eyes around the room as if someone could have overheard her.

Rebecca couldn't help smiling, which made Darlene frown fiercely. "Ask anyone here or in the village. They know, too. And about the missing girls."

"Missing girls?"

"Them that comes here are never seen again. Disappear off the face of the earth, they do."

These rumors were evil. No wonder the poor man didn't like to leave his house if the servants and villagers spread such tales. "You must cease spreading such gossip immediately, Darlene," she said kindly. "His Grace is simply a man who enjoys his privacy."

"He's a monster."

Despite the real fear the made her blood run cold, Rebecca forced a smile. "He is merely a man who…"

"Never goes outside. Will not allow light? Will not allow his servants to look at him? It's said he drinks the blood of virgins." The girl was very nearly hysterical.

"Please do stop, Darlene. You are speaking of my husband."

"God be with you, Your Grace."

With that, Darlene went to the bed and opened the trunk. In only a few minutes, she had put all Rebecca's belongings in the massive wardrobe that took up nearly an entire wall. Her clothes looked rather pitiful in the space.

Once Darlene had helped her undress and Rebecca had donned her nightdress, a sick feeling swirled in her stomach about what was to come that night.

"Will you need anything else, Your Grace?"

Rebecca sighed. "You may go, Darlene." She watched with some bemusement as the girl ran from the room, leaving her in darkness. Utter darkness. Feeling her way, she went to the window and opened the drapery, but the overcast sky did little to brighten the room. If only it were a moonlit night, then at least she would be able to walk about the room without tumbling over something.

"Close it."

Rebecca gasped and whirled around, her eyes almost aching from straining to see something, anything, in dark. "Your Grace." She took a bracing breath. "You frightened me. I did not hear you knock."

"I did not knock," he said, his voice low. Rebecca would have deemed it a pleasant voice under different circumstances.

A terrible thought occurred to her just then. Was the man standing in her room the duke? Was it possible it was Mr. Winters? Her skin crawled at that thought.

"I did not mean to frighten you. I apologize." No. Not Mr. Winters. Her frantic mind had her hearing things. This was the voice of a younger man, smooth and melodic.

"If you did not wish to frighten me, then I daresay you should have knocked."

She wondered if he smiled or frowned at her words. Oh, it was maddening not to see him. Was he so terrible, such a monster, that she would run from the room screaming if she saw him? She could not imagine it being so. Once, a traveling troupe had come to St. Ives, one that displayed freaks of nature. She hadn't been allowed inside the tent, but pictures of impossible creatures had been painted on the outer canvas. Was he like one of those poor souls?

"I do not need permission to enter any room of my house. Including yours."

"Then do not apologize for frightening me, for that was clearly your intent."

"No," he said harshly. She could hear him moving, pacing perhaps? How could he see where he was going? He knocked into something and cursed, and she smiled. He could see no better than she in the dark. "I did not want to give you the option of denying my entrance," he said finally, softly. "I do know that this must be rather terrifying to you."

"It is," she said, and bit the side of her mouth when she felt her throat close. She would not grow hysterical. She would not weep. No matter what he was, he was only a man. And her husband.

Oh, God. He didn't feel like her husband. He was nothing but a voice in the dark. Nothing could be less comforting than that.

"I will endeavor to make this as pleasant as possible for you."

Rebecca furrowed her brow, not understanding what he meant. "This?"

She could hear him breathe in, breathe out, as if she were trying his patience. "The consummation of our marriage," he ground out.

"Oh." Rebecca worried her hands together. *Oh, God.* Of course, she knew that marriage entailed certain activities with one's husband, but she had been hoping it would not occur the very night of her arrival. Perhaps after a conversation or two with her husband. Or after she'd actually seen the man. Surely he could not expect to demand his husbandly rights this night? What sort of man was he?

"I don't..." The pacing started again. "I don't wish to frighten you or harm you or do any ill at all to you. I wish you to be my wife."

"I am your wife," Rebecca said, trying to sound reasonable even as she backed away from the sound of his voice. She could run, escape, if only she could find the door.

"Not until the marriage is consummated. Surely you understand that. Did not your mother explain?"

"I understand a wife has certain...duties," Rebecca said, feeling her anger grow.

"Good. Allow me to introduce myself. I am the Duke of Kendal. Your husband."

The word "husband" seemed to linger in the air. "And I am Rebecca Caine. A nobody. A commoner."

"It matters not," he said, slight irritation in his voice.

"Why me?"

"I thought you pretty."

Rebecca couldn't stop herself. She snorted.

"You are amused?" he asked, his words fraught with tension, as if she had greatly insulted him.

"I suppose I am pretty. Many women are. But you are a duke and I am the daughter of a squire. Surely someone of a higher rank than I would marry you. You're a duke," she repeated.

"I am aware precisely what I am. Please get on the bed."

He'd said *please* but it was clearly an order and his voice was so cold, Rebecca had to suppress a shiver. This was wrong. How dare he treat her like some brood mare, without even the decency of a conversation. How could he expect her to lie in a bed with him, to allow him to touch her in places no man had, as if she were nothing, an object he'd bought and now wanted to play with. More than anything, his arrogance made her seethe with anger. Not one to hold back her anger or hide her feelings—that was the stuff of a true lady—Rebecca decided to let him know precisely what she thought.

"How can you make such a demand of me? Is it not enough that you have threatened my family? How could you think I would give myself to such a man? Yes, I married you, but I did so only to save my father from prison. Did you think I would go willingly to bed with you, a person who tore me from my family, who used such evil means to coerce me into this devil's bargain?"

The silence that ensued was so long, Rebecca thought perhaps she'd frightened him away. Or made him so angry he couldn't speak. Her eyes strained for a shadow, her ears for the sound of him pacing or breathing.

"It seems," he said, his voice so low Rebecca had to tilt her head to hear him, "that Mr. Winters used extreme measures to get you to agree to this union. I was not aware, I can assure you. I ask only that..." Rebecca thought she heard him utter a low curse. "Yes, I can understand how this happened. I imagined a girl like you would jump at the chance to become a duchess."

"I was never given a choice, Your Grace, though I am certain I would have declined had Mr. Winters come to me with such a proposal. Do you not realize how awful it is to be married to a man one has never seen? Who hides in the darkness even on his wedding night? Whatever it is that is wrong with you, it is better to know than to allow my imagination to run amok."

He ignored this last. "What did Mr. Winters do to convince you?"

Rebecca hugged her arms around herself. "He won a great sum of money from my father playing cards, then threatened debtors' prison if my father did not agree to give me to you."

"Ah. Mr. Winters is excellent at exploiting a person's weaknesses. Still, no one forced your father to lose such sum. You can hardly blame Mr. Winters or myself for your father's failings."

Anger rushed through her. "Do you not care that you and your whims have ripped me from my family?"

"It was hardly a whim," he snapped. The pacing began again and Rebecca stepped back lest he collide with her. "Get on the bed."

She gasped. "No."

"This marriage must be consummated."

"This night? This hour?" Rebecca hated that her voice trembled. "I don't even know your given name." Hot tears pressed against her eyes.

"Oliver."

She heard him move toward the bed, the sound of the mattress sinking beneath the weight of him, and she stood still, her muscles aching from her stillness.

"This is not what I imagined," he said. "I thought if it was dark, it would put you at ease. I imagined this going far differently."

"What did you imagine? How could you have thought any girl would feel at ease in such a situation?"

She thought she heard a chuckle. "You are a duchess."

"I never had such lofty aspirations. I want…" *I want to go home.* Her throat ached so, she knew she would be unable to speak for several moments.

Movement, the sound of fabric shifting. "Tomorrow night, then."

And then he was gone and Rebecca sagged with relief. Tomorrow night. Please God, she would be gone from this place, from this marriage. No one should be asked to endure such a thing. She bit the side of her cheek to stave off tears. But no, she could not leave, and that realization left her defeated. Such an act would be disastrous for her family. She must endure. She stood there for several long minutes, partly to make certain he had indeed left her room, and partly because she could hardly bring herself to move. She stood where she was, her arms clutched around her, and tried with all her being not to crumple to the floor and cry. "Oh, Papa," she whispered, her heart aching. "See what you have done."

After several minutes trying to get hold of her emotions, she shook her head as if to clear it. Then, hands in front of her, Rebecca searched for the pulls that would bring a footman to her room to start a fire; she was about to scream out her frustration when she finally felt the thick velvet rope. She pulled, hard, and tried to control her emotions. A fire would calm her. It was the utter darkness that made everything even more frightening; she would feel better with a cheery fire in the grate.

Tomorrow night.

Oh, God, how could she do this thing?

Chapter 4

Oliver strode to Mr. Winters' suite, growling at a maid who ducked her head and skittered out of his way, annoyed that yet another female was frightened of him. When he reached Winters' door, he stopped to collect himself, then gave up on the effort and slammed his fist against the wood.

"Winters," he shouted. "Open immediately."

He did so, calmly. "Yes, Your Grace? I must say I am surprised to see you so soon. Did it not go well?"

Oliver pushed past him, ignoring Winters' mocking tone. "It did not go at all…" His voice faded when he spied the secret passageway access, slightly ajar. Oliver turned, his fists clenched tightly by his sides as rage filled him. Winters quietly closed his door and turned to him, his eyes flickering to that gap in the secret panel. He wondered if Winters knew how close he was to violence. He could not, given the bland questioning look Winters was now giving him. "You are never to look at her when she is in her chambers. *Never.*"

"I did not," Winters said with excruciating care.

"But you were there, were you not?" Oliver had known Winters long enough to understand the nuances of conversing with him. Winters had not *seen* his wife, but he had most certainly heard her—and him—from the secret passageway. The wave of humiliation that swept over Oliver was nearly staggering.

"We know nothing of this woman," Winters said, tugging on the sleeve of his jacket. "She could have been bent on murder for all I knew. Someone has to protect you."

The thought that Winters had been there, listening, was beyond mortifying. "You will not do so again. In fact, I shall board the entrance up."

"There are dozens of entrances, some we likely aren't even aware of. I hardly think that is practical."

Oliver took two long strides toward Winters and grabbed his lapels, thrusting him violently against the door. Winters' eyes widened, but other than that small movement, he gave no indication that he was alarmed. By God, Oliver thought, Winters would be alarmed if the man knew what he was feeling at that moment. "I shall have the entire system of passages removed."

"Calm yourself, Your Grace," Winters said with maddening composure. "Think of how much more difficult your life would become without the passageways."

Oliver dropped his hands and stepped back, disgusted with himself for exhibiting such behavior to a man who'd been more father to him than his own father. "I want your word, then. You shall never watch her or listen to her while she is in her chambers. Or mine."

Winters frowned, as if Oliver were being unreasonable. "May I speak frankly to you, Your Grace?"

"When have you not spoken frankly, Winters?" Oliver asked darkly.

"This was a mistake, Your Grace, this marriage. On the journey here, I became convinced that she is not suited for you." He paused, as if trying to get a bad taste from his mouth. "She is more suited to be a maid in this house than its mistress. She comes from a large brood of children, sired by a wastrel and a woman as common as a barmaid. Her blood will taint any children you have. As you have not consummated the marriage, you can still have it annulled. Then, if you wish to make her your mistress, so be it. But to have her here, acting as duchess, it is untenable."

"Take care, Mr. Winters. Your position here has never been more precarious."

Winters' face tightened imperceptibly. "You would choose a girl you don't know, who is nothing, over me? I have been loyal to a fault. I have protected you, taught you, made your life as rich as possible, given your affliction. I tell you, Your Grace, that this woman is common in the most basic definition of the word."

"Yes, Mr. Winters, I would choose my *wife* over you. Over anyone." Winters paled, clearly shocked at Oliver's words, and Oliver sighed. "You have been a loyal friend, but we are discussing my wife. You have not given me your word."

Winters pressed his lips together as if trying to stop himself from speaking. Finally, he smiled. "Of course, Your Grace, I will not spy on your lovely new bride." He hesitated only a breath. "You have my word."

"Then I bid you good evening, sir." Oliver left, his body still thrumming with anger.

Winters could not know what was behind his fascination with his wife; he could hardly understand it himself. His wife was as lovely as he'd imagined she would be. Thanks to the intricate and expansive passageways in the house, he'd watched her arrival, seen her look around herself with dismay at the dimly lit entrance, the long gloomy hallway. Though his poor eyesight made it impossible to make out details from any distance, he could see her lithe form, that delicate face he'd stared at for weeks. And he'd heard the maid tell her that anyone who looked at him would turn to stone.

He actually hadn't heard that one and had laughed aloud. Vampire. Ghost. Devil. But never some sort of demon who was so monstrous he would turn an innocent victim to stone. No wonder the servants refused to look at him; then again, he was glad they did not, so perhaps he should let things be.

Still, he had to wonder where such outlandish stories had come from. As he reached his room, he looked down at his hand, starkly white against the dark wood. A hand made of marble. Or ice. Ah. Of course. He supposed in a certain light it did look as if he were made of stone. He stood there for a long moment, staring at his hand as it gripped the doorknob; it almost seemed to glow in the darkness. Shaking his head once, a sharp, angry gesture, he pushed into his room and slammed the door. And realized he'd forgotten to confront Mr. Winters about the nefarious scheme he'd used to force Miss Caine into marrying him.

With a sigh, he removed his banyan and threw it on the end of his massive, ducal bed. Only three women had joined him there, local prostitutes, Winters had said, who were used to servicing clients no matter their appearance. The first time he'd been sixteen, skinny, and excessively excited and nervous about losing his virginity. Winters had suggested he keep the room dark and he had. But afterward, when the girl was affectionate, he'd thought perhaps he'd be able to invite her back, so he'd lit a small lamp.

A mistake, that.

"My God, it's true," she'd said, looking at him with horror. "Yer the devil himself." She'd fled the room in tears, and realized only after she was out the door that she was unclothed. Thankfully, Winters intercepted her and retrieved her belongings before sending her on her way. Winters had probably been behind his wall listening, then watching. It was a disturbing thought.

Oliver's grandfather had been a bit of a nefarious character, smuggling in French goods. He'd been in league with a mean group of locals who'd used Horncliffe as their headquarters. Indeed, the house had been built for the purpose of smuggling, with a vast labyrinth of passageways beneath the house, long since closed up, that had once led to the sea. Part of the building plans included the secret passageways that allowed one to travel from the top floor to the basement without being seen by the occupants or guests of the house. It was a clever design and one Oliver appreciated. He would dislike closing the passages up or destroying them, but he could not be certain Winters would keep his word.

And he would dislike even more having to walk the hallways, exposed to prying eyes.

Now that he was married, he knew things would have to change. Servants might accept the strangeness of the household, but a wife would not. Perhaps that was why Oliver had married, to force a bit of normalcy onto his home. Normal. It was word that pierced his heart.

He thought back on what Winters had said of her background: sired by a wastrel and a lowborn woman. Based on his brief conversation with his wife, he did not believe this to be the case. While she didn't have the diction of a lady, she certainly carried herself well and had been exceedingly poised, given the situation.

She was fierce and lovely. Angry. Thank God there had been no tears, even though he thought he'd detected the slightest trembling in her voice. Damn it, he didn't want her afraid of him as so many were. He wanted... God, it was so *stupid*. He wanted her to love him.

Oliver laughed aloud.

The sound of tapping on the door that adjoined his suite at first startled him, for no one ever had walked through that door.

"Your Grace?"

Hastily, he blew out the lamp that offered dim lighting in his chambers. He had a merry fire blazing in the hearth and it was still far too bright in the room to admit a visitor, especially his new wife. "Yes?" He stood there, taut, waiting for her response.

"I pulled on the rope and no one came. My room is cold, sir. And dark." A silence. "And then I pulled harder, thinking I hadn't pulled hard enough, and the entire thing came off. So..."

"You would like me to send for a footman to light your fire."

"I would, yes."

Oliver strode to his bell pull and gave it a sharp yank, then walked to the adjoining door and laid a palm upon it, imagining he could feel her warmth on the other side. "I've called for a footman; he should be up shortly."

"Thank you."

Oliver stood there, trying to hear whether she'd moved away. "Rebecca?"
"Yes?" She was still there, separated from him only by an inch of door.
"I apologize for everything. For bringing you here. I was unaware of
Mr. Winters' scheme. But you should know I am still glad you are here. I
don't wish for you to be frightened of me."

"I'm not," she said quickly. Then, "Perhaps a little. This is all strange
to me. A large mansion like this. We lived in a manor house with twelve
rooms and thought we were quite the thing. This is a palace in comparison.
And it's so…dark."

"Ah. My eyes, you see. I cannot tolerate bright light. It is painful for me."

"I should like to go home." There, her voice closed on that last word,
and he knew she was fighting back tears.

"You cannot. You are my wife." There was a small sound and he prayed
she was not crying but knew she was. "Please do not cry, Rebecca."

"I'm not crying," she said in a voice that told him she was.

He smiled and stared at his pale, pale hand splayed on the door. "No
matter what you may have heard, I am not a monster. I am just a man who
wants a wife."

A long silence followed. "Then why not allow me to see you?"

Because you would most certainly leave. "It is not possible. Not now."

A knock sounded on his bedroom door and he strode to it. "Her Grace
requires a fire and a lamp. See to it."

"Yes, Your Grace."

Oliver returned to the door and listened to the quiet murmur of his
wife's voice as she instructed the footman.

"Oh, a lamp. Thank you."

She said this last more loudly, and Oliver knew she was directing the
gratitude toward him. That she should thank him for something as simple
as a lamp bothered him. That she suspected he was still at the door listening
bothered him even more.

Her room was beyond lovely. Holding the lamp in front of her, she
walked barefoot on the softest carpet she'd ever tread upon. It was a light
pink with blue and white flowers and covered much of the cold stone floor.
The walls were gold, the trim white, the ceiling painted sky blue with soft,
billowy clouds. Indeed, it was so far from what she'd expected when she'd
been standing in the dark, she let out a giggle. This was not a monster's
lair with gargoyles and dark, heavily carved paneling, but a room fit for
a duchess. Which was what she was.

Oh, goodness.

It was more than a room, but rather a suite of rooms that included a sitting room with ceilings that soared above her. The furniture was feminine and well-crafted, with soft tufted seats in the palest pink, a large settee in gold and white, and another plush carpet on the floor. She spied another door, left ajar, and wandered over to it, curious what it could lead to, and smiled when she realized she now had a private bath. It was a ridiculously large room, larger, in fact, than her old bedroom at home, and contained modern conveniences she'd seen only in the posh hotel she and Winters had stayed in on their journey here. It included a washing basin with running water and a large tub. The commode was an impressive piece of furniture with a comfortable-looking seat and a clever little door where the chamber pot could be removed. But the most wonderful part of the water closet was the bathing tub, pristine and white, with brass spigots for filling. It couldn't be...

Rebecca tiptoed over to the tub and turned the spigots, first one then the other, gasping when after a time, hot water began spewing out, steam rising from the bath. Why, she'd nearly be able to swim in hot water when she bathed. Everything in the room appeared new, and she realized it had been created for her.

Turning the spigots off, she sat on the edge of the large, deep tub and thought about her predicament. She was not a prisoner, and even if she were, this was certainly a pretty cell. Yes, this marriage was odd, but the duke hadn't forced himself on her. Hadn't ranted and raved like a madman, even when she'd said she wanted to go home. In fact, something in his tone had held a plaintive note, as if he were fully aware of how awful this experience must be for a provincial girl like her. *No matter what you have heard, I am not a monster. I am just a man who wants a wife.* Such an odd way of going about it, but here she was, married. A duchess. *A duchess.*

With a determined step, she walked back to the door that adjoined her suite to the duke's and tapped lightly.

A moment later: "Yes?"

"My rooms are lovely, Your Grace."

"I am glad. Have you eaten?"

Rebecca had been so overwrought she hadn't given food a thought, but as soon as he'd mentioned it, she could feel her empty stomach calling to be filled. "No."

She heard a curse, then footsteps. "You shall have dinner brought to you shortly."

Though she didn't want to put the cook to the trouble, she *was* hungry. Now that she gave it some thought, it was odd that no one offered her anything to eat. "Thank you. And good night, sir."

"Good night."

Rebecca awoke when a maid entered her room to tend the fire. The drapes were still closed, but a sharp slice of sunlight split the room and Rebecca smiled. Surely nothing too awful could happen when the sun was shining so brightly.

"Good morning."

The maid turned around, startled. "Good morning, Yer Grace," she said, and made a quick curtsy. It seemed strange to have someone curtsying to her, but she'd get used to it eventually, she supposed. "I didn't mean to wake you." In the Caine household, the servants were more like family than employees, quick to give their opinion or disapproval. Perhaps it was that she was unused to dealing with staff in such a lofty household, but Rebecca sensed an underlying disquiet amongst the staff that went beyond fear of their eccentric master.

"Please do not worry. I am used to waking early. I grew up in the country and rise with the sun every day."

The maid, a thin, pale thing with her blond hair pulled tightly up under her cap, gave her a strange look that was quickly masked.

"What time is it?"

"Just past the noon hour," the maid said.

Rebecca let out a laugh. "My goodness, I must have been more tired than I thought. I haven't slept so late in years, and then I was ill. What is your name?"

"Sally, Yer Grace."

"Sally, could you please find Darlene? And someone who can repair my bell pull? I yanked it clear off last night."

Sally quickly gathered up her things, including a bucket of coal that looked far too heavy for her to carry, and, after another quick curtsy, left Rebecca alone. The sunlight beckoned her, and Rebecca threw off the covers and ran to the window, curious about what the estate looked like in the daylight. Pushing aside the curtains, Rebecca gasped at the sight before her.

A large lawn stretched to a thick forest, that now was brilliant with the colors of fall, and a small lake sparkled, its surface dotted with water fowl. In the distance, the glimmer of the sea made her smile. She hadn't realized Horncliffe was so close to the shore and it made her feel a bit closer to St.

Ives. If she wanted to go home, all she had to do was walk along the sea until she reached St. Ives. It was a silly thought, but comforting just the same. She hadn't known anything about this place, not how cold it would be, nor how beautiful and different from her home.

With a sharp pang, Rebecca realized she had no one to share the view with. Her sisters would have delighted in it, would have run down the stairs and ruined their shoes on the wet grass just to dip their toes into lake. No doubt, the water was icy cold this far north, and Rebecca wondered if anyone ever swam in it. If she were home, Eliza would have been at her door, begging to go for a walk. Alice would have bundled up her little baby and let her play in the colorful leaves that covered the lawn.

"Stop it," Rebecca said aloud. No good came from feeling sorry for oneself. And what did she have to feel sorry about? That she was a duchess and living in a mansion with a household of servants who were willing to do her bidding? Most women would give anything to be in her position. Well, perhaps not married to a man the servants and villagers feared, one who refused to show himself, who lived in shadows because…because of something horrible.

The knot in her stomach that had begun to unfurl tightened once again.

Bundled up and wearing her oldest boots, Rebecca headed outside to explore the grounds. She hadn't counted on air so cold it stole her breath and made her teeth hurt when she smiled. The wind went right through the wool coat she wore, a coat that had been more than adequate on the coldest days in St. Ives. Still, she was a hearty soul and refused to allow a bit of cold air to push her back into the house.

As she neared the edge of the forest, leaves rustled beneath her feet with each step she took, a comforting, familiar sound that only made her homesick. No one was about and the world was silent; not even a bird sang and Rebecca suppressed a shudder that had little to do with the cold.

Looking back at the house, she frowned. Rebecca had hoped Horncliffe would seem more inviting in the daylight, but if anything, it was even more formidable. The roof was all angles, with windows and dormers, towers and peaks, created without a thought to symmetry or beauty. The dark stone and mullioned windows, all covered with heavy drapes, did little to make the mansion more inviting. A madman might have designed it, so incongruous were its angles. Her gaze went from one end to the other, stopping at a gargoyle guarding a tower room, and she let out a giggle. A gargoyle? Poor fellow was alone in his vigil, and Rebecca wondered if there had once been a pair of them glaring down at whomever should dare approach. A slight movement brought her eyes to the window in the tower, but she saw nothing except the dark drapes. Was the duke up there looking down at her? She was too far away to see. Mr. Starke had mentioned that the duke spent much of his time in the tower. Or was it Mr. Winters? With that thought, she turned away, pressing down the sudden apprehension that threatened to ruin her day.

The forest was thick and dark, the sort Little Red Riding Hood would have skipped through, unaware of a lurking wolf. Were there wolves at Horncliffe? Or other creatures that could harm her? Something rustled in the brush, and, with her heart beating hard in her chest, Rebecca turned away from the woods, scaring herself into thinking something—or someone—was watching her. What silliness. Honestly, she must learn to temper her imagination. But walking toward the house did little to stem her fears, for the mansion loomed large and threatening, as if it were warning all to stay away. It was easy to understand why the locals were so afraid of the place, for it was a rather frightening vision and Rebecca couldn't imagine who would have designed such an ugly thing.

"You don't frighten me," she whispered, her eyes narrowed in an attempt to find a bit of bravery.

With determined steps, she walked around the entire manse, marveling at the ugliness of it, so unlike anything she'd ever seen. It was as if whoever created it had done so on purpose to repel. Hardly was there a straight wall, but rather false entries, doors and porticos and angles that made little sense. The grass around the building was well-kept, but she saw no whimsy, no beauty, no organized garden. Perhaps this house needed a woman to plant some flowers to soften the look of the dark stone.

The west side wall was nearly covered with ivy that climbed to the roof, the vines crawling into every nook, even covering one of the windows entirely. Suppressing a shiver, Rebecca backed away, as if the ivy was somehow malevolent. She laughed at her silliness, knowing she was allowing Darlene's words the previous evening to influence how she felt about the place. It was stone and wood, nothing more. A house could not be menacing, and ivy was lovely. Still, in the spring, she thought she might direct the gardener to remove it.

Despite the unusual architecture of the place, by the time she reached the front again, she'd begun to feel sorry for the house. Rebecca tended to do that, give human emotions to inanimate objects, something that made throwing anything away difficult.

"You need me," she said to the great house. As silly as it sounded, she felt it was true. "You ugly old thing, all you need is someone to love you."

She let out a laugh, amused by her thoughts, but not enough to discard them entirely.

After going inside, her cheeks pink from the cold and near freezing to the touch, she headed to her rooms to write home. She would write to her sisters about the grounds, about the house, and her journey, but she hadn't any idea what she could say about her new husband. They were, she had little doubt, anxious to hear whether he was ugly or handsome. To their naïve minds, all dukes must be handsome. How could she tell them when she still didn't know? She realized she would have to write a vague description that would not hint at the strangeness of her marriage thus far.

She pulled out the rosewood writing desk her father had given her as a wedding present, moving her hands over the smooth surface before opening it up to the felt-covered interior. It had been his mother's and she knew how much it meant to him, for no one had been allowed to touch it. She'd cried when her father had given it to her, knowing it was his way of saying how much he would miss her, how sorry he was for his mistakes. Inside was a pen and ink pot, several pieces of expensive paper, and a wax and seal—everything she would need to stay in touch with everyone she was missing. She couldn't tell anyone the full truth; they would worry too much. After sitting at her desk, staring at a blank bit of paper for several minutes, she gave up, leaving the letter-writing to another day.

She was waiting for him in the dark, likely fearful. Or angry. Oliver liked her anger far better than her fear. Her maid had tapped on his door not ten minutes prior to tell him Her Grace was prepared. The larger question—was he prepared?

He was certainly physically prepared, he thought with chagrin, his cock already standing at half mast at just the idea of some relief. It had been more than three years since Winters had brought him a girl, an event that had filled him with such shame and self-loathing, he'd asked that no more be brought. She had been willing, yes, but she'd had a strange odor about her and had talked during the entire event about her husband of all things. She'd lifted her skirts and spread her legs. "Come on now, Yer Grace, let's get this done, now. I've got supper to make."

While his body had been sated, his mind had been completely repulsed by the idea of bedding another woman he had to pay, and one with a husband waiting at home. He couldn't bear to think of another woman even though his needs grew each day; it was humiliating.

"Never again," he'd told Winters, who had given him an odd smile, one tinged with disbelief.

"Was she not to your liking, Your Grace? I can find a better one next time. I did not realize she was married. Entirely unsuitable."

Oliver never asked for Winters to bring him a woman; they just appeared, all willing enough. Still, the arrangement left him feeling unsettled.

Rebecca was likely a virgin, and he wasn't certain he was glad of it or not. Some primal element inside him was fiercely glad, but he was still bloody uncomfortable with the idea. He prayed she knew a bit of what was to come. Hell, he hardly knew. Winters, seemingly amused by his ignorance in such matters, had told him virgins experienced some pain and bled their first time, an idea that was horrifying to Oliver. How was he to know such things, having spent most of his life within these walls? The only things he knew of the outside world he found in books, and books hardly discussed deflowering virgins.

All day, she had invaded his thoughts; his mood had been mercurial, veering from stark fear to giddy anticipation. That morning, he'd watched her outside even though the light had hurt his eyes. At that distance, she was nothing more than a blur to him, but he knew it was she. Who else would be taking a stroll around the grounds, who else had such vivid auburn hair? At that moment, he wished he were a normal man, the sort who could have courted her, could have joined her on her walk.

Tonight, in the dark, he could be a normal man, lie with his wife and make her forever his. If she would have him. No matter what Winters said, he would not force her.

With a sigh, he opened the door that connected their suites and walked in, swallowing any uncertainty he felt. "Good evening, Rebecca."

"Good evening, Your Grace." Her voice was smooth and strong, and he could detect no hint of unease.

He began walking toward the bed, only to smack his shin on some piece of furniture that should not be in his path.

"My apologies, Your Grace, I hadn't thought to move the ottoman." Did he detect laughter in her voice? Had she purposely placed obstacles in his path? It was nearly a certainty that she had, he realized when he slammed into a chair not a moment later.

"I am wholly amused," he said, without even the hint of amusement in his voice. His shin hurt like the devil.

"There is only one more," she said, and this time he could clearly hear the laughter in her voice. Despite himself, he smiled, though he was glad it was dark and she could not see it. By now, his eyes had adjusted enough so that he could discern the vaguest shadows, and he easily side-stepped her obstruction.

"You are in the bed?" he asked.

"I am not."

He closed his eyes, dreading that this was going to be battle. "Please get in the bed, madam. I promise I will not harm you."

"I fully intend to fulfill my wifely duties," she said, and this time her voice was not so strong. "But I should like to touch you first. If that would be permissible." This last was said in a rush, as if she feared angering him.

"You wish to touch me?" He ought to do a jig and shout out that of course she could touch him. Whatever was he here for if not that? But something in her voice told him she was far more frightened than she was letting on. He could only imagine the stories she had heard about him from the servants. She would likely touch his teeth to make certain he had no fangs.

"Yes, Your Grace."

He had not anticipated such a request. He'd imagined her lying on the bed, fists clenched, while he touched her. "Very well. I am at the end of the bed, near the post."

He heard the faint sound of her bare feet on the carpet, her soft breath, the rustling of her nightdress, and then he caught the subtle scent of lavender and he smiled. "Did you enjoy your bath?"

She gasped. "You... How did you know I bathed?"

"I can smell the lavender." He let out a low chuckle. "I assure you I was not spying on you."

"I did enjoy my bath, Your Grace. I believe it is my favorite part of Horncliffe." She stood there before him, silently, for a space of three breaths; it seemed like an eternity. "I am going to touch you now."

"Very well." He closed his eyes even though he could hardly see her, only the slightest of shadowy outlines, and then he felt the warm pressure of her hand on one shoulder and he had to stop himself from inhaling harshly. It was a simple touch, nothing more, but his body was alive and straining and all he could do was fist his hands and close his eyes and try to maintain some sort of control. She smelled so damn good. Too good, and he cursed himself for providing her such sweet-smelling soap, a scent that would linger, that would forever remind him of this moment. Her hand rested on one shoulder, tentative, and all he could think of was that he wanted her to touch his flesh, to warm his skin. "Shall I take off my banyan?"

A small hesitation. "If you like."

In one fluid motion, it was off and on the floor, leaving him naked in front of her. "You may touch me again now."

She let out a small sound, a little laugh, and he found her ability to find amusement in what was likely a highly unusual moment for her, rather admirable. "Very well," she said, echoing his earlier words.

Again he felt her hand on his shoulder and was unable to stop his shaking breath. How could she know what this was like for him, a man who had never been voluntarily touched by a woman in his life. The others had been paid, and it was entirely different. This woman was his wife. It was a bit miraculous.

Her fingertips feathered up his shoulder to his neck, to be joined by her other hand in exploring his face, and he gripped the bedpost hard to keep from moving, to keep from sinking to the floor. His jaw, his nose, his brow, and then his hair, light touches that were serving to make him mad with lust. His member was fully erect and when her nightdress brushed against him, the slight touch nearly made his knees buckle. She ran her fingers through his hair, up and around to the back of his neck, then down to his chest.

"My God," he whispered, when her fingertips grazed his nipples. He shuddered beneath her hands, then finally clasped them in his own, stopping her movement. Her wrists felt impossibly delicate beneath his hands and he immediately loosened his grip.

"I don't understand," she said.

"I want to be gentle with you. I don't believe you realize what your touch does to me. This is your first time?"

"Yes."

"If you continue to touch me, I shall lose the small amount of control I have and I fear I will not be as gentle nor as considerate as I should be."

Rebecca laughed. "That is not what I meant, Your Grace. I do understand men a bit." Now, that was a lie, given she'd grown up in a household of mostly females. But she had three married friends who had hinted at what occurred between a man and a woman. She rested her hands on his chest, her fingertips on the curve of his clavicles, and his large hands held her wrists lightly. She could feel his chest moving in time with his breaths, strong and sure and slightly accelerated.

"I…I don't understand why you will not allow me to see you. You are not fat or bald or an ogre." She let out a small laugh. "You are an ordinary man." In fact, he seemed more of a man than many she'd seen. He was tall, sturdy, muscled. He had no lumps or bumps or scars that she could feel. He was strong and lean, the angles of his face chiseled.

"You know nothing." Anger edged his words, and Rebecca felt a small fissure of fear. She knew nothing of this man, after all. He sighed, and she felt his breath on the top of her head. "Now, may I touch you?"

"I supposed it's only fair." She said the words lightly, but her stomach clenched. This was it. She was about to bed a stranger, allow him all sorts of liberties, allow him to touch her where no one had before. The urge to run was almost overwhelming, but she stood her ground. She was this man's wife.

His hands touched either side of her neck, then moved up into her hair. "Ever since I saw the painting of you, I have wanted to touch your hair," he whispered. "It is far softer than I imagined." He drew her to him and kissed her softly on her forehead, an oddly tender caress and one that made her smile. She'd feared he would make her get on the bed and spread her legs, then have his way with her. His hands still in her hair, fingers moving restlessly against her scalp, he kissed her cheeks, first one, then the other, the way she'd seen Frenchmen do when greeting a friend.

And then, he pressed his lips, firm yet soft, against her mouth, before laying his forehead against hers, his breath harsh. "Will you remove your nightdress?"

No no no. "Yes. Of course, Your Grace."

"Oliver."

"Oliver." With hands shaking from the cold or from pure nervousness, she pulled at the bow at her throat, then undid the buttons, one by one, until she could shrug the garment off. It fell to the ground with a little thump that sounded overloud in the darkness. When he laid his hands on her shoulders, she shivered.

"Are you frightened or cold?" he asked.

"Perhaps a bit of both."

"I am sorry we cannot have a fire this night. As soon as we are done, I shall ring for a footman to light one for you. Get into bed, then, and under the covers with you."

For a moment, Rebecca thought it was over, that he would leave, and she wasn't certain whether she was relieved or frightened when she felt him get into bed next to her, under the covers. He lay there for a long minute, close enough for her to feel his body heat, but not close enough to touch. Then, she felt him kiss her shoulder, then a large, warm hand just beneath her breast. She was so taut, so nervous, she could hardly breathe, and she willed herself to relax.

"How old are you, Rebecca?"

The question startled her. "Twenty-three."

"And why are you not married? You are beyond lovely. Is everyone in St. Ives blind?" He kissed the side of her breast, gently, casually.

"You have only seen the painting. Perhaps I am spotted and crone-like."

She felt rather than heard him laugh, as he kissed her breast again, and then he found one peak, and sucked, and Rebecca's eyes flew open and her breath caught. What was *that*? A low growl sounded from his throat as he continued to suckle her, and Rebecca's hands, with a mind of their own, apparently, moved to the back of his head, holding him there.

For the first time in her life, Rebecca felt a sharp stab of desire, a liquid pooling between her legs, and she moved restlessly beneath him as he moved to her other breast. How was it possible she had lived twenty-three years and never realized the pleasure one could rouse with a kiss? She let out a small sound, unable to remain silent, and he lifted his head, allowing the air to cool her breast. Then he kissed her mouth, fully, with lips and tongue and teeth and Rebecca, who had never been kissed like that before, found herself lost in the sensations, the sounds, the feel of a man making love to her. He tasted of mint and he felt like velvet steel beneath her wandering hands. His back was broad and unblemished, his manhood hard and long against her thigh. She knew what it was, pressing against her, moving in a rhythm even someone as innocent as she could recognize.

He stopped, pulled away, his breathing harsh. "I need to slow," he said, then brought his head down for another drugging kiss. "Tell me about your family," he said, but he'd moved one hand between her legs, to where she burned, and she could not speak. "Later, then." He chuckled, then found the center of her, and Rebecca let out a sound she'd never in her life emitted before.

"What are you doing?"

"I haven't the foggiest, really."

"You seem to be doing well enough."

He kissed her jaw and she sensed he was smiling. "I'll muddle through."

"Yes," she said on a hiss, when the feeling between her legs intensified. "Muddle away."

Then her world shattered in a seizure of pleasure, a bit frightening but wonderful too.

"Rather good muddling," he said, laughing, obviously pleased with himself.

Rebecca was liquid and drowsy, but tensed when he moved, pushing her legs gently apart and positioning himself between them. "Shh," he said, and she felt something between her legs, quickly realizing what it was. Some primal urge overcame her at that moment, and she lifted toward him. It was the oddest thing, as if her body knew better than she what it needed. He pushed inside her in one fluid movement, and she cried out at the unexpected pain. She'd known it would hurt, her mother had told her as much, but she hadn't expected it to hurt quite so much.

"Oh, God, I'm sorry," he said, and kissed her cheek, her nose, her lips. He was still, rather like a human statue, and she could feel him inside her. "I have to..." He pulled out slightly, then eased in, and though Rebecca braced herself for pain again, she felt little more than a burning sensation.

"It's all right now," she said, and rested her hands on his shoulders.

"Good, good. Because I'm afraid if I don't move, I shall die."

He began moving, thrusting in and out, his arms shaking, and Rebecca was uncertain what she should be doing. She lifted her knees and he let out a sound that told her whatever she'd done was a good thing. "Wrap your legs around me," he said, his voice hoarse. She did, and his movements became faster, harder, and not entirely unpleasant. In fact, his movements were beginning to produce rather nice feelings and the need to move her own hips. And when she did that, he arched his back and found his release, letting out a sound so primal, Rebecca couldn't help but smile and feel just a bit heady with feminine power.

He lay atop her, most of his weight on his arms, for a long moment, his breathing harsh, his head pressed against the pillow. "I am sorry I hurt you," he said finally, and shifted, pulling himself out of her.

"It was only for a moment," she said, turning her head toward him even though it was black as pitch. "We are officially married now."

"No escaping."

She smiled, but thought it an odd thing to say, as if he knew she'd wanted to run away. It was possible, she realized, that he knew how strange this marriage had been so far and felt sorry for it. She couldn't help but wonder how long they would continue this way. He couldn't mean for them to not see each other forever, could he?

"May I see you in the morning?"

He immediately sat up. "No." And then he left the bed. "I'll ring for a footman to light the fire."

"Am I never to see you, Oliver?"

Silence met her words. Just when she thought he must be gone, he said, "I don't think I could bear it."

Chapter 5

Rebecca did not see nor hear her husband the next day. She spent her morning writing to friends and family, making things up for she hadn't much to say that wouldn't leave them worrying about her. She certainly couldn't mention what had happened the previous evening, even though it had gone quite a bit better than she could have hoped. Just thinking about it made her blush, made her feel hot and achy. How could making love to her husband have been so pleasant when she was still so uncertain of him? Was he so different from other men that he had to hide himself? He certainly hadn't felt different—or at least as different as she imagined a man would feel.

Instead, her letters were filled with descriptions of her journey and Horncliffe, but she knew everyone would want to know what the mysterious Duke of Kendal was like. What should she say? What could she say? That he knew how to touch her to make her writhe with pure pleasure? That he was a skilled lover in bed and had been considerate of her? In the end, she decided to include a vague description that would hopefully put her family and friends at ease while satisfying their curiosity.

The duke is a shy fellow, charming and kind. He is taller than I, which is a relief, and has a head full of thick hair.

Variations of that description filled her letters. She'd finished with her correspondence by noon, and after taking a light lunch, again in the breakfast room and again alone, Rebecca went to her rooms and sat at her writing table, lost in thought. She'd yet to write to Eliza, for she was debating whether she should tell her dearest friend the truth about her situation. The servants were so convinced the duke was a monster, and yet the man she'd been with had seemed rather ordinary. Perhaps even better than ordinary, given how his touch had made her lose herself. If not for the fact he would not allow her to look at him, she would think him no different from any other man. How was it that the superstition around him had grown to the point where an entire village lived in fear of crossing Kendal?

After a time, Rebecca grew bored. Nothing would be proven nor accomplished sitting in her room feeling sorry for herself. She considered taking a walk around the grounds, but decided instead to explore the house a bit. As disjointed as the outside had been, the inside was even more of a puzzle. Only the public rooms were accessible. Room after room, in each wing of the house, was locked. It was a maze of hallways and stairs, some that seemed to lead nowhere but to a small window. It was as if a madman had designed the place. Though she was tempted to go to the tower room, where she suspected Oliver was spending all his time doing God knew what, she did not. The one time she walked in that direction, Mr. Winters intercepted her.

"His Grace is working," he'd said, then had gently taken her arm and led her away.

Everything in the house was immaculately clean. Silver polished to a high sheen, furniture gleaming from beeswax. The stairs, the very floors, were spotless. Even a chandelier, unlit since she'd been in the house, held not one speck of dust. Yet no one ever used the rooms. No one, as far as she could tell, even walked through them. The dining room lay empty, a china cabinet filled with unused plates. The music room, with its pianoforte, piano, and harp, seemed to be frozen, waiting for someone to fill the room with sound. When she'd first seen it, she'd thought perhaps His Grace played an instrument, but she hadn't heard a note since her arrival. It was almost like walking through a meticulously maintained museum.

When she found a library, she felt her spirits lift and hurried to the first shelf, her eyes scanning the titles. Most of the books were written in Latin or French and those that were written in English were scientific treatises that she could hardly make sense of. Did the duke read anything for pleasure? Disappointed, she was about the leave when she spied a series of small tables, each holding what appeared to be a tiny dollhouse. Above them were a series of landscapes and portraits of women, all beautiful. A quick scan showed that her painting was not among them, so Rebecca turned her attention to the tiny houses.

Walking to the first, she couldn't help but smile, for the detail of the creation was remarkable. It was a small cottage with a kitchen, main room, and two bedrooms above. If she could shrink herself down, she would live quite comfortably in a homey little cottage such as this, and she felt a sharp pang at the realization she never would. No, she would live in this rambling monstrosity of a place with cold marble floors and soaring ceilings, a mansion that smelled of beeswax and little else.

Rebecca reluctantly moved to the next table, then to the next, delighted by the creations. It was an astounding collection, unlike anything she'd ever seen in her life. Each detail was exquisite, from a tiny desk, some drawers left casually open and filled with tiny bits of writing paper, to sweeping staircases with intricate bannisters. She wondered who had been collecting the little wonders. It seemed such a whimsical collection to find in the otherwise dreary house. Despite the lack of a readable book, the library became her second favorite room in the house. Her bathroom could not be eclipsed just yet.

If the library delighted her, the portrait gallery did the opposite. A long, narrow room with thick, heavy paneling of some dark wood, it seemed to Rebecca to hold a malevolent air, though she couldn't pinpoint why. The paintings themselves were innocuous enough, the typical series of stern faces looking down at her with lifeless eyes. One painting of a duchess from 1751 included a charming little dog, which only served to remind her of the pets she'd left behind. Dates progressed to 1856 and stopped abruptly with the Fifth Duke of Kendal, Oliver's father. He was a handsome man, with long sideburns and smiling blue eyes, and Rebecca couldn't help but smile back at him. Like his son, he had thick, wavy hair, and Rebecca wondered if Oliver's shared the same rich brown color as his sire's. If he looked anything like his father, Oliver was a handsome devil, which made absolutely no sense to her. Oliver had the same sharp jaw, the same straight nose and masculine brow—at least based on what her fingertips had told her.

Oliver couldn't hide from her forever; she'd learn soon enough whether he resembled his father. The wall had many spots left, but the one next to the fifth duke was empty of either a duchess or the next duke, Oliver. She stood there a long moment, looking at that empty spot. She sensed it would likely never be filled with his likeness and wondered if her own portrait would ever hang in the gallery.

That's when she heard the hazy sound of a woman crying, a strange noise in the otherwise silent house, and she shivered. It was so faint and faded so quickly, she thought she might be imagining things or hearing the wind as it whistled around the angles and arches of the house. Straining her ears, she heard nothing more and decided it had been her imagination.

After wandering about for a time, Rebecca grew restless. Would this be the pattern of her days? Wandering alone with no one to talk to? Perhaps the village would prove to be a place where she might strike up a conversation. With that happy thought, she decided to explore the small place she'd caught a glimpse of when she'd arrived. A nice walk in the bracing air would do her good, as would seeing other people and perhaps visiting a few shops. She thought she'd seen a bookstore on the way in. A good book would help fill the long hours of the day when the only company she had was herself.

"Darlene, I wish for you to accompany me into the village this afternoon," Rebecca informed her maid after she'd finished lunch.

"I shall ask Mr. Starke to have the carriage readied," the maid said, and headed for the door.

"I think I'd rather walk, to be honest." One might have thought Rebecca had said she planned to fly to the village on the back of an owl.

"Walk? Goodness, no, Your Grace. You could never do that. Whatever would people think, the Duchess of Kendal forced to walk to town."

She smiled gently. "Perhaps they would think I wanted to take a walk?"

They took the carriage, an ornate affair from another decade, drawn by four identical black horses with red plumes on their harnesses. It was the type of vehicle that Rebecca would have run out to the street to watch pass by back home. When she saw it, she again wished they were walking, for it seemed garish and far too conspicuous. The inside was spotless and smelled of beeswax; soft, tufted leather covered the benches. It was by far the most luxurious vehicle she had ever been in.

The ride took all of ten minutes, and throughout the short journey, Darlene remained uncharacteristically quiet and tense, as if she wished she had not been asked to accompany Rebecca. When the carriage stopped, Darlene looked at her. "Are you sure, Your Grace? The villagers are a bit wary of the residents of Horncliffe."

Furrowing her brow, Rebecca asked, "What do you mean, wary?"

"They think Horncliffe and all who live there are cursed. Because they believe the duke—"

Rebecca held her hand up to stop the maid. "I'll have no such talk about His Grace. One of the reasons I wish to visit the village is to dispel such ridiculous rumors." Surely when the villagers saw her, saw that she had not been harmed, they would begin to wonder about all the evil rumors that surrounded the place.

"Very well, Your Grace," Darlene said, but her expression told Rebecca she greatly disapproved of this visit.

Rebecca had grown up in a small village and so understood how rumors and tales could grow out of hand. Likely, a tale or two had been told about the duke, given his reticence at being seen by anyone other than Mr. Winters. "I thought I noticed a bookstore when I was passing through," she said.

"Miller's Books that would be."

"I think that should be our first stop," Rebecca said with a firm nod.

"If you say so, Your Grace."

Darlene gazed out the small window of the carriage as if she feared a wild mob was about to attack them. Could the residents of this village be that fearful of Horncliffe's inhabitants? When they stopped, Rebecca waited for the footman to drop the stairs before standing. The door opened and wonderfully clean chill air filled the carriage. Rebecca stepped down, reminding herself that she was a duchess and trying to imagine how a duchess might act. In her limited experience—she had never met a duchess and only a handful of aristocrats—duchesses did not smile or shrug or speak too loudly. Her sisters and she had played pretend, of course, and because she was the oldest she'd always held the highest rank, but this was far different. She was an actual duchess, and she had no idea what to do. After a long minute of waiting for Darlene to join her, she realized her maid was not going to follow her.

"Darlene, I wish for you to accompany me."

"Yes, Your Grace, and I have."

"You actually mean to remain in the carriage?"

"I do, Your Grace." Indeed, Darlene didn't even deign to lean forward into the light, forcing Rebecca to speak into the shadowed carriage. Biting her lip, Rebecca wondered what a true duchess would do. Demand Darlene remove herself from the carriage? Terminate her employment instantly? In the end, she did nothing but lift her chin and scan the narrow, cobbled street for the book store.

The streets seemed eerily vacant for such a bright day. The air held a chill that portended winter, but it was not so cold as to prevent the souls who were used to the cold from venturing out. She'd expected to see more bustle. In St. Ives, one couldn't walk more than a few feet before stumbling into someone one knew. Or at least see a stray dog or cat. With one last look at the carriage, its bold crest gleaming in the sun, Rebecca made her way across the street toward the book store, an uncomfortable feeling of being stared at following her.

When she opened the door, it sounded unnaturally loud in the quiet, creaking eerily as she pushed it open. The place seemed deserted at first, but then Rebecca noticed some movement toward the back of the long, narrow shop and began walking that way. The store was divided into two long aisles, with a long, tall set of shelves dividing the shop. It smelled divinely of books, that wonderful combination of ink, paper, and leather that always sent a bit of a thrill through her heart.

"Hello?"

Silence. Utter and complete, but for the ticking of a clock somewhere.

Rebecca walked to the very end of the aisle, the room growing darker the farther she got from the door. When she got to the end of the aisle, she cautiously went around the center bookcase and looked back toward the entrance, only to see the shadow of a man slipping behind the counter.

"Hello!"

Letting out a sigh of frustration when she heard no response, she headed back to the front, stopping in front of the counter, where a portly gentleman wearing a bright green coat and yellow waistcoat sat upon a tall stool looking out the window. He was pretending to read, but his eyes, she noticed, were on the carriage that seemed far too large for the narrow village street. "You are the proprietor here? Mr. Miller?" Rebecca asked.

He hesitated a moment before turning his gaze toward her. "Indeed I am." He gave her a good long look before adding, "Visiting our fair village?"

"I live here. I am the new Duchess of Kendal."

The man pulled out a handkerchief and wiped his brow. That was when Rebecca noticed his entire face was covered with a fine sheen of perspiration. "There is no Duchess of Kendal," he stated boldly.

Rebecca laughed. "You are mistaken, sir, for here I am. His Grace and I were married not two weeks ago."

Mr. Miller craned his neck and looked again through the window to where the carriage sat, and it seemed as if his breath caught in his throat. "Is he..." He swallowed. "Is he waiting in the carriage?" His voice rose to a squeak when he uttered the last syllable.

"No, His Grace did not accompany me."

Rebecca wasn't certain whether the relief she saw on the shopkeeper's face was amusing or frightening.

"You've seen the duke, then?" he whispered.

What could she say? She hadn't actually seen the duke, but she certainly knew she was married to him. "I've been here for nearly a week," she said, neatly evading the question.

His eyes darted to her, and something in them caused a frisson of fear to move up her spine. "Then you know."

"Know?"

He swallowed, darted another look outside, then leaned forward and whispered. "The curse."

Despite herself, she couldn't stop the shiver that convulsed through her. Suddenly, the bookshop lost its charm. She knew it was all silliness, but it was difficult to dismiss talk of demons and ghosts and curses when she hadn't actually seen His Grace. Only touched him. And had him touch her. Had his hands been unusually cold? Giving herself a mental shake, she forced herself to smile warmly at the man. "If there is a curse, sir, I am not aware of it. I have been made more than welcome at Horncliffe and have..." She'd been about to say she'd seen nothing untoward, but that wasn't entirely the case. "I have nothing to report of a curse. I've come to purchase a book. It seems all the books in Horncliffe's library are scientific treatises, which do not interest me in the least. I was hoping to find something more to my taste in your fine store."

"Did he send you?" Rebecca could not ignore the real fear in Mr. Miller's voice.

"If you are referring to His Grace, no, he did not. As I said, I've come to purchase a book. It seemed as if this would be a good establishment to find one." He didn't appear to find her amusing in the least and frowned heavily at her.

"George, who are you—" A woman, as thin as the man was stout, appeared behind the desk from a small door that apparently led to stairs to the second floor. When the woman saw Rebecca, she stopped and stared at her. She looked from Rebecca to the man, immediately seeming to sense that all was not well. "George?"

"My name is Rebecca Sterling, Duchess of Kendal," Rebecca said gently, and watched with dismay as the woman, whom she assumed was Mrs. Miller, grew markedly paler.

"Did he send her?" she whispered to her husband.

"She says no."

"For goodness' sake, what are you two going on about?" Rebecca asked, not bothering to hide her exasperation.

"Did you tell her about Enid—"

"Hush, woman," the man said harshly, before turning to Rebecca. "Take whatever you like, Your Grace."

Did he mean for her to take a book without paying for it? "Please tell me why you seem so frightened of me."

"You've seen him?" This from the wife, who stared at her as if she, herself, was a demon.

"As I told your husband, I have been here nearly a week." The two of them looked as if she was about to pull out an axe and begin chopping them to pieces; they held a sense of inevitable horror. She sighed. "I am aware of the rumors surrounding His Grace, but please let me assure you he is all that is refined and gentle."

The two scoffed, and Rebecca felt her face heat, this time from anger. "If you would please recommend a book for me, I will be on my way."

The woman seemed to snap out of whatever had frozen her to the spot and wiped her hands on her dress. "What sort of books do you prefer, Your Grace?"

"I do rather like Jane Austen. Do you have anything by her?"

"We have *Emma* and *Pride and Prejudice,* but we could order anything you like."

"I've never read *Emma*, so that would be fine," Rebecca said. Feeling horribly uncomfortable, she waited in silence while the woman fetched the book and wrapped it for her. The man continued to look out the window fearfully, patting his forehead frequently with his handkerchief, as if he hadn't believed her when she'd told him the duke was not in the carriage. When the woman handed her the book, Rebecca pulled out her small purse, but the gesture seemed to shock the proprietress.

"Oh, no, Your Grace. Keep the book. Please."

"I cannot simply take this without paying. Will you bill His Grace, then?"

She might have asked if they could fly to the moon, for they both shook their heads adamantly. Not wanting to argue further, Rebecca thanked them, bade them good day, and left the shop, nearly on the verge of tears. What the devil was wrong with these people?

She returned to the carriage, book clutched in hand, the day ruined. She wasn't certain what she'd expected, but it certainly was nothing like what she'd experienced. The streets were still deserted, though now Rebecca had a stronger feeling people were looking at her from the shadows, and as soon as their carriage was on its way back to Horncliffe, the streets would be filled with terrified villagers. She could just imagine them all flocking to the bookstore to grill the Millers on who she was and why she was riding in the duke's carriage. They certainly would be surprised to find out they had seen the new duchess.

Once she was back in the carriage, Darlene, wide-eyed, said, "I told you, Your Grace. I knew it wouldn't go well."

"Something is terribly wrong with these people," Rebecca said hotly.

Darlene remained silent, clasping her hands tightly in her lap, her posture rigid.

"I have never in my life seen such ridiculous behavior from adults," Rebecca fumed. "No wonder His Grace remains hidden if this is what he must face."

Darlene's pale cheeks bloomed with two spots of color, but she did not respond.

It was an entirely upsetting experience and left Rebecca feeling angry and frustrated. She had a mind to fling the book out the window, but resisted only because she really did want to read it. And yet, those people obviously were truly afraid; they were not putting it on. What had made them so? She knew from experience that all rumors began from some sound foundation, yet she could hardly think she had married anything other than a man who was in some way terribly damaged. The entire incident only made her feel more fondly toward him.

Once they were back at Horncliffe, Darlene headed to the kitchens, no doubt ready to tell the staff what had happened in the village. Rebecca, though, went directly to see Mr. Starke. Surely he would be able to cast some light on why everyone seemed so terrified of His Grace.

She found Mr. Starke sitting at his desk, his chin on his chest as he napped, hands clasped over his rather large belly. Smiling tolerantly at the older man, Rebecca cleared her throat so as not to alarm him, but he started anyway, shot to his feet, then apologized profusely for sleeping during the day.

"Oh, don't be silly, Mr. Starke. We've all taken little cat naps. I need to speak to you, if I may."

"Of course, Your Grace."

She explained what had happened in town, but to her surprise, Mr. Starke didn't share her astonishment.

"It's because of Enid. She lived in the village and disappeared. Rightly or not, they blame His Grace. But it's more because of the maid, Your Grace. He turned her to stone, he did."

Rebecca pressed her lips together to stop from smiling. "Are you telling me you believe His Grace turned a maid into stone?"

"We are never to look at him, you see, and she did, bold as brass, she did. Molly Holly. Cute as her name, she was. Pretty little thing. She looked at His Grace. Said he looked like a demon, she did. She come down to the kitchens crying, her whole body shaking like a leaf. Said he bellowed at her to get out and never come back. Well, she left all right. She disappeared. And then, a month later, the gardener was out for the first time since the winter and there she was."

"Molly was in the garden?"

"Not the girl. A statue. It's still there today—you can see for yourself. The spitting image of her, it is."

Rebecca furrowed her brow and couldn't stop the tingling of fear she felt run through her. "You think His Grace did it?"

"We know he did," Mr. Starke said, his voice a harsh whisper. "He was cursed at birth, he was, or so the story goes. His own mother never held him, ran from the house in terror. Not one person who was on the staff when he was born is still here today. They're all gone. Every single one of them. Not one soul from the time before the old duke died is still here. Some think he killed his own father."

Rebecca stood, anger coursing through her. "I can assure you His Grace did not kill his father. It is unconscionable that you would say such a thing."

Mr. Starke stood and hung his head. "I am sorry, Your Grace. But there's strange doings in this house. Strange noises. Some think the ghost we've all heard is Molly, poor little thing."

"I have heard your ghost, Mr. Starke, and I can assure you it is more likely the wind whipping around this house." Even as she said the words, Rebecca found herself a bit spooked. She'd heard the dim cries, the sound of a woman, so faint it might be the wind. But Rebecca had never heard wind that sounded quite so peculiar.

Even though she knew the story was the stuff of fiction, a story made up by some servant as a prank, Rebecca couldn't stop herself from calling for her cloak and heading back outside for a stroll in the garden. When she'd explored the grounds previously, she had not bothered with the garden, for most of the flowers were long past blooming. Now, though, she walked out to the back terrace and headed down a stone path, dead leaves crunching beneath her feet. The garden did not seem at all well maintained, nothing like the gardens at Costille House back home; the earl had one of the most spectacular gardens in Cornwall and she had visited them on more than one occasion. Perhaps this garden was lovely in the spring and summer, but now it had an abandoned, almost neglected look.

Rebecca headed down a path toward the sound of what must be a fountain, hidden behind a high hedgerow. Though it wasn't a maze, it was difficult to see the garden in its entirety thanks to the height of the bushes that lined the path. Off to one side, a bench sat, hidden in a small alcove, and Rebecca wondered if anyone ever sat on it. It was the perfect place for lovers to hide from prying eyes, for when one sat on the bench, Horncliffe was entirely invisible.

Above her head, the leaves rattled noisily in the wind, though where she stood was well-protected from the crisp breeze. Other than the sound of the wind and a gentle gurgling, it was silent. Turning one corner, Rebeca came upon the fountain, an impressive affair with a man on a rearing horse surrounded by urns that overflowed into the fountain's pool. On its surface leaves floated, pushing by a breeze, a tiny regatta racing on the water.

It was odd. Normally, walking through a garden would be a lovely thing, a settling and calming experience. But something about this garden with its high hedges, its neglect, the pure isolation, had Rebecca on edge. No matter that she tried to tell herself she was being silly, she couldn't help feeling somehow threatened, as if the hedges would move in and trap her.

"Stop it," she whispered, shaking her head. Overhead, the sun was lost behind a large cloud, and the garden suddenly darkened and became a place of shadows. She fought the urge to turn around and chastised herself again for her cowardice. Taking a bracing breath, she circumnavigated the large fountain, giving the fierce warrior atop the horse a wary look—just in case he decided to come alive—and continued down the path in search of Molly's statue.

The pathway narrowed, leaving little room on either side, until she reached another clearing, this one set off to the right of the path, and there she was. Rebecca shivered, then laughed aloud. It was a statue, nothing more, carved by some skilled artist from marble, now pitted and with a bit of moss growing on the figure's dress. The sculpture stood directly on the grass, the lady's dress acting as the base. No, not a lady, for the figure was that of a maid, complete with cap and apron and an exquisitely rendered feather duster in her hand. The artist, whoever it was, had done a remarkable job with the detail. Rebecca stepped forward, taking in the fine work, noting how carefully each element had been carved, from the feathers in the duster to the fine lines on the woman's fingers.

"You can hear her scream sometimes at night."

Rebecca let out a shriek and turned around, frightened to nearly fainting. Her heart hammered in her chest as she whirled about to see an old man behind her at the entrance to the clearing. He wore rough clothing and a cap that covered most of his gray hair and his face was clearly in need of a shave. In his hand was a fierce looking tool made of metal, curving and sharp, and Rebecca felt her entire body quake in fear.

The man looked from her to the tool, then laughed, a sound so incongruous that Rebecca was momentarily stunned. "I'm the gardener, Mr. Corcoran."

The relief that flooded her was so immense, Rebecca sagged, resting a hand on the maid's arm, the one that held the feather duster. Laughing lightly, she said, "You startled me, Mr. Corcoran. I am—"

"I know who you are, Yer Grace." He moved into the small clearing, his eyes on the statue. "She was a pretty little thing, she was."

"Who?"

"Miss Molly." He jerked his head toward the statue. "That's her."

"That, sir, is a statue. While it is a fine bit of artistry, you cannot mean it is actually a young woman turned to marble."

The old man narrowed his gray eyes, his abundant brows drawing together. "Beggin' yer pardon, Yer Grace, but I was here when they found her. I been working this estate since soon after the old duke died. There weren't no statue here. And then Miss Molly disappeared and this statue appeared. How do you explain that?"

"I'm not sure I can," Rebecca said. "But I am quite certain His Grace does not have the ability to turn anyone to stone."

He lowered his head but kept his gaze steady on her. "You've seen him?"

Rebecca wanted to lie, but could not. "I have had several conversations with His Grace. He is a bit shy about being seen."

Mr. Corcoran shook his head. "'Tisn't shyness. You should leave here. Leave before he does the same to you."

"Mr. Corcoran, while I do think *you* believe what you are saying, I do not. His Grace is simply a man, a man who does not have the ability to turn anyone or anything into stone. Goodness, what would make you think such a thing?"

"You're new here. You don't know what goes on." His eyes lifted toward the mansion, even though it was still hidden behind the hedgerow. "Let me ask you this, Yer Grace—why did he have to go all the way to the end of England to find a bride?"

Rebecca swallowed down her irritation, and to be honest, a tiny bit of fear that everything she was hearing was true. Oh, not that the duke could actually turn someone to stone, but that he had caused some sort of ill to befall the poor girl. What did she know of her husband, after all? "His Grace did not have to travel so far, but it is where I lived, sir. I do wish all of you would cease these flights of fancy."

Mr. Corcoran looked at the statue for a long moment, then back to her. "God protect you, Yer Grace." Then he tugged at the brim of his cap and left.

When his footsteps had disappeared, Rebecca let out a long, shaky breath. It was all a bunch of nonsense. All if it. Still, she could not stop her stomach from twisting. These people had worked and lived in Horncliffe far longer than she had. What if they were right? What if the duke wasn't some sort of fictional monster, but worse, a monster who was living among them, who might just harm her.

Rebecca looked at the maid again, found herself trying to read her expression, but it was just a pretty girl, her eyes vacant, her thoughts frozen. No matter how many times she told herself people were daft to believe such tales, she had to acknowledge that something was wrong in this house, something was dark and maybe even dangerous. And if everyone thought that dark and dangerous thing was the duke, wasn't it at least possible they were right? Could they all be wrong?

Later, when she was getting ready for dinner, as casually as possible, she asked Darlene about the sound she'd heard in the gallery earlier that day. After Mr. Corcoran's story about Molly, she had to admit she was beginning to feel a bit on edge.

"It was the strangest thing today. When I was exploring the house, I thought I heard a woman crying. Did one of the maids receive some bad news?"

"Were you in the gallery?"

Surprised, Rebecca nodded. "I was."

"That would be Molly. She was a maid here before I came but one day she disappeared. I know you don't like to hear tales about His Grace—"

"I do not," Rebecca said. It was ridiculous. Oliver certainly had not turned some little maid into a statue. But no matter how many times she told herself how silly it all was, Rebecca couldn't stop the tiniest bit of doubt that crept into her mind. If she hadn't heard the woman crying, it would have been easy to dismiss all the talk. But she had heard something ...

Darlene shrugged. "Molly haunts the place, don't you know. At night and sometimes during the day, you can hear her wailing. Gives you the shivers, it does. Everything about this house gives me the shivers. You've felt it too, haven't you, Your Grace."

Rebecca chose to let that go unanswered. At any rate, it was more of a statement than a question. "If this place is so frightening, why don't you find another position? Surely there's another great house you could work in."

Darlene seemed horrified by the idea. "And be cursed my entire life?"

It was a nonsensical response, but Rebecca let it pass. It seemed as if someone here was filling the maids' minds with ridiculous stories, and she wondered if it were Mr. Starke. Every time she spied a maid, the servant was skittering about from one place to another, as if being chased by a phantom. Perhaps she ought to talk to Mr. Starke about addressing all the rumors and superstition, though he was likely the one who was perpetuating them.

Darlene pushed a final pin in her hair. "There you are, Yer Grace. Do you recall the way to the dining hall?"

"Will His Grace be joining me?"

"Oh, goodness, no. His Grace takes all his meals in his rooms."

Odd that she felt a stab of disappointment. "Then I will dine alone?" The dining hall was a massive room and the thought of sitting at the long table by herself was absurd.

"Mr. Winters will be joining you."

Rebecca forced herself not to frown, but her appetite swiftly diminished. Mr. Winters clearly held her in contempt; why would he lower himself to dine with her? With a sharp twinge of homesickness, Rebecca wondered what her family was having for their dinner. Meal times were a rather noisy affair at the Caine house, as one might expect in a home filled with five women chattering all at the same time. Her mother had never insisted on silence during mealtimes unless she was vexed with them. Were they thinking of her, wondering what she was doing? As Rebecca made her way down to the dining hall, her stomach in a bit of a knot, that unbearable urge to flee, to go home, struck her again and she wished fervently that none of this had ever happened. She would fly into her mother's arms and her sisters would gather around and tell her how glad they all were that she was home.

Rebecca stopped before the entrance to the dining hall and gave her head a firm shake. Such thoughts would only serve to make her miserable. At least the duke was not cruel. Thus far. There was that. But was it not cruel to extort her father and force her into marriage? *Stop, Rebecca.*

Mr. Winters was already seated and the moment she entered the room he stood, pulled out his watch, and frowned, even as a clock behind her finished chiming the hour.

"Am I tardy? I do apologize."

"Meals are served promptly in his household, Your Grace," he said, his tone rather harsh for such a slight transgression.

Rebecca glanced at the large mantel clock, which likely still vibrated from its marking the hour.

"It is two minutes off," he said, then flicked a hand toward a waiting footman, who immediately hurried to the clock to adjust the time.

"You could have started without me if you were so hungry," Rebecca said with exaggerated cheerfulness. She would not allow this man to get under her skin. Winters looked annoyed by the suggestion and Rebecca felt a bit of triumph. "I'm surprised you wish to dine with me at all, considering my very existence repulses you."

The footman, who had completed adjusting the clock, hurried forward and pulled out her seat. Rebecca sat near the head of the table and Winters across from her. The table was meticulously set, the china gleaming, the cutlery polished to a high shine. At one time, the Caines' settings might have looked so fine, but years of use had left them with chips and scratches. What lay before her looked as if it had never been touched.

"His Grace insisted I give you company."

"His Grace should offer his own company," Rebecca said.

"That is not possible."

She wanted to ask why, but she truly did not want to engage in conversation with the man. If the duke could take his meals in his rooms then the duchess could as well. In fact, she planned to refuse to eat anywhere but her rooms until Oliver joined her. What that would accomplish other than a bedroom that smelled of food, she did not know. But Rebecca found the thought of even that small rebellion satisfying.

A footman brought out a tureen and proceeded to ladle a creamy soup for each of them. Resisting the urge to sniff it first to determine just what it was, Rebecca instead took a small taste, then smiled. Celery soup, one of her favorites.

"I do hope your experiences here thus far have not been too unpleasant." Rebecca snapped her head up to stare at Winters, who looked at her blandly but with that disturbing, mocking air just beneath the surface. He had put the slightest emphasis on the word "experiences;" could he possibly be referring to her time with the duke? She felt her entire body heat with outrage and embarrassment. "I imagine the temperatures here are much colder than you are used to."

"I have never experienced such cold before, but I am certain I shall get used to it." She smiled politely at him, refusing to allow him to bait her. "In fact, all my experiences thus far have been exceedingly pleasant."

He returned her smile with one of his own, but something in his eyes was frightening, holding a malevolence that she prayed she was imagining.

The rest of the meal held little conversation, and when it came time for dessert, Rebecca declined, for she was more than ready to return to her rooms. She stood and he slowly followed suit. "Thank you for your company," she said. "Have a good evening."

"Good evening."

As Rebecca left the hall, she could feel his eyes on her and had to stop herself from hurrying her steps. If not for Mr. Winters, Horncliffe would be tolerable. But his presence cast a pall on the entire household, and she wondered how she could remove him. She didn't think she could bear spending time alone with the man.

Rebecca didn't pass another soul as she made her way to her room, her muted footsteps on the thick carpet the only sound. Just before she entered her room, she paused. Would it be in darkness, indicating her husband planned another visit to her bed? As pleasant as the experience had been, it had been so distressing to have a man do such intimate things to her body and not know what he looked like. She recalled Eliza had said the villagers called him the Ghost Duke. For one fantastical moment she wondered if he were, indeed, a ghost and not a man at all. Could ghosts be solid?

Letting out a giggle at her foolishness, Rebecca pushed open her door and sighed a breath of relief when she saw a cheery and vibrantly burning fire in the grate. So, no, he would not impose himself on her that night. Within minutes of her entering her room, Darlene arrived to assist her in undressing, her face slightly red as if she'd run all the way from wherever she'd been, no doubt urged by Mr. Winters to attend her.

"We'll have to be getting you a new wardrobe, we will," she said with a tsk. "Something worthy of a duchess."

Rebecca did not see the point if they were to have no visitors nor leave the house, but she nodded. The thought of new dresses in the latest style seemed pointless if no one but Mr. Winters and the staff saw them. When Rebecca was in her nightdress, she put out her lamp and crawled into bed to stare at the fire.

"Rebecca?"

Her heart hammered in her chest at the sound of the duke's voice on the other side of the door. "Yes, Your Grace?" she called. It was so long before he answered, she wondered if he would.

"Tell me about St. Ives."

The question made her smile, and she climbed out of bed and walked to the door. "St. Ives?"

"That is where your portrait was painted, was it not?"

"Yes. I posed for several artists. Which painting did you see?"

"You are sitting on a large boulder looking out to sea."

Rebecca knew the one; she'd been quite taken aback by the artist's suggestion that she remove her shoes and allow her bare feet to poke out beneath her skirt. It wasn't really improper, but it had seemed that way at the time. "Last summer," she said, her voice wistful. "I've lived in St. Ives my entire life. I don't think I fully appreciated how beautiful it is until I left. I had no idea, for instance, that the sea wasn't that brilliant blue everywhere. The sea here is so dark. Forbidding. But in St. Ives, the color is warm and beautiful."

She went on to tell him about her village, the colorful houses, the steep cobbled streets, the scent of bait fish, and the beach with its soft sand. He listened, asking infrequent questions, and just let her talk until she was there, could picture herself on a summer's day, a soft breeze bringing in gentle waves, the seagulls floating above her. At one point, she excused herself to gather a blanket around her and sit on the floor. He must have followed suit, for the sound of his voice seemed to be at the same level. She leaned against the wood and imagined him doing the same, heads separated only by an inch of mahogany.

"We should go there some day," she said finally. "So you could see for yourself."

That remark was met by silence. "You are settling in?"

"Ah, the change of subject." The soft sound of his chuckle made its way through the door. "I'll allow it this time. Yes, I am settling in nicely."

"And you..." He cleared his throat. "...are not suffering any ill effects from last night?"

"No, Your Grace." Something about his tone touched her, his real concern, his hesitation.

"I believe I requested that you call me Oliver."

Rebecca grinned. "No, Oliver."

"Good night, Rebecca."

"Good night, Oliver."

Oliver knew the moment his duchess retired for the evening the next night for he could hear the murmuring of voices—hers and her maid's—and then her door close as her maid left. His nerves were a bit frayed for he'd been thinking of her all day, remembering her smooth skin, her female scent, her heat. Her laugh.

Waiting to touch her again was far more difficult than he would have thought. His body screamed for him to walk through the connecting door, to touch her, sink into her, find the blessed relief from the agony of his desire. It had not been this way with the others. Yes, he'd needed to find release but he'd found the entire process of having Winters supply him with a woman humiliating and found other ways to slake his lust that, while not as satisfying, worked to keep him from going completely mad.

And now he had Rebecca. Who had cried out when she came, who had turned soft and drowsy and had touched him as if she wanted to, not because her profession demanded it.

He let out a long, shuddering breath as he stared at the door knob. Thinking about her beneath him would only leave him painfully hard, so he forced his thoughts away from visions of her naked body. Before that night, he'd judged a week was a considerate amount of time for her to heal and become used to him. That was, he realized now, entirely unacceptable. He'd never make it. Tomorrow, he would make love to her again.

"Rebecca?"

He heard the rustling of sheets, then the sound of her hurrying to the door, and he couldn't help but smile. His wife was just a few feet away. *His wife.*

"Yes, Your Grace?"

"How was your day?"

"Lonely. I'd like to have spent it with my husband."

He shook his head, smiling. "Perhaps one day."

He heard her sigh, then a rustling sound as he realized she had sat down on the floor, readying herself for a nice long chat, so he followed suit. "Tell me about your childhood," she said. "It's only fair as I told you about mine."

"Very well, although it's not a pretty story. My mother left a month after I was born and died five years later in Italy in her lover's villa, which was destroyed in an earth quake. My father died when I was six. We were at the breakfast table."

That should suffice, he thought, and waited for her to respond.

"You're not much of a story teller, are you?" she asked, a smile in her voice. "What was your father like? I saw a portrait of him in the gallery and he was a handsome man. Devilishly handsome."

Oliver closed his eyes, trying to picture the flesh and blood man who had been such an influence on his boyhood. "He was. My father was a heroic figure to me. My nanny was appalled that he allowed me to eat with him, but he insisted we be together for every meal. When he died, I was relegated to the nursery, a change I was not happy with. We went to London once, to see a physician to find a cure for my affliction. I remember little of that visit, but I do recall how fascinating the buildings were. The smells and people. It seemed impossible to me that so many people could exist in one place."

"Oliver?"

"Yes?"

"I'm resting my head against the door. Here." He heard two light taps. "You should do the same."

He found himself oddly moved by her suggestion and moved closer so that his head rested precisely where hers did.

"I was terribly angry with my father because of what happened," Rebecca said softly "When I left, I could hardly look at him and I know it broke his heart. I think I shall write him a letter to tell him all is forgiven."

"A good idea. I am forever grateful that my father and I were having a pleasant morning the day he died. We were laughing about something Winters had done. What was it... Ah, Mr. Winters likes things just so, and his face turned nearly purple when a footman served him buttered toast. He loathes butter, if you can imagine. My father took one look at the toast and one look at Winters' face and burst out laughing." He frowned, recalling how angry Winters had been, how even when his father had been stricken, he'd seemed unconcèrned. At least initially. "Moments later, he just dropped to the floor and was dead."

"That is a terrible thing for a child to see."

"It was." It was. Even as a lad he had recognized that his life would change irrevocably and that change had been immediate. Mr. Winters had been appointed his guardian, a job the man took on with surprising dedication. Even now, the older man took it upon himself to shield Oliver from anything or anyone who might harm him. He'd let it happen, to his great shame, relinquishing all decisions, all management of staff. Marrying Rebecca had been his most important decision, and even that he'd relegated to Mr. Winters.

It had not happened in one day or one year, this realization that he was monstrous to others, something to fear. He knew not how it had all started, how the rumors about him were spawned—devil's child, ghost, demon—but he'd learned at a young age to do anything to avoid being ridiculed. If that meant living his life within the walls of Horncliffe, never venturing beyond the boundaries of the estate, never seeing the world he'd longed to explore, then so be it. No visitors called on him, no invitations were issued, and he told himself he was glad of it.

How could he risk the small joy of talking with his wife by allowing her to see him?

"Are you still there, Your Grace?"

"Lost in thought," he said.

"You must have been very lonely to marry someone you'd never met."

Desperately so. "I require an heir," he said instead.

This time, she was silent for a long stretch. Finally, she spoke. "If that's all you require, then why are you speaking to me at all?"

"You want me to admit that I am some pathetic creature who was wasting away from loneliness when that is hardly the case," he said, bristling a bit, even though it was mostly true.

To his surprise, he heard her softly laugh. "I see it is quite easy to stir your ire. I shall enjoy myself immensely."

"Are you saying that you enjoy making me angry?"

"A bit. It is my natural tendency when confronted with an aristocratic boor," she said lightly, as if she hadn't just insulted him.

"Was I acting boorish?"

"You were."

"Shall I apologize?"

"Would that not be like the sky apologizing for being blue?"

He stared at the door in astonishment, as if he could see her. Then he started laughing, an odd rusty sound he had not heard in a long time. It sounded rather like croaking.

"Are you quite all right?" He could hear the smile in her voice.

"That was a laugh. Apparently I have not done enough of it lately for my throat wasn't sure how to respond."

She laughed then, a musical, easy sound that told him she laughed often.

They talked long into the night, talked until he could hear Rebecca yawning every few minutes. He'd never talked and laughed so much in his entire life and he told her so just before bidding her a good night.

"Good night," she said. "And Oliver, I think you and I shall get along famously."

Rebecca spent another long, lonely day seeing only Darlene and the occasional servant moving silently through the house. There was none of the usual chatter she'd become used to at her home and the homes of her friends. The silence came from more than a stringent sense of propriety, she thought. It was more oppressive. Dark. She ate breakfast and luncheon in the breakfast room, alone but for two footmen who stood at attention throughout the entire meal unless they were serving her. Her single attempt to make conversation with the one serving her was met with a startled expression and silence. Rebecca couldn't help but wonder if her husband, who spent so much time alone, was even aware of the general gloom that shrouded the place.

She'd explored most of the house, getting lost more than a few times before making her way back to the main section of the mansion. Again, as she was walking by the gallery, she thought she heard a woman singing or crying, but it was only a whisper of sound that gave her chills. Could the place be haunted? She stood outside the dark room, straining to hear something, but whatever she'd heard—if she'd heard anything at all—was now gone. After a brief meeting with the housekeeper, Mrs. Cutter, a severe-looking woman in her fifties whom she'd seen only once, Rebecca resigned herself to going back to her rooms for the evening. She had no intention of eating alone with Mr. Winters in the cavernous and dark dining hall. Just thinking of the man made her stomach hurt.

Turning a corner, she saw ahead of her Mr. Winters himself and one of the maids. Immediately, Rebecca sensed something was wrong, for the maid's head was down, her body stiff, and Mr. Winters appeared to be chastising her about something. While she watched, Mr. Winters pinched the girl hard enough to make her let out a sound, and Rebecca's blood turned hot.

"What is wrong, Mr. Winters?" she asked, finding small satisfaction when Mr. Winters whirled around in surprise before quickly composing himself.

"I ask very little of the staff, Your Grace, and when one member takes it upon herself to disregard my instructions, I find it unpleasant."

"What terrible thing did Sally do?" The girl lifted her head, clearly surprised that Rebecca recalled her name. Though Rebecca had not been formally introduced to the staff, she'd made a point of learning the names of those she saw or interacted with. Sally was the little maid who cleaned out her hearth.

Mr. Winters pulled out a piece of wood from his inside jacket pocket, and Rebecca would swear Sally flinched. It was a ruler. "Vases are to be six inches from the edge. Not four. Not seven. One vase is to be on the left, one precisely in the middle, and one on the right. Symmetry is pleasing to the eye, Your Grace."

Rebecca could feel her cheeks heating. She had rearranged the vases herself, making a small arrangement on the side table in her boredom. Symmetry, obviously, had not been pleasing to her. She hadn't thought such a small change would bother anyone and she certainly would never have touched the vases if she'd known one of the staff would be punished.

"I'm afraid I rearranged the vases to my liking," Rebecca said, trying to remove any sense of apology from her tone.

Mr. Winters's expression tightened subtly. "I suppose that is to be expected," he said enigmatically. "In a household such as this—" He slapped the ruler onto the table, making Rebecca and the maid jump, and placed the vase six inches from the edge. "—symmetry is preferred."

Sally stared wide-eyed, looking from one to the other, as still as a deer in the forest confronted by a hunter. Rebecca forced a smile, though her heart beat rapidly and her skin felt hot. "This is my household, Mr. Winters. And while I would never question your sense of decoration, for everyone has their own opinions, I prefer the arrangement I made." She couldn't help but wonder if she sounded like a duchess or a frightened girl.

Mr. Winters froze, his hand about to place the second vase down precisely in the center and six inches from the edge. He turned his head slightly, just enough so that he was not in full profile. "You are dismissed, miss," he said with lethal softness. Sally darted her a frightened look, then hurried away.

When Sally was gone, Mr. Winters faced her fully and Rebecca had to fight the urge to follow the maid. Instead, she schooled her features and prayed she didn't look as frightened as she felt. He stared at her a long moment with hooded eyes, long enough that Rebecca nearly lost her composure. It would have been far easier to let the man have his way, but something inside her, that stubborn part that loathed backing down whether she was right or not, kept her in place.

"You really are a fool," he said with contempt. "His Grace does not like change. He cannot tolerate it. If you think you are going to come into this house and exert your influence, you are mistaken. The damage you can do here is insurmountable and I will not allow you to destroy his world. Have a care, little girl."

Rebecca had never hated another person in her life, but she found she was beginning to hate this man. "If I see you abusing another servant, I will make certain you have no contact and no influence over the staff. The staff is the purview of the butler and housekeeper. Not some unwanted distant relation." His mouth tightened and Rebecca felt a surge of triumph. "His Grace trusts you, yes, but do not underestimate me, sir. I am not easily frightened nor easily discouraged." The impact of her words was perhaps slightly diminished by the trembling in her voice and Rebecca prayed Winters thought it was anger and not terror causing it.

With that, Mr. Winters placed the final vase six inches from the farthest edge, bowed and left without saying another word. When he was gone, Rebecca sagged and fought the terrible urge to weep. Something about his emotionless, dead stare frightened her to her core.

This could not continue. Surely Oliver should have some inkling of what a tyrant Mr. Winters was, and if he did not, she would happily enlighten him. A bit of anger toward the duke flared, for it was unfair that she'd had to face Mr. Winters on her own. When they spoke this evening, she planned to tell him he needed to help her deal with Winters.

By the time she reached her rooms, Rebecca's nerves had settled down, but when she opened her door, they immediately went all a-jumble. Her room was dark, the curtains pulled, and she could see the barest shadow of a man standing by her bed.

Chapter 6

"Who is there?"

Rebecca hadn't realized just how rattled she was from her encounter with Mr. Winters until she spoke. Her voice trembled and she sounded on the verge of tears.

"I am sorry, I didn't mean to frighten you." Oliver. The relief she felt made her sag, and she closed her door. Had she truly thought Mr. Winters had somehow made it to her room before she had simply to terrorize her?

"I thought… It is not important."

She sensed rather than saw him step toward her. "What happened? Something has upset you."

All the stories, all the fear and doubt she felt, seemed to disappear. This man was not cruel or a monster. She could hear the real concern in his voice, which made all the tall tales she'd heard even more ridiculous.

"I know Mr. Winters is dear to you, but I find him loathsome." To her horror, she felt hot tears press against her eyes. She disliked feeling such animosity toward another and it was not in her nature to complain, but it was all too much for her to take.

"What has he done?" His voice was nearer still, low and somehow soothing. In the last two nights, they had become friends of sorts, and Rebecca felt the urge to fall into his arms for comfort. She nearly laughed, thinking about how her imagination had run wild after her visit to the garden. The gardener had frightened her more than she'd realized. Now, though, Oliver was acting as a husband should, and that thought made her want to cry even more for some reason.

"It's more of what he says than anything. Or perhaps the way he says it. He holds me in contempt. He believes I am unworthy of you."

A long silence, as if he were carefully considering each word. "He has said that?"

Rebecca thought back to the carriage ride, to Mr. Winters staring at her with his cold, brown eyes. *Your very existence repulses me.* He'd said nothing directly insulting to her since, so Rebecca decided not to tattle like a child. "Not in so many words. He called me a fool for thinking I could exert change in this household."

"Did he? I fear he will be proven wrong," Oliver said, and Rebecca smiled, feeling as if she had a bit of a champion in her husband.

"I found him chastising a maid about the position of some vases on a table. He pinched her hard enough for the girl to let out a yelp." Rebecca sighed. "It seems like such a small thing now. He has a way of looking at a person that makes one feel small."

Two large, warm hands touched her shoulders, making Rebecca stiffen slightly. He dropped his hands immediately. "No, it's all right," she said. "I was startled."

"I should not have been waiting for you. I've upset you."

"No. But I do wish you would enter a room like a normal person by knocking."

"I do not need to knock to gain entrance," he said, sounding rather ducal. "But I also do not wish to frighten you." He sighed. "I shall knock next time."

Rebecca smiled. "It would be nice of you."

He chuckled, as if the idea of his being nice amused him. "If I am to be perfectly honest, I was growing impatient." He put his hands on her shoulders, this time drawing her close to him. "You have bedeviled me, duchess. I have thought of nothing else all day but you." She felt his lips on her cheek and she wondered if he'd missed his intended target. But no, he kissed her jaw, her neck, her chin, making her giggle.

"Have you forgotten where my lips are?"

"I am searching, madam." He kissed the corner of her mouth, then her cheek, and Rebecca laughed.

"Here," she said, putting her hands on either side of his face and slowly drawing him to her mouth. She kissed him, a brief, almost chaste kiss, but he would have none of that. With a low groan, he pressed his lips against hers, then licked at the seam of her mouth, silently requesting entrance.

How odd it was that just three days ago, she had been terrified. But now, she welcomed his kiss, relished it.

"Can I tell you something?" he asked, feathering kisses along her jaw. "You must promise not to laugh."

"I cannot make such a promise, sir. What if what you tell me is amusing?"

"You must not," he said, this time his tone almost angry.

Rebecca stilled. "Then I will not."

He sighed, then kissed her again. "You are the first woman I have ever kissed."

"But…"

"But?"

"But you are rather good at it, sir. I may not have a vast amount of experience, but I can tell that you seem to be well-versed."

He chuckled. "I believe I need practice, in spite of your praise. I find I rather enjoy the activity. Among other things."

And so he kissed her, as if they had all night—which they did—taking his time, exploring, soft and hard and drugging. After a time, when Rebecca's knees were weak and her entire body felt as if it were burning, he stopped, his breath harsh. His hands had not wandered, he had not pressed himself against her, but rather made love to her mouth with his. Just those kisses had Rebecca wanting to crawl out of her skin—or at least her clothes—and beg him to kiss her everywhere.

"Are you still tender from our first night?"

"No. At least, I don't think so."

"Then please do undress. I'm about mad from wanting you and unless you want a madman in your bedroom, we should make haste."

Rebecca laughed until a rather disturbing thought occurred to her. That morning, Darlene had pulled a dress from her wardrobe that required no assistance to put on. Or off. That had not been the case the two days prior. The fire had not been stoked and allowed to die. She realized, with burning embarrassment, that the servants were aware her husband would be visiting her this night long before she was.

"Your Grace, did you instruct my maid which dress to pull out this morning?"

"I have little direct interaction with the servants," he said, but Rebecca thought she detected a bit of caution in his tone, as if he knew she was displeased. And, she noted, he did not directly answer her question.

"Who would have told Darlene to pick out a dress that I could easily remove by myself? Who would have told the footman not to keep my fire lit?"

"You are angry."

"Not yet." He was silent. "Mr. Winters then."

"Mr. Winters deals with the servants, yes."

"Everyone in this household except for me knew you would be coming to my room this night. Is that what you are saying?"

"You make it sound nefarious when I was simply giving instructions so that I might spend time with my wife," he said, and Rebecca didn't miss his defensive tone.

"Do you not think it odd that I am the last to know when you will be in my bed? Why did you not simply tell me and let me plan accordingly?"

"I—"

"Do you have any idea how embarrassing this is? Mr. Winters knew you would be sharing my bed this evening. God. Mr. Winters!"

"You need to get over this enmity toward Mr. Winters."

Rebecca gasped. "And you need to leave, sir."

"You wish me to leave?" he asked, sounding incredulous. "I am your husband. I have thought of nothing else this day but taking you to bed and I planned accordingly. Your dislike of Mr. Winters is causing you to act irrationally."

Anger, hot and swift, made her blood boil. "This has nothing to do with Mr. Winters and everything to do with my insufferable, inconsiderate, and scheming husband." She spun around and stepped away from him, wrapping her arms around herself. It was cold and she had no fire and she wished her husband to perdition.

"So I shall leave?"

"Yes. Please do."

She could sense him standing there, no doubt fuming at the turn of events. "Very well, Your Grace."

Rebecca didn't let the tears come until she heard the soft click of the adjoining door.

Of all the... How dare she refuse him? Who cared what the servants knew? What did she suppose they thought was going on between them at night? He ached for her, he was still hard, still mad from needing her, but he found himself alone in his room with an angry wife on the other side of a closed door. She was being irrational. And cruel. Yes, it was cruel to leave him in such a state when he had been all that was kind to her. He could have demanded his husbandly rights every day had he wished. But no, he had been considerate of her feelings. And this was his reward? To be rejected so blatantly?

He paced in his room, silently railing against his wife, before leaving, slamming the door with satisfying force and heading directly to Mr. Winters' room. Winters answered the knock at his door almost immediately and was obviously dressed for bed. Oliver didn't care.

"A match, if you will," he said, then turned about and headed directly to the ballroom, where he donned his fencing garb. His eyesight was poor even when he did not have his mask on, and it was worse with it. Over the years, he'd mastered the art of predicting what his opponent would do. When he was younger, he'd had a fencing instructor who excelled at the sport. Mr. Winters was a challenging opponent, but had slowed down a bit in recent years. Ideally, Oliver would have liked to face an expert who would push him beyond his abilities. He wanted to sweat and make his muscles scream.

God, he still ached for her. He hadn't been lying when he'd told Rebecca making love to her was all he could think of that day. He'd worked in his studio for long hours, trying to stop himself from thinking of her, to stop his body from wanting her.

Before Winters entered the ballroom, he'd donned his uniform and practiced his thrusts on a hay-stuffed dummy that he practiced with when no one was available. "Bloody idiot," he said, thrusting his rapier into the dummy.

"I don't believe he can hear you," Mr. Winters said dryly from the door.

"Sod off, Winters."

"Shouldn't you be making sweet love with your wife, Your Grace?"

Oliver turned, swiping his sword so it produced a whistling sound as it cut through the air. "You should take care, Mr. Winters. I am in no mood for your wit."

With a beleaguered sigh, Winters went to the equipment and donned his fencing clothes. "You do have your tip on, I hope," he said, as if Oliver might actually skewer him.

"I do. En garde."

Winters was a worthy opponent for perhaps the first two minutes, then the older man began to visibly tire. He tried valiantly to defend against Oliver's onslaught, but it soon became apparent the match was one sided. Oliver scored point after point until Winters was spent, bent over, hands on knees, trying to catch his breath.

Instead of feeling sympathy for the older man, as he usually did, Oliver felt nothing but impatience—and was then disturbed by his thoughts. He'd never questioned Winters and yet just five days after Rebecca had entered his life, he was beginning to wonder whether Winters had been given too much power within Horncliffe's walls. Now that he could think with something other than his cock, he realized he *was* a cad and had quite possibly irreparably damaged his fragile friendship with his new wife.

Still catching his breath, Winters said, "Not quite as good as a swive, but it'll do for now, eh, Your Grace?" He chuckled, and Oliver looked at him with distaste.

"Do not speak so, Mr. Winters. I warn you, my hold on my temper is a fragile thing."

Winters looked up as if surprised by the harshness of his words. Then he smiled and shook his head. "I thought it would take longer than five days for her to set you against me. I have to give Her Grace credit."

"You know nothing of which you speak. No one has turned me against you, sir, but I am beginning to believe I have removed myself too far from the happenings in this house. It is high time I began to act like the man my father hoped I would become."

Winters straightened slowly, his expression growing cold. "You bend so quickly," he said softly. "I am disappointed." He gave Oliver a thoughtful look. "Good evening, Your Grace."

At one time in his life, Oliver would have run after the man and apologized. His old friend was correct, however. Something had shifted in his life since Rebecca had come to Horncliffe. For the first time in his memory, he felt the weight of responsibility for another person. It occurred to him, with shocking awareness, that as duke he should have felt such weight long before now. The servants, his properties, his tenants—everyone tied to the Kendal title was his responsibility. Of course, he'd always known this on some level, but it had been so much easier to allow Mr. Winters, who seemed to manage everything so deftly, to carry on.

"It is high time I began to act like the man my father hoped I would become."

Those words, spoken aloud, pierced him. What would his father think of him now, a man who lived in fear, who hid away each day and created a world of fantasy? Still, the thought of going out in the world, of suffering the stares, the whispers. How could he?

"Courage," he whispered. It all came down to that, didn't it? He walked to a mirror at the end of the room and stared at himself for a long moment. He did not look into mirrors often for it was difficult to view his reflection without wanting to bash his head against the glass. This time, he looked, long and hard, until his throat ached and his eyes burned. Any courage he had leeched from his body, leaving him desolate. "Stupid fool." He watched his mouth move as he spoke and imagined someone else had uttered those words. That thing in the mirror could not be him, yet it was. Courage.

I cannot.

Defeated, Oliver walked back to his room and, once there, disrobed and cleaned the sweat from his body. He ought to send his wife back home. How could he have sentenced a beauty such as she to live a life of solitude and isolation? But the thought of being alone again…

He walked to the door and pressed his forehead against the cool wood. "Rebecca?"

During the long silence that followed, he could hardly breathe.

"Yes, Your Grace?"

"Oliver."

He heard her sigh. "What do you want?"

"To apologize. I'm not entirely sure what I did wrong. I wanted to make love to my wife and I planned accordingly. All day, you were all I could think of. Please, Rebecca. Forgive me. I've never been a husband before and apparently I'm doing a terrible job of it."

"As much as I hate to admit this, I was also in the wrong. I allowed my emotions and my animosity toward Mr. Winters to influence my judgement. But I would like to ask something of you."

"Ask."

"From now on, Oliver, talk to me. Please, do not involve anyone else in our marriage. If you want to be with me, tell me." A small pause. "Did you think I would deny you?"

"Perhaps. Or perhaps I am so unused to thinking of someone else's feelings, I acted rashly and selfishly. You call me Your Grace when you're angry."

Rebecca laughed softly. "I was angry, yes."

"I do realize this is not what you expected in a marriage. I do know that much."

"It hasn't been so terrible. I am tired this evening, but perhaps tomorrow you will join me?"

He closed his eyes and smiled. "I should like that. Good night, then."

"Good night."

On the sixth morning, the sun shined brightly, and Rebecca, flinging open her window and feeling only the slightest chill, knew that it was warm enough to venture outside. Feeling her spirits buoyed, she dressed, foregoing the assistance of her maid. She chose her dress knowing her husband would be the one taking it off that evening, and a sharp thrill of anticipation filled her, surprising her. Over the past nights, she and her husband had become friends of sorts, and she did wish for them to get on.

Love was something she hadn't considered yet, but the new day gave her hope that her strange marriage could somehow be happy.

As she was about to open the main door to walk outside, a man burst into the grand entry, clearly upset. From his dress, he was a working man, and from his expression, he was close to weeping.

"Sir, what is wrong?"

He looked up, startled. "Nothing, miss."

Rebecca smiled. "I am the new duchess here."

The man stopped as if he'd walked into a wall, then snatched the cap from his head, revealing a thick head of curly, salt-and-pepper hair. He gave an awkward bow. "Sorry, Yer Grace." He stared at her a long moment. "You're not jesting?"

Laughing, she said, "I fear not. Now, what has you so upset, sir?"

"You married His Grace?"

Was the man daft? "Yes, mister…"

"Bentley." He seemed distracted, and looked behind him as if making certain no one was listening. "We've been tenants to Kendal for generations. My father raised sheep here and his father before him. We've never missed rent. Not once. But this year we lost more than half our herd. I could only pay half rent and Mr. Winters is evicting us. Just like that. I'm sorry, Yer Grace, but it isn't right. It isn't. What am I to tell my wife? Where are we to go?" The man's eyes were suspiciously wet. To drive such a man almost to tears was unconscionable, and Rebecca would have none of it.

"How many sheep were affected, sir?"

"As I said, half the herd. Two hundred fifty."

That was a terrible blow, but if it was negligence that caused the sheep's death, Rebecca knew there was little she could do. "And how did they die, sir?"

"Bluetongue, it was. You know of it?"

Bluetongue was as terrible disease and could wipe out an entire herd. "I do. And you could not have prevented the disease, nor stopped its progress. That you only lost half your herd is an indication that you effectively separated those infected from the healthy sheep." Mr. Bentley looked at her with the oddest expression. Rebecca supposed not too many duchesses had ever heard of bluetongue, never mind understood its implications. But she had grown up in a small village where news of such catastrophes spread quickly; everyone knew the dire consequences of a herd infected with the disease.

"You are not to worry, Mr. Bentley. You are not evicted from your farm and you will pay your back rent when you are able and not before."

"But Mr. Winters—"

"Mr. Winters is overruled," Rebecca said firmly. "I will make certain he is aware of my decision. And I'll make certain His Grace is informed as well."

"You're an angel, you are," Mr. Bentley said, his eyes glittering once again. "Thank you, Yer Grace."

He bowed a few times as he made his way to the door, and the moment it closed, she heard Mr. Winters behind her. "You know nothing of estate matters. The Bentleys will be removed from their farm immediately. If you give their kind leniency, they will take advantage of your kindness."

Rebecca turned slowly around, swallowing when she saw how very angry Mr. Winters was but determined not to show how he unnerved her. "It is not kindness to understand that Mr. Bentley had absolutely no control over the loss of his sheep. Had it been the result of neglect or even ignorance, I would not have been as lenient. Would you throw a family from their home if they lost all in a flood or another act of God?"

"Firstly," he said, stepping toward her, "it is not *their* home, it is the duke's. Secondly, yes, I would. If rent is not paid, the tenant loses the privilege of living in a home. We are not a charity. Your Grace."

Though her heart beat rapidly, from a mixture of anger and fear, Rebecca would not be dissuaded. "You are not in charge here, Mr. Winters. His Grace is."

Then he smiled and gave her a mocking bow. "In that case, Your Grace, my decision stands. His Grace gives me final say in all estate matters and will continue to do so. His mind is incapable of such complex thought."

Rebecca furrowed her brow. Nothing in her interactions with her husband had led her to believe Oliver was a simpleton. "My mind, sir, is completely capable of such complex thought and you will abide by my decision."

The man had the audacity to laugh at her. "I think not. Good day, Your Grace."

I think not? She would see about that. Surely, Oliver would agree with her. How could he possibly allow a family to be evicted for such an unavoidable infraction? He wouldn't, at least not after she convinced him. And there was no better time than the present, when her ire was piqued and her resolve strong. With determined steps, she headed toward the tower.

Oliver moved the candle farther away from where he worked so it would not glare so strongly in his eyes. His London townhouse was nearly complete. All he needed to do was hang the drapery and lay down the rug when they arrived from the village, where a seamstress had been commissioned to make them. Leaning forward, he examined each room, each bit of furniture, to make certain everything was as it should be. He frowned at one cane-backed chair, whose angles seemed a bit off. Reaching in, he picked it up to take a closer look, turning it in his hand to determine what it was that was off about the piece.

It was just his imagination. He placed the chair back in its place and was reaching for the architectural journal, which held the drawing for his next project, when the door to the tower room opened. His door never opened, at least not without someone knocking and waiting for him to bid entry.

So startled was he, he stood and backed up to the wall, the stool he'd been sitting on falling noisily to the planked floor. The door to the tower was not visible from his work table, and he stood still, staring toward it, frozen. "Who is there?"

"Rebecca." And his wife walked in, all color and brightness, and a nightmare come to visit him. He pressed himself against the wall and looked away from her, insanely wondering if he should hide or try to run past her. His heart beat wildly in his chest, and the odd thought, that this must be how a rabbit felt right before a hawk swept down, came to him. What the hell was she doing here and why had no one stopped her? His entire body heated with humiliation, with the horror that she should see him before he was ready. It was too late, she was walking toward him silently, studying him, and he simply wanted to die.

"Oliver?"

God, she was so close. Close enough to see him even in the dim light of the candle. He wanted to scream out his anguish. He wasn't ready yet. Not yet. He'd wanted her to have some sort of affection for him before... this. And then she was next to him, and he could see her from the corner of his eye while he stared, desperately, at the tiny house. Would that he could disappear inside it. His jaw was clenched so tightly, it ached. He could hardly breathe as she studied him like some oddity she'd never seen.

"That's all?" she whispered.

He darted a quick look at her, then immediately looked away, not wanting to see what was in her eyes.

"Oliver. Oliver, look at me," she said softly, then reached up and cupped his cheek, exerting a small pressure to force him to look at her. Pity. Worse than fear. He could not look at her. God, why, *why* had she come up to the tower?

"Oliver, please."

Feeling as if he was sentencing himself to a lifetime of desolation, he did look, defiant. Angry.

"Your eyes," she said, gazing at him as if he weren't monstrous. "They're beautiful." She reached for the candle and held it up, forcing him to pull his head back and squint against the brightness. "I apologize; I forgot you are sensitive to the light."

"Please leave."

"Why ever for?" she asked, placing the candle back on the table. "I cannot tell you how relieved I am, not that I put too much stock in appearances. Still, I was a bit worried, I must confess, after everyone in this house acted as if I'd married the devil himself. I don't understand the fuss, really. What is *wrong* with everyone in his house? I think they're all mad." Her voice was perfectly calm, as if she were completely unfazed by his appearance. It made no sense.

"What are you talking about?"

"It's only that you are an albino. I confess, my imagination came up with something much more frightful."

His brows drew together. "A what?"

She tilted her head at him, studying him, her lovely face—and it was as lovely as he'd imagined—holding only curiosity, not horror, not repulsion. "Don't you know? Has no one ever explained to you your condition?"

"My condition?" he repeated stupidly.

"You have albinism. A fisherman in Penzance had the same condition. He would come to St. Ives on market day…" Her voice trailed off.

"Others?"

"It's not terribly common, no. But certainly nothing to fear. I suppose some people are not kind. That is usually the case when one is different. When I was a girl, I was made fun of terribly because of my hair. It was far brighter when I was young. I do realize it's not the same, but still, it is as if everyone has gone quite mad."

Oliver let out a deep, shuddering breath. He could hardly believe what she was saying. Her reaction, her words, were so far from what he had dreaded, it made no sense. "Others are like me?"

She laughed, not unkindly. "Yes. It's not so uncommon in nature. Our neighbor had an albino cow. Not that I am comparing you to a cow. I'm just pointing out that the condition is far more common than you were apparently led to believe."

All this time, all these years of feeling like a freak, a monster… He wasn't certain whether he wanted to scream out in anguish or joy. "Then why…" Why, indeed. Why had everyone in his life feared him? Why did the servants not look at him? Why did the villagers run inside and make the sign of the cross when he passed? *Why had his own mother left him?*

"You are wrong. You are simply being kind, though I cannot imagine what your motive could be."

She dropped her hand and he fought the urge to bring it back. "You think I am lying to spare your feelings?"

"Yes," he said harshly. Then, "No." He clutched his thick hair in frustration.

"I adore your hair," she said, ignoring his confusion and putting her hand atop his head, grazing his hand as it clutched his hair. "It's quite lovely. So white. And your brows, too. And lashes. Your lashes are spectacular. You're rather remarkable, Oliver."

Rebecca stepped back to get a better look at her husband, who still stood pressed against the wall, though some of the tension had left his body. He looked at her with his beautiful lavender eyes; she had never seen another person with such eyes. Other than his eyes and his lips, he was white, as if dipped in powder. The result was striking and not at all unattractive. That everyone in this household treated him as if he were some oddity, some horrid creature that was not quite human, was unforgivable.

"Why are you treated so badly in this house? Surely the servants' superstition comes from someone." She paused, trying to understand why, how it could have come to pass that Oliver was treated like some monster. And then she realized there could only be one person who could instill such fear into the servants. Only one. "Mr. Winters—"

"No. Mr. Winters has done nothing but protect me since the day my father died."

Rebecca wanted to argue but thought better of it. She would get nowhere by criticizing a man Oliver clearly loved. She had her own opinion of the man and one day hoped to open her husband's eyes to Winters' true nature, but now was not the time. Still, she wished to throttle anyone who had made this man think so ill of himself that he locked himself away from prying eyes.

"Very well. But someone has poisoned these people's minds. And it's terrible. There is nothing wrong with you, Oliver."

He looked down at his hand, so pale in the dim light, and frowned. "Why did you come up here?" he said, his tone detached.

"Oh. I was quite vexed with you and I came up here to give you a piece of my mind."

"I made you angry? I haven't even spoken to you since…"

Rebecca felt her cheeks blush. "I was angry because Mr. Winters was attempting to evict one of your tenants and I strenuously disagreed. He refused to listen to me, saying that you leave all matters pertaining to the estate up to him. But—"

"He is correct. I have little involvement in the estate's operations. And from what I can tell, he's done an excellent job."

"Do you know Mr. Bentley?"

"Is he the tenant you are referring to?"

Rebecca could feel her temper rising again and took a calming breath. "Yes, he is. He lost his herd to disease through no fault of his own and was only able to pay half his rent. That he could pay even that much is a testament to the man's skill at raising sheep. His family has been on the same farm for three generations, Oliver. He has a wife and several children. Babies." This last was manufactured, but it might be true. "It is unconscionable to evict them. Surely you are not that sort of man."

His face tightened. "I am not a man at all to them," he said dismissively.

"Only because you allow it." She'd raised her voice, then inwardly chastised herself when he visibly flinched. How many times had her mother told her that shouting didn't make people hear your words better; it did the opposite. "Oliver," she said calmly, walking to him and placing a hand on either side of his face. "Evicting the family is wrong and only you can stop it." She leaned toward him and kissed him, shamelessly using her wiles to get her way.

"Are you trying to manipulate me with a kiss?" he asked sardonically. And Mr. Winters had implied he was simple.

"Of course I am. Is it working, do you think?"

He smiled, and it was a beautiful smile. Rebecca found herself fascinated by his lips, masculine and sculpted, but the loveliest shade of pink. She kissed him again, this time lingering, and only withdrawing when he brought his hands up and around her back. "Well?"

He laughed. "I knew you would bring me joy." The muscles in his jaw bunched, but Rebecca could tell he was not angry. "Mr. Winters does not like being thwarted."

"All the more reason to thwart him, then," she said on a laugh, then grew serious. "You are the duke, Oliver, not he."

"I've never felt such. Are you enchanting me, Rebecca?"

"I hope so." She looked at him again, and knew he felt uncomfortable under her scrutiny. "Have you no mirror? You are very handsome, Your Grace. How could you think otherwise?"

That compliment only produced another frown, and Rebecca kissed him again. "Do you still wish for me to visit your chamber this evening?" he asked, sounding hesitant, as if he feared she was repulsed by his appearance.

Her heart ached for him, but she would never allow him to see how it hurt her to know what had been done to him. She could be fierce but she would try never to show the pity she felt in her heart. "Yes, Oliver. And tonight, I shall have a fire if you agree."

He hesitated just a breath before he gave her another smile. "I agree."

Rebecca dropped her arms and gave the room where her husband spent so much time a better look. Like all the other rooms, it was made dark by the heavy, velvet drapes that covered each window, allowing only the barest of light into the room. But in that dim light, she saw another miniature house sitting on the table, surrounded by bits and pieces of wood, small pots of paint, and brushes. She'd been so distracted, she hadn't been aware of the strong smell of paint and turpentine.

Furrowing her brow, she leaned in closer and held the candle nearer. "This is like the ones in the library. By the way, you really should get better books. I couldn't find a single one to hold my interest."

"I have many more books in my rooms that may be more to your liking. You may borrow any that you like."

Rebecca smiled, her eyes still on the small house, marveling at the intricate detail. "Did you make this?"

"And the ones in the library. It is what I do with my time."

"It's marvelous. You're a true craftsman. An artist."

"Thank you." He stood where she'd found him, still pressed against the wall, still rigid. What must he be thinking? She found out moments later.

"May I look at you? My eyesight is quite poor and I haven't really seen you in the light." Rebecca straightened and turned around. "Closer please." She was very nearly stepping on his toes, but he moved closer still, leaning his head until Rebecca thought he was simply vying for a kiss. But no, his gaze moved over her features, taking them in, one by one, until he straightened and smiled. "I thought you would be lovely," he said.

"And am I?"

He chuckled. "You exceed my expectations." He frowned suddenly. "I am sorry that I cannot possibly exceed yours."

Rebecca laughed—she simply could not help herself—and Oliver gave her a startled, almost hurt, look. "Oliver, you have far exceeded my expectations. Do you not realize that I had created a rather monstrous image in my head thanks to your proclivity for darkness and the ridiculous behavior of the servants. You are lovely, sir. A happy surprise."

"You are not patronizing me."

"No, I am not." She leaned forward and kissed his cheek. "The only thing you are missing is color." She tilted her head. "But your eyes are a lovely lavender, quite unlike anything I've ever seen before. You said they are quite sensitive to light?"

"I cannot bear the sunlight, and everything is a bit of a blur if it's any distance away. You're a bit blurry now, as a matter of fact."

"Have you ever thought of purchasing tinted spectacles? They would protect your eyes from the light and allow you to go outside."

"Tinted spectacles?"

"We can go to London and visit a jeweler who can manufacture some for you. Then you'll be able to see better and perhaps even go out into the sun."

He looked toward the draped window, squinting even against the small sliver of light that managed to find its way past the dark material. "The sun burns my skin. When I was a boy, my father took me fishing. He covered my eyes with some material that I could hardly see through but protected them from the light. But my cheeks became blistered by the sun and it hurt like the devil."

"Then we shall take precautions and limit the time you spend in the sun. Oh, Oliver, I should think it would be wonderful to get out and about."

"Rebecca…"

"Cooped up inside this house for years, I'd imagine you would like a respite. We can visit museums and the zoo. I've never been to the zoo and I would very much like to see the elephants. Perhaps we can visit—"

"Stop, please," he said harshly. "I cannot. I…" His breathing was uneven, his features taut.

"I'm sorry, Oliver. I only wish to help."

"I wasn't ready for you to see me." His voice was dull, his expression unreadable and the earlier magic of the moment was gone. "Please leave me. I have much to think on."

"Of course." She walked to the door and looked back. "I shall see you this evening?"

He'd been staring blindly at the floor, but at her words, lifted his head, his expression bleak. "You shall."

After she'd gone, Oliver resisted the urge to sweep his latest miniature off the work table. He'd done that once—he couldn't even remember what had made him so angry at the time—and had deeply regretted it. Righting his chair, he sat down, cautiously, as if doing so would cause him pain, and stared blindly at his little house. It was all too much to consider, but the one thing he could not push away was this: He was not a monster, according to his wife, and yet all his life he had been treated like one. She must be wrong and yet…

Others were like him, she'd said. She had a name for it. Albinism. Perhaps his condition was rare, but yet common enough to have a name assigned to it.

Instead of leaving the tower through the main door, Oliver proceeded to the narrow secret door toward the back of the room and followed the stairs down to the main level where the library was. He rarely ventured to the main level, particularly during the day. Why should he? But he remembered as a boy seeing book after book on scientific studies and animal husbandry. Surely he could find something about his condition in one of them.

Once in the library, he strode to the entrance and shouted to the nearest servant, "I am not to be disturbed," then slammed the door. For hours, he pored over books on husbandry and volumes on human pathology. Articles, yellowed and crumbling, were cast aside in frustration. Not a word could he find, and the pile of books and articles, pamphlets, and journals at his feet was growing. Perhaps three hours after he'd begun he heard a timid knock on the door and shouted for whoever it was to go away.

Was she lying? Making words up because she pitied him?

Then he took down a flimsy bound book with a promising title: *Lectures on Physiology, Zoology, and the Natural History of Man* by Sir William Lawrence. And there he found it in the index: Varieties of colour of man and their causes. Listed second, was the word: Albino. Page 243. Heart beating hard, he pulled the book close to his eyes and flipped the pages, past descriptions of animals and humans of various races. He stopped when he saw the word. A word that made him real.

That singular description of human beings called Albinos, possesses a skin of a peculiar reddish, or an unnatural white tint, with corresponding yellowish white or milk-white hair, and red or at least very light blue or grey eyes.

"My God," he whispered.

The hair on all parts of the body is unusually white, light yellow or flaxen appearance of the fair-haired (blondins Fr.) German variety : but it is compared to that of milk or cream, or of a white horse. The eyebrows, eyelashes, beard, the hair of other parts, and often a soft down covering the whole body, are of the same colour. The iris is of a pale rose colour, and the pupil intensely red : these parts, in short, are exactly similar to the corresponding ones in white rabbits and ferrets. The characters of the Albino arise...*

It went on, but his eyes were blurred by tears, and he dashed them away and kept reading, fascinated to learn about himself. Reading for any length of time was difficult, tiring to his eyes, but he squeezed them shut and continued on, his heart racing, his mind filled with more and more questions. Albinos had been seen in nearly every continent, every country. Including England. Yes, he was unusual, just as Rebecca had said. But enough people existed in this world like him so that he was not alone. *Others.* That word, that one word, brought indescribable joy.

"Sir?" Mr. Starke called to him from the other side of the door. Oliver had little doubt his unusual trip to the first floor and to the library, of all places, had stirred some curiosity among the staff. He looked around and was a bit surprised at the extent of the mess he'd created while looking for answers. Books lay on the floor, the reading table, stuffed haphazardly back onto shelves.

"Yes, Mr. Starke, please enter."

The old butler entered, his eyes cast downward, and Oliver felt that old irritation mixed with humiliation.

"I am albino," Oliver said. "I am not a ghost or a demon. I am a common man with a condition."

"Yes, Your Grace."

"You knew?"

"Oh, no, Your Grace."

Still, he stared at the carpet, his cheeks ruddy. "Why do you not look at me?" he asked quietly.

Starke lifted his head, but his eyes were trained above Oliver, at the wall. "We are forbidden to, Your Grace. And the curse—"

Oliver stood still for the count of three, letting those words—and their meaning—settle in. "By whom were you forbidden?" Though he knew the answer, dreaded the answer. Starke looked as if he might be ill. "By whom, Mr. Starke. Who sentenced me to this existence? Who?" This last was a shout.

"I did." Oliver snapped his head toward the door to see the blurry outline of Mr. Winters. "It was to protect you, Your Grace. The staff had been disrespectful. You were quite young and perhaps you do not recall, but they would stare at you. They already feared you and I simply took advantage. You were unaware of it because of your poor eyesight, but I saw the way they looked at you. I corrected it, as I do all things that offend me. Certainly, you can recognize how well this household now operates. Fear, Your Grace, is the ultimate motivator. Fear is why I know I can run my finger along any shelf in this room and be sure it will come back clean. Fear is why they are respectful. They are simple creatures who only understand one thing, and I have taken advantage of this."

"I don't want them to fear me. I—"

"If I may, Your Grace, you know little of the day-to-day operations of running a great house. Please leave this to me."

"I will not be made to feel like a monster in my own house," Oliver shouted, and saw Mr. Starke back up a pace, which only enraged him more.

"You are becoming overwrought, Your Grace," Winters said with maddening calm.

Two breaths. Three, and he regained control of his emotions. Oliver took up the book he'd been reading. "Look, Mr. Winters." He jabbed a finger, humiliatingly desperate, to the page. "I am an albino. Others are like me. I am not alone. Rebecca said—"

"Ah, Her Grace is behind this hysteria? I should have known. I am certain she means well, but she knows little about you, about this house. Just this day, she attempted to countermand a decision. You must keep her in her place and not allow her to interfere."

"Why?" Oliver asked with deadly calm. "She is mistress of this house and I am master. As a matter of fact, Rebecca mentioned the dispute and I must say I agree with her position. Apparently that family has been on Kendal land for generations. Missing one month's rent certainly does not justify eviction." How foreign it felt to defy Winters—and how oddly freeing.

"If you give them an inch, they will take a mile. With all due respect, if you do this, Your Grace, every tenant on your lands will begin taking advantage of your soft heart. Horncliffe is one of the most profitable estates in all of England. It is this way because I have ruled with an iron hand. The tenants should be grateful, not come begging for hand-outs, not rewarded for failure. Simple creatures understand only one thing."

"Yes," Oliver said softly. "Fear."

Mr. Winters smiled. "Precisely, Your Grace."

"I should like to meet the staff."

Those were his first words when Rebecca entered her room. He sat by the window, velvet drapes pulled closed, the book from the library on his lap. He'd read every single mention of albinism in the tome, whether it was a discussion of humans or rats. He read and he thought, something he hadn't done in far too long. For years he'd accepted his fate, his life. No deviations from his routine, no conflict, no decisions. A full accounting of his life only filled him with self-loathing of a different sort from what he'd ever experienced, the deep, raw emotion of a man who realizes he's not a man at all. The fire was the only light in the room and he watched with the slightest bit of anxiety as his wife began lighting a few lamps.

"Your eyes can accept this amount of light?"

The question caught him off guard, and he found himself inordinately pleased by her consideration. "Yes. It is the sunlight that is most bothersome. Rather like shards of glass stabbing my eyes."

She wrinkled her nose. "Now, then, we can converse like husband and wife," she said, taking a seat in the chair adjacent to his. "Much better, don't you think?"

"Much."

"What is that book?"

"It's a scientific treatise on the human race. It contains quite a lot of information on albinism."

She beamed him a smile. "And did you find it interesting?"

He glanced down at the book, rubbing his thumb along the leather binding. "It is difficult for me to express how profoundly grateful I am to you. How profoundly you have altered my perception of myself, my life. How others have treated me. How I have allowed them to treat me."

"Is this why you wish to meet the servants?"

He looked up at her, frustrated by how blurred her image was, so he dragged his chair closer. "They fear me."

She dipped her head. "Yes, I know. I believe…someone has poisoned their minds."

"Mr. Winters."

Obviously surprised, she looked at him and tilted her head. "You know?"

"He admitted as much. As misguided as he was, he meant well. He thought to protect me from their stares, you see. I realize Winters is a difficult man to understand, but he is all that I have had of family since I was six years old."

"He is cruel."

"Only because he believes that is the only way to maintain control of the staff. And to protect me, though I do believe the need for protection has long past. I am not a child nor have I been one for quite some time. He does mean well. I must believe that."

Rebecca stood and stared into the fire but she was too far away for him to read her expression. "You agree with him, then?" she asked.

"No, I do not. And that is why I wish to meet the servants. I want to show them that I am simply a man."

"Not just a man," she said, a smile in her voice as she turned to him. "But a duke."

"Yes."

Rebecca returned to her chair, but this time sat on the very edge, so that her knees touched his. She could not know what such a simple thing as that, touching him without coercion, without repulsion, meant to him. "I'm sorry about earlier. I cannot know how difficult this is for you, how difficult your life has been. We shall do whatever you wish, whenever you wish, but I shall not give up on you, Oliver. I will not allow you to hide anymore. And I will not allow anyone to mistreat you or malign you."

He reached for her hands and pulled until she was on his lap and laughing. "Take down your hair."

She reached up, such a feminine thing to do, and undid the pins in her hair until it fell, thick and beautiful, down her back. Picking up a lock, he held it to his nose and breathed in. "Lavender?"

"Yes. I made good use of my wonderful tub today."

He held her close, breathing in the lavender, enjoying the sensation of having a feminine form on his lap, in his arms. "Should I let you go?" he whispered.

"I'm quite comfortable," she said.

"That is not what I meant."

Rebecca stiffened slightly, then relaxed. "If you should let me go, I would not go far, Your Grace." A pause. "Do you wish for me to go?"

"I do not. But I am fully aware that the manner in which we were married was hardly honorable."

She toyed with the collar of his banyan. "That is the second time you've told me I may go and the second time I have told you I wish to stay." Pulling back, she looked at him, but she was close enough so he could see the exquisite details of her face, her long lashes, her flushed cheeks, her expressive brows. "Do not ask again, Oliver, else I'll begin to believe you wish me gone."

"Never." He pulled her close and kissed her, letting out a moan when he tasted her. His heart felt too large for his chest at that moment. As he deepened the kiss, he came close to pulling away, simply to tell her that he loved her. Did he? He'd never loved another person other than his father, but what he was feeling at the moment was far, far different from anything he'd ever experienced. The love of a child for a parent was something else entirely. This was new and cruelly wonderful.

Love had never been his reason for wanting to marry. Sex, children, companionship, yes. The romantic notion of love was something that lived in poems and that he'd never experienced in his life. How was he to know he was in love if he had never seen it?

Sighing, she ended the kiss and rested her head on his shoulder, and that more than anything she'd done moved him. "Are you certain you are ready to meet the staff, Oliver? I don't want to push you. It is only that I am so happy you turned out to be so dashing." She laughed and he joined in.

"Did you truly think me some sort of monster?"

She trailed a finger beneath his banyan, touching bare skin and making him hiss in a breath. "I think I knew after I touched you that you were not a monster, though I could not imagine what all the fuss was about given your fine...physique."

"You think my physique fine?" he asked, his ego puffing up exponentially. Other than the lightness of his skin, he'd never given any thought to his appearance. He supposed he was fit, given his long hours of fencing, but hadn't realized his wife might find his muscles pleasant.

Laughing, Rebecca flattened her hand and explored his chest, making his cock stiffen painfully. "Rather fine, yes. Not a bit of extra flesh on you. So pale." This last was whispered, more with wonder than aversion.

"Would you like to see all of me?" he asked, cocking one brow, reveling in this feeling of being admired.

She ducked her head and at first he thought she was being shy, but then felt her tongue on his flesh. "I should like that."

Rebecca was shocking herself probably as much as she was shocking her new husband, but she knew her attention was pleasing him. Well, she could feel how she was pleasing him, given that she was sitting on his lap, but it was more than that. Surprising her with his strength, he lifted her easily off his lap and stood. Though she had lit three lamps, it was a large room and much of it was still cast in shadow, lending an air of hominess. She settled on the chair and looked at Oliver, who suddenly seemed uncertain.

"You cannot back down now, sir, not after that bold question."

He glanced at the fire, squinting his eyes a bit, as if he were looking at the brightness of the sun. "No one has ever seen me," he said softly.

"Then it is good that the first person who does should be your wife," Rebecca said lightly, though inside her nerves were a-jumble, not for her but for him.

In one swift movement, he untied the belt and dropped the robe and for a long moment, Rebecca could not speak. He was utterly perfect, a man made of the purest marble, muscles taut and sculpted, torso flat and ridged, his chest covered lightly with the whitest hair. He was beautiful. To think he'd been made to feel like a monster.

"Oh, Oliver," she said, her throat closing slightly with emotion. "You are spectacular." Her eyes dipped below his waist, and she smiled. That part of him look rather angry and red at the moment.

"Would you mind very much undressing for me? It's only fair. It's rather cold and I'd like to get to the good parts."

Rebecca giggled. "You hound," she said, then turned around so that he might undo her buttons.

"Good God, am I expected to do this?" he asked, running his hand down the length of her dress, his fingers following the line of buttons.

"Only if you want to get to the good parts."

With a quick growl, he began tackling the buttons. In short work, she was down to her chemise and he was on the bed, under the covers. "I don't usually go around unclothed in the autumn. Come here and warm me, Rebecca."

After unclipping her stockings from her garters and tossing them aside, Rebecca slid the garters down and ran to the bed, diving on top and under the covers he held open for her. "I don't think I shall ever get used to this cold," she said, snuggling into the warmth of her husband.

"I don't think I shall ever get used to your icy feet."

She tucked them up against his calves and he laughed. "But you're so warm. It doesn't get cold in St. Ives, not like this, but on the coldest winter nights, my mother would heat bricks by the fire, then wrap them up and put them in our beds so that when we got in, it was all cozy and warm. You shall be my heated bricks."

"I should like to be more than that," he said lazily, bringing one hand up to tease a nipple through the thin cloth of her chemise. "Why are you still dressed?" He dipped his head and licked her and Rebecca let out a small gasp of pleasure.

"I'm hardly dressed, Your Grace."

"Oliver."

Laughing lightly, she untied the ribbons on her chemise, sighing contentedly when he pushed the material down and took her nipple into his mouth, sucking lightly. It was fascinating to see how pale he was against her rosy skin. She sank her fingers into his soft white hair and pulled him closer, reveling in the feel of his tongue, his mouth, his teeth on her stiffened peak. "I could let you do that for hours," she whispered, and he chuckled, a low and wonderfully masculine sound.

A noise from within the room made Rebecca stiffen. "Oliver?"

"Hmmm."

"Did you hear that?"

He stopped immediately and looked down at her. "What?"

"I heard a noise. I swear it sounded as if it came from within the room."

"Wait here," Oliver said, in a commanding tone Rebecca had never heard before. He tore off the covers, strode to the adjoining door and disappeared into his room. Rebecca stayed in bed, sitting up, ears trained for any unusual sound, eyes wide, heart pounding. Whatever she had heard, obviously Oliver had an idea what it was.

And then an object leapt onto the bed and Rebecca screamed, the sort of scream one emits when confronted by some horrible wild beast. In this case, though, it was a black cat, one Rebecca had never seen before. Within seconds, Oliver was back in the room, running toward her until he spied the object of her fear.

"Satan," he said. "What the devil are you doing in here?"

"S-Satan?"

"My cat." He plucked the creature off the bed and tossed it into his own room before shutting the door.

"Yes, I could see it was a cat," Rebecca said dryly. "I haven't come across it before."

"He usually is in the tower with me, but he was not there today. I expect he was outside as the weather was a bit warmer today. A wonderful mouser, he is. Harmless fellow."

"Harmless." Rebecca let out shaky laugh. "Are you hiding any other beasts in this house, sir?"

"Only this one, and he is hungry." He looked down toward his manhood and Rebecca laughed.

"He is, is he?"

"Ravenous."

"We shall have to feed the poor fellow," Rebecca said, wrapping her hand around him, feeling him for the first time.

"I rather like that."

"I rather like that, too."

Chapter 7

Since his father's death, Oliver frequently used the secret passageways in Horncliffe rather than risk running into the army of servants Winters managed. As a boy, the passageways were an endless source of fascination, a wonderful secret only he and a few others even knew about. Winters always said if the servants were aware of the passages, they would begin to secretly use them for all sorts of nefarious purposes. Oliver never asked what those nefarious purposes could possibly be, and when he was eight years old, he didn't even know what nefarious meant. He only knew that the passages were lovely and a grand secret.

As he got older, they were a means of staying hidden and separate from the inner workings of the house. The older he got, the more imperative it was that he not be seen, until he sometimes went months without meeting another soul except Winters. It simply was the way he lived and he'd never considered questioning it. His affliction made such a life necessary. When he was eighteen, he'd ventured into the music room only to find a young maid there; she had let out a screech and run from the room. Deep humiliation had left him burning and he'd made sure such a mistake never happened again. The girl had been pretty, not much older than he, and she had run from him in fear, as if he were the very devil himself. Later, Winters told him the maid had been dismissed, for she'd grown hysterical, repeating her encounter to anyone who would listen.

"You see why I must protect you, Your Grace," Winters had said.

Oliver had wanted to scream at him that he did not understand. But he did. Since his father's death, he'd come to realize what he was, why others feared him. No one else had strange eyes and shocking white hair. No one else had pale, pale skin. He was the only one. Alone but for Mr.

Winters. Over the years, he accepted his fate and gave little thought to how his rooms were cleaned, how his clothes were washed, how his food was prepared. From the earliest memory, everything was simply…done. Of course, on some level he knew that servants were busy somewhere in the household, doing something.

It did not help that on the rare occasions he did walk the halls of Horncliffe and happened to run into a hapless maid, she froze on the spot, clearly terrified. Every time, he would feel that awful mix of humiliation and anger. And shame.

Those same servants were now lined up by rank, no doubt shaking in fear that the master of the house was, for the first time, going to greet them. It simply had never occurred to him to do so. Mr. Winters handled all that, and Oliver had happily let him. Why subject the servants to his presence when they were so clearly frightened of him?

On this occasion, Mr. Winters had acted as his valet, for he'd had no need of one up to this point. At least, he hadn't had need of one prior to getting married. He'd had no need of formal clothes or even of ordinary clothes, and so he'd had one of Mr. Winters's suits altered for him on this occasion. Oliver was quite a bit taller and broader than Mr. Winters, so the results were not ideal but it would have to do for now. He realized that if he were to go out into the world, travel to London to get his spectacles manufactured, he would have to have a valet. And new clothes. Certainly, Rebecca needed a wardrobe befitting a duchess. The dresses he'd seen were more suited to a governess than a duchess, according to Winters.

While Winters tugged and adjusted the ill-fitting suit, Rebecca watched, perched on the edge of a chair, giving silent encouragement with her smiles. He was certain she could not know what a monumental thing this was, to expose himself so openly to a group of people who feared him. Indeed, he was feeling rather frightened at the moment. He never had liked people staring at him or worse, looking away so as not to stare. When he was young, he'd had all manner of tutors and all of them had avoided looking directly at him. It had never seemed strange or hurtful; it simply was. He wondered, now, if this was also Winters' doing. Had he ordered them not to look at him? He was not unique, but his condition was rare and it was possible few if any of his tutors had ever seen a person with albinism. His father had mentioned that it was his eyes that made most people uncomfortable. They were violet and translucent, a color not found in ordinary folk, and could be disconcerting to people who did not know him. Rebecca had called them beautiful.

"How many servants do you have now?" he asked.

Winters answered, "Thirty-one, Your Grace."

"And that is adequate?"

"More than adequate, Your Grace.".

"Do you believe Horncliffe to be overstaffed?" Rebecca asked. "It seems to be a rather large number of servants for two people."

Winters hesitated a moment before saying, "In order to maintain the high level of cleanliness I require, I do believe Horncliffe is adequately staffed. Many grand houses have more. That does not, of course, include the outdoor staff. I thought this day, it would suffice to see only the indoor staff."

"Yes, I agree," Oliver said, though he hadn't any idea what the outdoor staff did. Kept the grounds, perhaps, and took care of the cattle. How long had it been since he'd ridden the lands? He'd only done so at dusk or before dawn, as he was unable to bear the harsh light of day. No wonder the servants thought him a ghost.

"Perhaps if we begin entertaining, we shall require a larger staff," Rebecca said uncertainly.

It ought to terrify him, all this change. Instead, he found himself surprised to feel excitement mixed in with the terror. Uncertainty, excitement, change. He had brought this all upon himself when he'd decided to take a wife, and damn if it didn't feel a bit grand.

Mr. Winters gave his cravat one sharp, almost painful, tug before stepping back. "I believe you are ready, Your Grace. I shall make certain the servants are all gathered and presentable, shall I?"

"Yes, Mr. Winters. Please do. The duchess and I will be down momentarily."

Mr. Winters was about to leave, but stopped. "Remember, Your Grace, they are simply ignorant servants. Do not expect too much of them."

"I expect them only to not run away in fear," Oliver said dryly.

"Yes, sir."

After Winters had gone, Rebecca rushed over to give him a peck on the cheek. "You look dashing."

"Do I?" Oliver asked with clear skepticism.

She looked him over and he could tell she was frowning slightly. "You've shaved," she offered. "And had your hair cut, I see."

He spread his arms out. "And the suit?"

"It will do for now, but I do believe, Your Grace, that a visit to the tailor is warranted. I have no idea who would be best for a man of your rank, but I shall find out. My dear friend Alice is the granddaughter of a duke and she knows such things. I shall write her and ask all sorts of questions. Do you think you'd be able to make a trip to London?"

He went to her and drew her against him. "If only to see whether I could find some spectacles so I can stare endlessly at your beauty."

As he thought she would, Rebecca burst out laughing. "Go on with you," she said, giving him a playful shove. She was close enough he could see her expression go somber. "Are you ready for this? I can't imagine it will be easy for you."

"If I cannot do this, I am not much of a duke, am I?"

She smiled and tucked her hand in the crook of his arm. "Then let us face the lions together, shall we?"

"I hardly think the servants are as ferocious as all that." He laughed, but inside, he was more than nervous. These were people who had worked for him for years, who had skittered away in fear, heads down, whenever he'd happened upon one of them. Today, he would ask that they look at him, acknowledge that he was an ordinary man, or at the very least, an ordinary duke.

"If they run from the room screaming, shall we let them go?" Rebecca asked, laughter in her voice.

"I know you think are you amusing…"

"I am amusing." He chuckled and she squeezed his arm. "See? I was amusing."

He was still smiling when he walked down the long, sweeping staircase to find a line of thirty-one servants standing at attention with Mr. Winters facing them, his arms behind his back, one hand clasping the other wrist. He looked, Oliver imagined, like a general facing his frightened troops right before a battle they were certain to die in. When Oliver reached the gleaming marble floor of the great hall, Winters bowed deeply and stepped back.

He was suddenly and ridiculously nervous. His footsteps sounded overloud on the marble floor, somehow menacing. They stood there, each with eyes cast downward, stiff and terrified. Good God.

"I would like to introduce myself," he said, his voice sounding overloud. "And my duchess. I am Oliver Sterling, Duke of Kendal, and this is your new duchess."

Not a single movement.

"Curtsy and bow," Winters boomed.

In a flurry, each, depending on his or her gender, did as Winters demanded, and Oliver winced.

Oliver gave Rebecca a sick look, and she responded with an encouraging smile. "I am not a ghost, nor a demon," he said, his eyes moving down the line. He couldn't help but notice more than one maid shrinking away, as if he were about to pounce. "I have a condition called albinism. I was born with it and there is no cure. It affects only the color of my skin, hair, and eyes. My vision is weak, but my mind is sound. Other than that, I am simply a man. You need not fear me. You need not avert your eyes. I have no power over you other than to dismiss you. Please look at me and you shall see there is nothing to fear."

Not one servant looked up, and Oliver felt his frustration and anger growing. He didn't realize how angry he was becoming until Rebecca gently squeezed his rock-hard arm. One little maid began weeping, her squeaking sobs bouncing off the floor and ceiling. *Bloody hell.*

Mr. Winters stalked behind the line and went directly to the maid. Taking his hands, he clasped her jaw on either side and forced the girl's head up. "His Grace said to look at him," he said harshly, and the maid began to sob in earnest, her eyes squeezed shut. Oliver's face heated with humiliation and it took all his resolve not to spin about and leave. He might have done so if he had not felt Rebecca give his arm a reassuring squeeze.

"Enough, Mr. Winters," he said. "You may leave us. I fear your presence is only making matters worse."

Winters' face paled, but he dropped his hands and gave Oliver a small bow—a very nearly mocking bow—before leaving the hall, his body stiff with anger. He'd left red imprints of his fingers on the maid's pale skin, and Oliver frowned heavily, disturbed by Winters' actions. Oliver watched his progress, remaining silent until Winters had reached the stop of the stairs and disappeared down the hall toward his rooms. Meanwhile, the first maid was still crying and another next to her had begun. Good God, they were all terrified. He felt himself heat with humiliation. This could not continue, not if he were to have any semblance of a normal life.

"Your Grace," he said finally, loudly. "Please face me and stare into my eyes."

Rebecca turned to him, the gentlest of smiles on her face, but her eyes held something he could not identify. And then she contorted and froze. As one, the servants gasped. Within seconds, Rebecca swept her hand over her mouth to stop herself from laughing aloud, but her entire body was shaking with mirth, her eyes half-moons of delight. The little scamp.

"I-I'm sorry, Oliver, but it's all so silly," she said, hardly getting the words out, she was laughing so hard. "To th-think they believed I'd actually turn to st-stone." She glanced at the servants, who stared at her slack-jawed.

"For goodness' sake, he can't turn me to *stone*. He's just an ordinary man. Actually, not ordinary, but extraordinary."

Oliver couldn't help himself, he started laughing too, until he could hardly stand upright. When Rebecca kissed his cheek, a rather shocking display in front of the servants, he blushed red.

"Your Grace," Mr. Starke said, "on behalf of myself and all the servants, we pray you will forgive us our outrageous behavior."

"I knew it," his wife's maid said beneath her breath, and beside him, Rebecca let out a small laugh.

The little maid who had gone into hysterics looked at the two of them warily and hiccuped softly.

"I can hardly blame you for believing such tall tales," he said. "I certainly did nothing to disabuse you of the notion and for that, I apologize." It might not be the thing for a member of the peerage to apologize to his servants, but Oliver didn't see the harm, not if it meant they could somehow turn Horncliffe into a somewhat normal household. "I do not wish to hear another tale or wild rumor that I am possessed by the devil or even the devil himself. That, I would not take kindly to."

Rebecca touched his hand as if to remind him he should not be too frightening, especially to the younger servants, who still did look a bit wary.

"Would you all introduce yourselves?" she asked, and walked to Mr. Starke, who, as butler, was the highest ranking servant. Oliver joined her, intensely aware that the servants were likely dreading having to step forward. Next to Mr. Starke was the housekeeper, a sour expression on her face, but she stepped forward, curtsied, and introduced herself.

Down the line they went, the braver among them, including his wife's maid, daring to look him directly in the eye, though letting out a surreptitious sigh of relief when they were not immediately struck down. Even the maid with a tear-stained face managed to dart a quick look at him.

"Well done," Rebecca said, as if they'd each accomplished some monumental task. He supposed they had. She gave him a small un-duchess like shrug and, by God, he had to stop himself from kissing her until she got all melty in his arms. He did like that.

Later, as Rebecca was readying herself for dinner—her first in the company of her husband—Darlene chatted about below stairs and how the staff was reacting to the excitement of the afternoon. "They think you've bewitched him," she said.

"No," Rebecca said with disbelief. "You must be jesting."

Darlene laughed. "Not a true bewitchment, Your Grace. Just the normal kind that a woman can do with a man who's in love."

Rebecca let that sentence pass. She was quite certain the duke did not love her, but rather was grateful to her for her assistance.

"We're so pleased, Your Grace," Darlene said as she took up a brush and began dragging it through Rebecca's thick auburn hair. "It's almost as if a dark cloud has been lifted from the old place. It's the strangest thing, it is. Walking down these dark halls, all of us feared that the duke would jump out at any minute and catch us unawares. And now, it's all changed. We all feel a bit bad about the duke. All these years of treating him so. Even the gallery ghost seemed happy today."

Rebecca raised a skeptical eyebrow. "Oh?"

"Missy, that's the one what started crying after Pamela's waterworks, swears she heard her laughing."

"I wouldn't think that a ghost had very much to laugh about," Rebecca said.

"Not in this old place, I wouldn't think." She paused in her brushing. "You never were afraid of him, were you?"

"Not like you mean, no. Coming here, not knowing a soul, not having met my husband... It was all a bit frightening. But as soon as I met His Grace, or rather soon after, I concluded he was nothing to fear."

Darlene placed the brush on her table and gave her a pensive look. "Sally told me what happened with Mr. Winters. You thought she'd gone, but she stayed around the corner. We all think you're an angel, Your Grace, come to save us. Including His Grace, poor soul."

"His Grace is not a poor soul, but I thank you for your compliment."

Darlene pressed her lips together and it was obvious to Rebecca that she wanted to say something more. "Out with it, then."

"I got to thinking, he is a bit...unusual, isn't he? Not an ordinary man at all. That white hair and his eyes are so striking, aren't they? I was trying to imagine what it would be like, to have people stare, to be so different."

"I imagine it is rather difficult and it would take a good amount of bravery to do the simplest things. Like going down to dinner tonight. From what I understand, he hasn't done so in years."

Darlene braided Rebecca's hair, then swept it up and began putting hairpins in until she'd created a pretty effect.

"You make a fine lady's maid," Rebecca said, turning her head this way and that to admire the work.

"Thank you, Your Grace," Darlene said, giving a small curtsy.

It was still strange to have servants bowing and curtsying and Your Gracing her. In another life, she might have been friends with Darlene, and that thought brought a pang of sadness for the friends she'd left behind in St. Ives. It was too soon to expect a letter from anyone—her letters likely hadn't reached her friends yet—but Rebecca couldn't help but wish she could speak to them. Alice's baby was probably crawling around, and Harriet might already be carrying the heir to an earldom. Would Eliza find a gentleman and fall in love before she even met the man? Perhaps after their trip to London, she could invite her to visit.

"Darlene, are there other members of the peerage living nearby? I confess, I am not at all familiar with this part of England."

"There's a high number of toffs here and about," she said. "I could get the old duchess's address book for you. Before His Grace was born, I hear Horncliffe was always filled with the aristocracy for one ball or party or another. That was before my time, though."

Rebecca smiled. Wouldn't it be wonderful if Eliza met someone here and fell in love? Then she'd at least have one friend nearby. Harriet's sister, Clara, had married Baron Alford, and when they were at his country estate, she wouldn't be too far to visit. A day's travel or so, she supposed.

With those happy thoughts in her head, Rebecca headed for the dining hall, only to have her mood dashed when she reached the room and found her husband sitting with Mr. Winters. The two immediately stood when they saw her. The gas sconces were lit, but the flames were low, light and shadow giving the room an almost cozy air. A large fire warmed the room, periodically snapping and showering the hearth screen with sparks. If not for the oppressive presence of Mr. Winters, Rebecca would have looked forward to the meal.

"Did His Grace tell you about our plans to go to London, Mr. Winters?"

By the surprised expression on his face, it was apparent Oliver had not mentioned the trip.

"His Grace is unable to travel," he said.

"His Grace is looking forward to the trip," Oliver said, letting out a laugh. "Rebecca and I both need a new wardrobe, and we plan to visit a jeweler to see if I can get special spectacles fitted."

"Ones with tinted lenses so His Grace can go outside without too much discomfort," Rebecca said, then took a spoonful of her potato soup and frowned.

"You don't care for it?" Oliver asked, amusement in his eyes.

"Perhaps more salt. And pepper," she said, taking the small salt cellar in front of her and adding some to her soup. "Dill would likely help as well. I do like to put a bit of bacon fat in, as well. Gives it such a nice flavor."

"You cook?" Winters asked, the way one would say, "You run about barefoot in the snow?"

"We had a cook, but yes, I do like creating recipes and I would often take over when she was off with her family. Of course, my father was horrified until he tasted my apple pie."

"I do like apple pie," Oliver said, hinting that she should make him some, and Rebecca gave him a grateful smile. It would be rare fun to bake again.

"I should think it would be unheard of for Her Grace to set foot into the kitchen, never mind cook," Winters said, the 'k' echoing throughout the room. The older man turned toward Oliver. "Surely, you cannot condone such behavior, Your Grace."

"I only said I like apple pie, Winters. I hardly directed her to run down to the kitchen and begin preparing it."

Another simple conversation turned into a confrontation. Rebecca was unused to such tension at the dinner table, and felt a rush of longing for the friendly chaos of meals with her sisters.

"Perhaps for our first ball, I shall make enough pies for all our guests," Rebecca said, only to vex Winters. Oliver, who seemed to suspect what she was up to, gave her a smile but subtly shook his head.

"Ball?"

"Our first ball. I should think we would want to introduce the Duke and Duchess of Kendal to the ton, though it might be better to wait until after the winter but before the season. Or do you have a townhouse in London? That might—"

"Rebecca," Oliver said, laughter in his voice. "May we discuss the plans for the ball in private?"

"Very well." He was being so charming, Rebecca felt a small surge of warmth in the region of her heart. She simply could not stop herself from looking at him, and she realized he was becoming quite dear to her. More than that, perhaps.

"You cannot seriously be considering a ball."

The couple, who had been staring at one another rather like lovesick youths, turned their eyes to Winters.

"Only for three hundred or so guests. Can the ballroom accommodate that number?" Rebecca, who had no experience at all planning a ball, grabbed a number from thin air in hopes it would be large enough to give Mr. Winters apoplexy.

Winters' eyes grew arctic and he slowly placed his fork down so carefully, it didn't make a sound when it touched his plate. The air grew thick with tension.

"I believe Her Grace is teasing you, Winters," Oliver said, and Rebecca could tell he was trying not to smile.

"I was indeed," Rachel said. "I think a ball would be too ambitious, but I do believe a small dinner party would be acceptable. Would it not, Your Grace?"

"Perhaps someday."

"Did you hold many formal dinners at your home?" Winters asked with feigned interest. In fact, the Caines had held no formal dinners and, if Rebecca were honest, were a bit unruly at the table, something she suspected Winters fully knew. He'd eaten with the family, after all, and even then Rebecca could sense his disgust of the family. They'd barely had the funds to feed their large brood, never mind to invite the local gentry. The only reason Rachel could be reasonably confident she was equal to dining with the aristocracy was thanks to her friends Alice and Eliza. Finishing school, lessons in deportment, seasons in London were things Rebecca had never been a part of.

"No, but it is my understanding that the aristocracy eat in a similar fashion to the gentry." Lord, she loathed the man.

He smiled tightly. "You forget, I have seen your table manners, Your Grace."

"Enough!"

Winters did not react overtly to the command shouted out by Oliver, but the look he gave Rebecca had her suppressing a shiver.

For the rest of the dinner Rebecca sat quietly, her entire body heated with humiliation and rage, as her husband chatted amiably with Mr. Winters about a new artist Oliver had an interest in. Rebecca knew nothing about art or artists, so she sat and forced herself to eat the tasteless meal. When the conversation slid into philosophy and the great debate over what is truth—an absolute or what someone believes is the truth—and throwing out quotes from long-dead people Rebecca had never heard of, she felt herself growing exceedingly bored. Two things bothered her. One, she was convinced Mr. Winters had begun the conversations about art and philosophy simply to illustrate how uneducated she was. And two, Oliver seemed completely oblivious to what Winters was doing. The two of them seemed entirely too engaged by the debate. It wasn't until dinner was over that she realized how very angry Oliver was. His answers were short, his tone clipped, his movements measured and precise. She hardly knew him, and had never seen him angry, but for some reason she sensed an underlying tension, a tautness, as if he were a snake coiled for attack. Mr. Winters, if he recognized Oliver's rage, either did not care or was pretending not to. "If you don't mind, Your Grace, I have something to discuss with Mr. Winters."

She saw a tension in Oliver's face that she hadn't recognized before, his sharp jaw tense, his eyes cold. "Of course," she said, looking uncertainly between the two men before turning and leaving them alone.

Oliver pushed his plate away and Winters motioned for the footman to remove it. Even that small gesture added to his anger, as if he were incapable of gesturing to the footman himself. These things that he hadn't noted before suddenly grated. "You are dismissed," he told the footman, then turned to the other servants in the room and asked that they also leave. Winters looked at him with that awful bemusement, one eyebrow raised.

"I would like you to leave Horncliffe, Mr. Winters. Tomorrow, if possible."

His thin lips separated briefly, the only indication that Oliver had perhaps shocked him.

"Ah." That one syllable seemed to hold so much. Censorship for siding with his wife, mockery for being so weak, a warning that he could not survive without Winters' counsel. So what he said next surprised Oliver. "I do not blame you for your anger, Your Grace. I was completely out of line, crass, and I apologize. I shall apologize to Her Grace as well when I see her next."

Oliver stared at the man he'd known nearly all his life, searching for mendacity and finding none. His anger deflated immediately. He was not at all unaware of how Winters had sacrificed his own life to stay with him. "Why do you find it necessary to insult her, not only to her face, but to me? I will not tolerate it. I am fond of Her Grace and no matter how our marriage came to be, I am glad for it."

Winters let out a sigh and nodded. "I cannot help how I feel, but I shall do a better job of hiding it." He hesitated for a moment, looking at Oliver with his dark brown eyes as if measuring how much he should say. "It is only that I think of you as a son. Or perhaps a younger brother, but if either were the case, I would be duke." He chuckled. "If you are indeed going to enter society, have a care, Your Grace. You must know I only think of your best interests. If I have been unable to hide my disapproval—"

"Hide it? You've been quite flagrant about it. It must stop. I do not make this threat idly, Mr. Winters. I will not have you insult my wife again. Is that clear? If you force me to choose, I choose her."

"Yes, of course," Winters said, looking chastised. He was acquiescing so easily, Oliver grew suspicious. Winters never acquiesced easily. "It is only that I fear for her, Your Grace."

"Thus far, the only thing she has had to fear is your censor," Oliver snapped.

"Yes, precisely. And I have apologized, Your Grace." The slightest bit of impatience entered his tone. "But do you think the ton will be kinder than I? It will be immediately evident to anyone who meets Her Grace that she is not of our class and certainly not worthy to be a duchess." He held up a staying hand when Oliver stiffened, his anger back in force. "I fear not only for you but for her as well. You have not been in society, and I admit I have not either in years, but it is an unforgiving place, a place that would take great delight in ripping Her Grace to shreds. Have you not considered this? That you will be mocked not because of your condition but because of your wife's low birth? Do you wish to be the subject of ridicule?"

Oliver's immediate reaction was to deny the truth of what Mr. Winters was saying, but he was not a fool. He knew little of society, or its cruelties, firsthand, but he was not so naïve to believe they would not be mocked. He would not allow that to happen to Rebecca. Everything was so new, he'd hardly given thought to anything but getting his delightful wife back into bed. All the tutors in the world could not have prepared him for society and he was woefully inadequate to train her.

"Do we have a relative, an aunt or cousin or such, who could train my wife in the social graces? I confess, I haven't noticed any egregious errors in her behavior or manners, but I am hardly a judge, having been so isolated from society."

A small glint appeared in Winter's eyes, as if he'd won some sort of victory. "Mrs. Habershaw would be ideal," Winters said after some thought.

"Habershaw," Oliver repeated, the name sounding familiar, though he was unable to recall ever meeting the woman. When he was young, his father would sometimes invite members of the ton to Horncliffe, but given his age, he'd not often been introduced.

"Your mother's sister, Your Grace. She has long been widowed. A more upstanding and uncorrupted woman you shall never meet." He chuckled. "She's a bit hard of hearing, but that might go in Her Grace's favor; more difficult for Mrs. Habershaw to hear Her Grace's atrocious speech."

Oliver frowned. "I hadn't noticed anything defective in her speech. And given my mother abandoned me as an infant, I hardly think someone from my mother's side of the family would be appropriate."

"Your mother came from impeccable lines," Winters said with a tight smile.

"My mother was not a race horse," Oliver countered dryly.

Oliver sensed his comment annoyed Winters, but the older man did not respond. "With your permission, I shall write Mrs. Habershaw immediately. In a matter of weeks, Her Grace will be up to snuff, intelligent girl that she is."

"Did you just compliment my wife?"

Winters opened his mouth, no doubt about to say something insulting, but remained silent. He stood and gave a quick bow. "If you will excuse me, Your Grace, I have a letter to write."

Oliver let him go, allowed him to write the letter that he himself should have written. He had been about to inform Winters that he would write the letter but stopped. The man was obviously attempting to make amends. Besides, Oliver's penmanship was atrocious. More importantly, he had a warm and willing wife waiting for him.

Chapter 8

"A tutor?"

"In a manner of speaking."

Rebecca's stomach knotted, knowing this idea must have come from Winters. Yes, she was a bit provincial, but she was hardly a scullery maid or a street beggar like Pygmalion. Did Oliver truly think so little of her?

She sat on her bed with her knees drawn up tightly against her body, her arms wrapped around her legs, and her head facing her husband, who lay there satisfied after their lovemaking, his hands tucked beneath his head. "I may not have attended finishing school, but I am hardly uneducated. We did have a governess." For six months. When she was twelve. But that hardly mattered. She'd been around highly educated friends all her life and had learned to emulate them. Alice was the granddaughter of a duke and Harriet and her sister had attended a finishing school, as had Eliza. No one had ever found fault with her manners or speech.

Unless her friends were simply being kind. It was true she'd received a spotty education thanks to her father's gambling.

"Who did you have in mind? Or should I rather ask, who did Winters have in mind?" She said this darkly and was gratified when Oliver's eyes darted away. "Ha! I knew he was behind this."

"The tutor was my idea," he said, surprising her. Hurting her, actually.

"Oh." She shifted so she was looking at the bump her feet made beneath the blanket. He laid a warm hand on her back but she continued to stare stubbornly forward.

"If we're to go out into society, we must be prepared. I had a long string of tutors growing up, who taught me all manner of things. I haven't had the chance to put many of them into practice, but it is all here," he said, tapping his head.

"Such as?"

"Such as a man keeps his gloves on at all times out of doors."

"Even I knew that," she said, unimpressed.

"And I shall need you, you know. I cannot see past my outstretched hand with any clarity." He held out his hand to demonstrate. "It's foggy and unclear. So I shall depend on you to tell me if someone has waved or said hello."

"You can hear," Rebecca said on a laugh. "Quite a bit better than I."

"Yes, but I won't be able to tell they are saying hello to *me*."

Rebecca sat up, then straddled him, leaning back. "Tell me when you can see my face." She began moving forward, slowly, watching as his eyes, darting slightly, stared intently at her. When she was perhaps six inches away, he said, "There."

"Truly?" she whispered. She hadn't understood the extent of his vision impairment, how even the simplest of things would be difficult for him.

"Truly."

"I do pray spectacles will help." She leaned forward even more and kissed him. "However can you fence?"

"Not easily," he said, laughing. "I listen, I can see general movement. I know when an opponent is going for a point by looking at the white blob in front of me."

"White blob?"

Oliver chuckled. "That's all I can see. But close up, I see quite well. It is tiring though."

"You never seem too tired to me," she said saucily, for she could feel him growing hard beneath her bum.

"My eyes grow tired. The rest of me is quite…energetic."

Mrs. Habershaw arrived within a fortnight, frowning heavily as she looked around the grand hall. "Where is my nephew?" she called out as she handed off her muff, cloak, hat, and gloves without looking at who was taking them. Rebecca swore she could feel the coolness of her sharp gaze when the older woman spied her. She looked down her nose through a pair of spectacles that perched, rather miraculously, near the very tip. "You there. Fetch His Grace."

Rebecca hid a smile and dipped a quick curtsy, realizing too late that she greatly outranked the woman before her. "I am the duchess." Even to her own ears she sounded unsure.

Mrs. Habershaw seemed to freeze on the spot—or rather turn to stone. "You?"

"I'm afraid so."

"Oh, dear." The woman's face sharpened imperceptibly. Her expression told Rebecca more than her words ever could. It said: Now I understand why my nephew sent for me. This girl is an impossible case but I shall forge ahead and do my best out of duty.

Oliver appeared then, walking into the hall, his eyes searching out Rebecca. "Your aunt has arrived, Your Grace."

Oliver came immediately to her side, then stepped forward to greet his aunt. "It is a pleasure to see you again, Aunt."

"You have not outgrown your affliction I see," she said matter-of-factly.

"Indeed, I have not."

"A pity," she said, and Rebecca felt herself bristle. She swallowed a retort, not wanting to be combative when she needed this woman to remain. "I last saw you when you were still in the cradle, shortly before my sister brought shame upon the family." She glanced at Rebecca. "I do hope we can avoid a repeat of such scandal."

"From what I understand, scandal is the only thing to brighten the ton's day," Rebecca said. "I do believe we shall cause quite a stir when we travel to London."

Mrs. Habershaw looked aghast. "Surely not for the Season."

"In two weeks. I would like to go and return before the holidays and before the weather becomes too harsh."

Mrs. Habershaw nearly staggered, but she did hold one hand over her heart, as if it were paining her. Stepping forward, the lady peered at her more closely. "Two weeks? I could not possibly get her ready to be presented in two weeks. You do realize she will have to be presented to Her Highness."

Rebecca felt the blood drain from her face. Presented to the queen? Oliver looked at Rebecca uncertainly, and she could almost hear his mind whirring—perhaps thinking he had miscalculated terribly in his choice of a wife. One might think she was standing there dressed like a... She looked down at herself and realized she was dressed more like a governess or a housekeeper than the lady of the house.

"We only wish to purchase a more suitable wardrobe and to obtain spectacles for His Grace on this trip. Then we will return and the lessons can begin in earnest." Twisting her hands together, Rebecca said, "Do I truly have to be presented to the queen?"

Mrs. Habershaw, wearing a look of rapt disbelief, said, "You are the Duchess of Kendal. It is one of the oldest and most respected titles in all of England. Of course you must be presented. And you must be presented in a manner that will not humiliate His Grace."

"I would never—"

A sharp hand motion from Mrs. Habershaw stopped her. "You are woefully unprepared, Your Grace. I could tell that immediately. You curtsied to me like some country miss. Girls who are presented to the queen have been trained in deportment all their lives. What they say, how they say it, their diction, their every movement is second nature. They are not—" She indicated Rebecca's entire person with a swirl of her hand.

"Her Grace is intelligent and far lovelier than any woman I have ever seen. I am certain she will make us all proud," Oliver said, his tone icy. Rebecca smiled inwardly, for she had never heard Oliver sound like the duke he was. And given his poor eyesight and hermit-like existence, his statement was likely true.

"I am humbled by your optimism," Mrs. Habershaw said. "Now, I am weary from my travels. If I could be shown to my room?"

"Oh, yes, Aunt, forgive me." Oliver nodded to the footmen to begin bringing her luggage to her rooms. It was rather a lot of luggage, judging by the large pile just inside the door, an indication that Mrs. Habershaw planned to stay for quite a while.

Rebecca had thought, at the very least, that her table manners were acceptable. It turned out, however, they were woefully inadequate.

"Why must you eat like a sailor on shore leave? You must cut a small amount of meat, lay down your knife, turn your fork thus"—Mrs. Habershaw turned her fork so that the tines curved downward—"and eat. Place your fork back onto your plate so that it crosses over your knife, then chew twenty times. No more. No less."

"But what if someone asks me a question on chew number six? Or sixteen?" She was only half-jesting.

"You must acknowledge that you have heard his or her question and continue to chew. I hardly think you'll encounter such rudeness at any rate."

Rebecca thought back to Caine family dinners, loud and boisterous affairs with much chatting. She could not imagine what dinners would have been like for her family had her sisters and she been required to chew twenty times before answering a question. It seemed silly to her.

"Your back, Your Grace."

She had begun to slouch imperceptibly and so straightened.

"And do not stare at your food so. Your chin should be parallel to the table. Parallel," she said, taking her hand and lifting Rebecca's chin.

For days it had gone on like this, with Mrs. Habershaw drilling her over and over again. She smiled too much and too broadly; she walked too quickly; her diction nearly made Mrs. Habershaw weep; her clothes were too common. Each time Rebecca entered a room where the older woman presided, she would look at Rebecca's outfit with a mixture of horror and deep sadness. More than once, Mrs. Habershaw said beneath her breath, "I cannot create miracles."

The list of things a duchess could do and could never do was lengthy and none of it appealed overmuch to Rebecca. When she'd told Mrs. Habershaw she'd never been on a horse, she thought the woman would faint.

"But it is imperative that a woman of your station not only ride but ride well. What about the hunt?"

"The hunt?"

Mrs. Habershaw had looked to Mr. Winters for commiseration, and the miserable man had simply shaken his head in disgust.

"You do know how to dance."

Rebecca had a feeling the type of dancing she and her sisters had done in their parlor would not count. "Not properly, no." She had danced a waltz more than once.

"And pianoforte? Violin? Do you sing?" This last was said with a tinge of desperation.

"We did not have a governess growing up."

She woman had actually gasped. "How were you schooled, then?"

"By my mother. I can read," Rebecca said, quite defensively. Indeed, her mother had come from a fine family that did have a governess. She'd had a Season in London and had the great misfortune (according to her grandparents) of falling in love with a vicar's son.

Mrs. Habershaw visibly paled and she looked to Mr. Winters. "You were not forthcoming, sir," she said sternly.

Winters' mouth tightened. "His Grace fancied the girl and it is always my duty to ensure he is content. The old duke made me promise to care for him and that is what I have done."

"But the consequences. If there are children, they will have her blood. Oh, it is unconscionable."

"I beg pardon, but I am not a street hoyden. I am a duchess, whether the two of you wish it or not. My father is a squire and my mother is the grandniece of a baronette."

"You cannot be so naïve as to think a well-born, normal man would have you," Mrs. Habershaw said cruelly. Perhaps worse, she had not meant to be cruel, she was simply stating what she believed to be a fact.

"It matters not. I am His Grace's wife and a duchess, which means, I believe, that I far outrank either of you." Even though she said the words coldly, her cheeks blushed. She did not honestly believe the words she spoke and almost felt silly saying them. Rank and position meant little to her—at least up until this point in her life. The Caines may not have been top-tier in St. Ives, but they were well-liked and well-respected. People loved her mother; they were less charitable to her father, given his penchant for the gaming table. Still, Rebecca had never felt ashamed of her family and had been secretly proud that her mother had come from such a grand lineage.

"She is correct, Mr. Winters. The deed is done and undoing it would create even more scandal."

"Scandal is not always a bad thing," Winters said enigmatically. "And a duke can withstand quite a lot."

Rebecca frowned, wishing she could tell him just what she thought about his opinions, but she was trying to be more pleasant to the onerous man for Oliver's sake.

"It matters not what I do, I fear," Mrs. Habershaw said. "If we cannot cleanse you of your low born accent, this will have been an exercise in futility. I have heard no improvement at all."

Was her diction so awful? She had not realized her Cornish accent was so noticeable.

"Every syllable, each letter, should be enunciated with care and precision," Mrs. Habershaw said, then brought out a book—the complete works of William Shakespeare—to have Rebecca read for her.

"Two households, both alike in dignity, In fair Verona, where we lay our scene—"

The older woman held up her hand. "Dignitee. Not dignitay. Each syllable, each letter, crisp and precise. Again."

"Two households, both alike in dignitee, In fair—"

"Stop. Fair. Not fayre. Repeat, please."

Rebecca swallowed. "Fair."

Mrs. Habershaw frowned. "Continue."

"In fair Verona, where we lay our—"

Mrs. Habershaw threw up her hands and gave Mr. Winters a look of desperation. "Impossible, Mr. Winters. The minute she opens her mouth everyone will know she is of the lower classes. If your mother was indeed the grandniece of a baronette, then she has failed you miserably."

Rebecca felt herself bristling but bit her tongue. It would do no good to argue with the woman, and Rebecca couldn't help thinking that her words held some truth. Her parents had done nothing to ensure she was educated, that she marry well. They both would have been completely content to have her marry a local shopkeeper, and there was a time when Rebecca would have been happy living in St. Ives with her shopkeeper husband. But thanks to her father's actions, she had been thrust into a world she was entirely unprepared for. Mrs. Habershaw was correct; her speech would give her common origins away even if she mastered all the other aspects of being a lady.

"What do you suggest I do?" she asked. "I am a duchess but I would not want to bring shame or embarrassment to His Grace."

Mrs. Habershaw gave her a thoughtful look that was very nearly tinged with admiration. "I suggest you say as little as possible."

"It will not work," Mr. Winters said. "People will be curious. They'll ask her questions. She will not be able to stand there like a mute. This entire trip is ill-conceived. Certainly she cannot attend a ball or any other public event. The family will be humiliated. If I had known things would carry this far this quickly, I never would have—"

"But you did," Rebecca interrupted. "And His Grace and I are happy."

Oliver, taking pity on her, had asked that Mrs. Habershaw relent for the evening meal so that everyone at the table could enjoy one another's company, but the old lady would not. "You have given me an impossible task, but I shall succeed despite it."

Rebecca had glanced over at Oliver and could see he was trying not to show his anger. They had agreed that while Mrs. Habershaw was a strict and unrelenting teacher, in the end it would all be worth it. Rebecca refused to embarrass her husband. Since Mrs. Habershaw's visit, they had seen little of each other except in the evenings.

"It's useless," Rebecca said two weeks after Mrs. Habershaw had arrived. She lay in bed beside Oliver, aching and sore and miserable. Her life had become a nightmare of criticism and endless drills; no matter how hard she tried, she failed again and again. Rebecca had thought herself, if not upper crust, at least presentable. It wasn't as if she'd never attended a ball; she had. One ball, but it *was* a ball and as far as she could recall, she had not embarrassed herself. Then again, other than the Earl of Berkley, the attendees were all from St. Ives, so no one was there who would have noted their provincial ways.

Even when Rebecca did well, she earned no praise. Rebecca hated to be suspicious of anyone, but she had a terrible feeling that Mr. Winters had poisoned Mrs. Habershaw's mind against her. At dinner, the two would talk quietly together, sharing smiles and looks that Rebecca couldn't interpret.

And Rebecca could not miss the looks of satisfaction Mr. Winters gave when Mrs. Habershaw corrected her.

"Mrs. Habershaw seems unreasonably strict in my opinion," Oliver said. "If she were a man, I daresay I would have called her out a dozen times."

Rebecca chose not to harp on Mr. Winters, though she longed to confide in Oliver. She was exhausted and grumpy and for the first time since she'd begun sharing a bed with her husband, she resisted his advances. She lay quiet, one arm flung over her forehead, and stared at the canopy above Oliver's bed, softly pink from the fire crackling in the grate. She hadn't slept in her own bed for days now, not since discovering Oliver's bed was far less lumpy. They'd become comfortable with one another, sharing stories of childhood in between mad and frenzied lovemaking. But this night, Rebecca wanted only to be held. "I'm a country girl and that's all I shall ever be." She turned to her side to look at Oliver. "Truthfully, I was glad that you were a bit of a hermit. All these rules, all those mannerisms. It seems so foreign and a little bit silly."

Oliver kissed the tip of her nose. "Perhaps we can concentrate on what's needed for the presentation. Surely you can muddle through it if you practice only that. I believe Mrs. Habershaw is attempting to do too much at once. All these lessons won't be needed when we go to London this time around. You'll have months to practice before the Season. Besides, I've no mad desire to enter society. I enjoy my quiet life."

"Must I be presented to the queen? I think I may be ill at her feet. Just the thought of it." She shook her head. "All the girls in England who wish to be a lady ought to go through what I've gone through and then they'd be happy to marry the butcher."

He scowled at her, his striking white brows snapping together. "Did you wish to marry a butcher?"

"No, silly," Rebecca said on a laugh. "But it would have been far easier." He growled and pulled her against him, making her laugh all the more.

"Do you think I am not terrified by the prospect of going to London? Of attending social events? I loathe the whispers. I may not be able to see well, but I can feel people's stares. People are either frightened by me or treat me as if I am an imbecile."

"At least no one will call you a fraud."

At those words, he bristled. "Winters was wrong to say that."

While Rebecca was glad of her husband's loyalty, she couldn't help but think that perhaps Mr. Winters was at least partly correct. In St. Ives, word that a member of the aristocracy was passing through created as much excitement as Christmas morning. The villagers would strain their necks and gawk, all the time hoping to catch a glimpse of whoever was in the ornate carriage driving by. When the Earl of Berkley took up residence in St. Ives, it was all the locals could speak of, as if some miracle had happened to their little village. Aristocrats were on the moon and the rest of the villagers were firmly treading on earth. Given how woefully unprepared she was to face the ton, it was becoming clear how ill-conceived their marriage was. But Rebecca realized she was fiercely glad they were married, just the same.

Rebecca was distracted from her thoughts by Oliver, who was nuzzling her breasts and whose hands were beginning to roam rather enticingly over her body. His warm hand, his breath on her neck, his big body stretched out beside her had her forgetting her weariness. It was always this way, a simple touch or even a look and she was ready for lovemaking.

She let out a soft moan as his fingers grazed one nipple, and any notion that she only wanted to sleep was quickly gone.

"You're not too tired?" he asked, then kissed her neck, which he knew drove her quite mad.

She giggled and turned toward him to get closer. "Not anymore."

He let out a manly sound of satisfaction and pressed his erection against her thigh as he kissed her. "Not a day goes by when I don't thank God for giving you to me," he said. "I adore you, you know."

"I'm rather fond of you, too," she said, then gasped when he bit her nipple lightly through the thin layer of her nightdress.

Suddenly, he stiffened, lifting his head as if he'd heard something.

"What is it?" she whispered. "The cat?"

Without a word, he flung off the covers and moved quickly, completely naked, to the far end of the room and then...disappeared. In the moonlight, it was easy to follow his progress, his skin ghostly white in the gloom. So when he suddenly vanished, a chill ran over her. It was almost if he'd walked through the wall. Like a real ghost.

Rebecca could feel her heart pounding madly in her chest as she stared at the spot where he'd been last. Sounds of scuffling, coming from somewhere indeterminate, drew her attention. Pushing off the covers, she stood and grabbed her robe, shivering in a cold draft coming from the area where Oliver had vanished. Wrapping her arms around herself tightly, she tiptoed across the room. "Oliver?" she whispered.

And then she saw it: a hidden door in the wall that had been completely solid not two minutes prior. Rebecca peeked in, seeing only utter blackness but hearing, somewhere in the distance, footsteps, which faded the longer she stood listening. Rebecca debated lighting a lamp and following him, but decided to simply wait for his return and question him about the passageway then. How exciting. A spooky house with secret passages. Her younger sisters would be mad with jealousy.

Rebecca returned to bed, pulling her knees up under her tented nightdress, and waited. It seemed an interminably long time before Oliver returned, quietly entering the room and doing something to cause the hidden door to close silently behind him. He began walking back to the bed, and paused when he realized she was still awake.

"Secret doors and passages?"

Oliver got into bed, the mattress sagging toward him a bit. "My grandfather was a smuggler. The house was built with that operation in mind. There's a labyrinth of passages, so many, in fact, that I can move from one end of the house to the other without ever setting foot in a common area. A feat of unimaginable engineering brilliance."

Rebecca lay down and Oliver drew her against him. "You're freezing," she said. Indeed, his skin was ice cold so she snuggled closer in an attempt to warm him. She let out a little screech when he tucked his feet against her calves.

"And you are warm," he said, chuckling as she tried to move away from his icy toes.

"Are the passageways a secret?" Rebecca asked, not liking the idea that anyone could be behind her wall, eavesdropping, spying.

"Only Mr. Winters and I know of their existence. Most of the staff were hired in the last ten years."

"No wonder the servants thought you were some supernatural being, appearing suddenly in rooms where no one had seen you enter."

He chuckled. "I imagine that did not help my reputation."

Rebecca was silent for a long moment. "You thought it was Mr. Winters, didn't you? Just now. In the passageway."

"Yes."

"My God," she whispered. "Do you think he's been listening? Watching?"

"I forbade it," he said tersely.

"You forbade it? That makes me feel so much better!" Rebecca sat up, anger making her blood hot. "I want him gone, Oliver. I know you feel obligated to him, though God knows why, but he clearly detests me. And now, he's been spying on us? Listening to our intimate conversations? To our…" She could not bring herself to mention it. The idea that Winters had listened to them as they'd made love, heard her cry out, known what was happening. It didn't bear thinking.

"He would not, Rebecca. He is a man of strict moral code and honor. If he says he would not, he would not."

He reached for her, but Rebecca moved away. "I think I'll go to my room," she said.

"Please, Rebecca."

"I am angry. And I have a right to my anger. Would you like to know what makes me the angriest? That you continue to take his side at all times."

Behind her, Oliver let out a growl. "I nearly beat him for not honoring you. A man I have thought of as a father. Let me make this clear to you, Rebecca. Should I have to choose between you and Mr. Winters, I would choose you without hesitation."

Rebecca, who had been striding toward her door, stopped. She stared blindly at the connecting door, debating what to do. "Would you truly?"

"I would. I have told Mr. Winters as much." He let out an audible sigh. "If Mr. Winters was behind the wall, it was only that he was traveling by, not spying. Like me, he prefers to travel unseen throughout the house. He says it keeps the servants on their toes for they never know when he will appear."

"If that is what you believe, then why did you chase after him?"

His hesitation told her all she needed to know. "Mr. Winters has always been inordinately protective of me, which is something that I cannot abide now that I am a man, but at the same time I cannot help but be gratified that he is. It turns out, he was not there. No one runs those hidden passages as quickly as I. I have been doing it since I was a boy. I know those hallways better than I know my own room." Rebecca still stood, just feet from the connecting door, and looked back at her husband, a pale outline in the large bed. *I would choose you.* Those words, more than anything, helped her decide. "Come back to bed, Rebecca. Please."

"Very well."

He chuckled. "It is not a punishment."

"Is it not?" she asked, with mock anger.

"No," he said solemnly, not allowing her to jest.

She climbed into bed, getting small satisfaction when he hissed in a breath as her cold feet touched his now-warm calf. "You need to warm me," she whispered.

"I shall be happy to do more than that."

Oliver leaned forward, inches away from the parlor of his tiny house and smiled. There on the floor was a homey rug, one that had not been there the day before. Rebecca must have slipped into the tower after he'd gone and laid it there. It was the sort of thing he imagined a mother doing, a simple kindness, something he had never experienced but even now, as a man grown, longed for. When he was a boy, he'd wondered what his mother was doing, whether she missed him. If she even gave him a thought. She never wrote, never sent gifts. Never came back to see him before she died.

Rebecca had only been with him for three weeks and already he could not imagine life without her. He was a different man altogether. Never would he have imagined traveling to London, but now he was willing, even knowing what it would entail. The last time he had been in public had been extremely unpleasant. He'd been twenty-one, having just reached his majority two weeks earlier, and invited to a dinner at Sir Robert Gilbert's home not three miles down the coast.

Mr. Winters had not wanted him to go. "They have a daughter and I believe they are hoping for a match, Your Grace. She is far below your station and it would not be a match anyone could condone. And your affliction…"

Oliver was damned sick of his affliction. He'd become used to himself, he supposed, and did not find his appearance all that objectionable. If the servants acted skittish around him, it was because he was a duke and not because his appearance was so grotesque. At least not entirely.

He accepted the invitation, feeling young and brash and sick to death of being alone and isolated from society. At twenty-one, most men had gone to university, had already attended balls and caroused to their hearts' content, while Oliver remained at Horncliffe growing more and more restless. Mr. Winters had wanted to accompany him, and Oliver had forbade it. He was not a child, after all.

Of course, it had been a terrible mistake. Even now, nearly seven years later, Oliver could feel the heat of humiliation of that night. The Gilberts, apparently, had been wholly unaware of his appearance and unable to conceal their shock when he entered their home. Mrs. Gilbert had uttered a single "Oh" before turning to her husband, an odd smile plastered upon her face. Miss Gilbert, a pretty girl with brilliant red hair and vacant blue eyes, had stared at him wide-eyed all night, flinching noticeably whenever he tried to make conversation. The social skills Oliver had been taught were worthless in such a situation, and he soon felt completely out of his element. He did not know the people of whom they spoke, could not recognize the subtleties of conversations, and was wholly unprepared—an awkward, strange-looking fellow with few social skills. Ten people sat around the table, including the Gilberts, their daughter, and a sullen son who said not a word during the entire evening. Another young man, introduced as Mr. Bagley, would not stop talking, and Oliver decided quickly he preferred the son. Everything Mr. Bagley said was met by a giggle from Miss Gilbert, and Oliver began wondering if there was something mentally wrong with the girl.

"I say, Your Grace, are you ill?" Mr. Bagley asked, then looked at Miss Gilbert as if to make certain she was listening. "You look rather pale." Miss Gilbert hid a smile behind her napkin.

"I am not ill at all," Oliver said, feeling his face heat. It was most humiliating when he blushed, for his face turned an unattractive pink.

"He's gone as red as a cardinal, he has." This was from the general, who'd had a bit too much to drink. He'd been a pleasant dinner companion up until that moment. The old man leaned back and took a good look at Oliver, his eyes widening a bit as if he'd just realized the man sitting next to him was unique. "Are you a foreigner? Maybe Finnish."

Oliver swallowed. "No, sir, I am English."

"Were your parents…normal?" This hesitant question came from Mrs. Gilbert, who no doubt was having second thoughts about tying her daughter to him, no matter his lofty title. He could feel the eyes of everyone at the table and for the first time was glad his eyesight was such that he could not discern the fine details of their stares.

Oliver smiled tightly. "My father, the fifth Duke of Kendal, was quite normal, madam. My mother took one look at me and fled in horror. But I understand she, too, was, as you say, normal."

"Then it's not a family trait? It's not a family trait, Cissy," she said cheerfully to her daughter, smiling encouragingly.

"Mother," Miss Gilbert said, shaking her head, her eyes tellingly going over to Mr. Bagley.

"Unfortunately," Oliver said, his pride stinging and his anger rising, "I do not care for redheads. And that, I believe, *is* a family trait." He looked directly at the woman's vibrantly red hair.

Mrs. Gilbert had gasped, and Miss Gilbert had the audacity to looked shocked. Oliver forced himself to remain until the meal was over, even though he felt as if he might lose his supper. Afterward, he declined the invitation for a smoke and a brandy with the men, and thanked everyone for a pleasant evening. He had, after all, been well-trained in politeness.

Now, Oliver was just as socially unready as he had been then. He rarely ventured off his lands and only in the evening when the bright light of day didn't burn his eyes. Until the day he'd seen Rebecca's portrait, he'd thought himself content with his lot. Some distant cousin could inherit the title or it would go into abeyance. He didn't care. At least, he hadn't cared. Now his dreams had been reawakened, his heart beating with hope that he could be a man who would make his father proud. With Rebecca by his side, nothing of his appearance mattered because it mattered not to her. He stared blindly at his little house, grinning like a besotted fool. In this very room, she had called him handsome.

His smile broadened when he heard a sound from behind the wall. Oliver's hearing was quite acute, and he heard Rebecca long before she managed to puzzle out how to open the secret door to the tower. When she finally burst through, her hair askew, her dress a bit dusty, a small oil lamp in her hand, he acted surprised.

"Ho, there, what is this? A fair maiden trespassing in my rooms."

Rebecca laughed as she caught her breath, then placed the lamp on a nearby shelf before blowing it out. "Goodness, why would anyone go through that," she said, pointing an accusing finger at the secret passage, "when one can simply walk through the hallways? It's like a maze. A dark maze filled with cobwebs and all sorts of creatures."

"Creatures?"

"I swear I heard something skittering all around me." She walked up to him, and he could see her cheeks were rosy from her exertion, making her look even more lovely than usual. Without a warning, she threw herself into his arms, laughing, her soft body pressed against his, and his arms went around her without a second thought. "I thought I'd never make it, that I'd be lost within the walls forever."

He looked down at her upturned face, a strange surge of joy filling him. By God, he must be the luckiest man on Earth. "I would have found you."

He kissed her, then, as if he would die if he didn't, as if she were the one thing that was keeping him alive, a desperate kiss. In all his life, he had never felt such a raw surge of desire come upon him. All at once, he burned for her, his cock hard and straining against his trousers, his hands working her skirt up because it had suddenly become necessary to touch her, to make her find her release. And so he knelt before her, her skirts bunched in his hands as she stood, panting, looking down at him with drowsy eyes.

"Hold your skirts," he said. "Higher." When she did as he asked, he pulled down her drawers, his palms sliding the soft material down her impossibly silky thighs.

"Oliver," she said, sounding hesitant. He looked up and kissed a thigh, smiling until she relaxed.

His eyes never leaving hers, he pressed his mouth to the apex of her thighs and tasted her. A gasp. She shifted, and for a second, he thought she would step back. But no, his beautiful wife spread her legs wider, welcoming him, and leaned against the wall. She was wet for him, her soft hair damp with her desire, and he stifled a groan when he slipped one finger inside her heat and found her ready. In the last few weeks, he'd learned what Rebecca liked, how to touch her, how to make her shake, her insides convulse around him, but he had never made love to her like this. It was heaven, tasting her, hearing her breath become labored, feeling her squeeze against the finger that caressed her hot wetness. She let out small sounds, unconscious little whimpers that encouraged him, that let him know he was pleasing her.

"Oliver. Oh." She convulsed, shaking, as she found release, letting out a high, keening that made him want to shout. She was still pulsing when he dropped his trousers and lifted her up, bracing her against the wall, and entered her. Had anything in his life ever felt like this? He was a god, an animal, a king as he thrust inside her. Rebecca wrapped her legs around him, and as he clutched her sweet buttocks and pressed his mouth against her neck, he felt an unexplainable need to taste her, feel every part of her. She smelled sweetly of lavender and he breathed in, trying to inhale her, make her part of him.

"Oh. Again," she said, breathlessly, and he felt her tighten around him as he drove into her again and again, mindless, seeking release. It seemed as if he'd become another creature entirely, one that was consumed with lust, with a desire so intense, he nearly screamed when he finally found his release.

For too long, he held her, finding his breath, trying to come back into the refined man that he was. What the hell had just happened to him? He slowly withdrew, afraid to look at her, afraid to see that he'd frightened her, and held her as she stood a bit unsteadily in front of him. Her chest was still heaving, her hair in complete disarray.

"That was—"

"I am so sorry, Rebecca. I lost my mind. You must forgive me."

Rebecca ducked her head and Oliver forced himself to look at her. "What are you talking about?"

"I was too rough," he said. "I could have hurt you. Did I hurt you?"

She bit her lip, and damn if he couldn't stop himself from staring at her kiss-swollen mouth. "That was perhaps the most wonderful experience of my life, Oliver. Don't you dare apologize."

His heart nearly swelled out of his chest and the words that had been hiding inside him for a few days, burst out. "I love you. God, I do. I love you so damn much."

Rebecca pulled back, her expression filled with what could only be described as surprise. Or shock. Or horror? And his heart hurt—not in a pleasant way at all.

"Then it's a very good thing I am your wife," she said, giving him a gentle kiss, strangely at odds with what had just happened. "And it's also a very good thing that I love you, too." The relief was profound. "Did you doubt it?"

He shook his head, more in wonder than anything else. "I suppose I did. You love me."

"It's rather difficult not to."

Oliver turned his head away, for he was desperately unsure whether he might cry. "I am glad." A vast understatement if there ever was one.

Chapter 9

"We're all delighted His Grace is gallivanting about," Darlene said as she took one last pin and speared her hair, narrowing her eyes as she did.

"I would not call a moonlight stroll gallivanting, but I am glad you are all delighted," Rebecca said. Darlene smiled at her warmly in the mirror. It was true; the household, which had seemed so dark and gloomy, now seemed light and filled with joy. The curtains were still pulled closed, the blinds drawn, but for some reason everything seemed brighter. Maids no longer froze or skittered away if the duke entered a room, and Oliver had taken to walking the halls rather than skulking about in the passageway. The servants were still nervous around him, for old habits were difficult to break, but Rebecca could tell they were all making an effort. To a one, they seemed happier, as if a great weight had been lifted from their shoulders. Imagine, living in fear each day, believing wholeheartedly that if they caught a glimpse of the duke, they would perish.

Rebecca would not have believed how quickly she would come to love the duke had someone told her the day she arrived. He was charming and thoughtful and made her laugh as no one had in a long time. Indeed, he reminded her a bit of her father—when he wasn't off losing a fortune at the gambling table. In the week since they'd giddily proclaimed their love, the two had been nearly inseparable. Rebecca had taken to sewing little pieces to put into his miniature houses, bits that gave each house a tad more comfort. A tiny blanket left on a chair, as if someone had just gotten up and would be returning shortly. A small strip of ribbon lying carelessly upon a bureau.

Her heart ached for him, watching him work, knowing he could hardly see the house in its entirety unless he leaned quite close. He had difficulty going down stairs if he was unfamiliar with them, not able to detect whether the ground was flat or the step dropped sharply. The few times they had ventured outside, always after dusk, he'd carried a walking stick. Rebecca learned quickly it was not an affectation but a needed tool to help him traverse the grounds. Even walking the uneven path that led to the gardens, he had to tread cautiously.

"How is it that you can run about the passageway but have difficulty on the garden path?" Rebecca had asked.

"I have memorized the passages. I rarely venture out of doors."

That would change, Rebecca announced after their first outing. "A person needs to breathe in fresh air once in a while. Even if it is ice cold." Compared to St. Ives, which rarely saw freezing temperatures, Horncliffe was bone chilling. She'd had to borrow one of the maid's thick coats to bear the weather. Mrs. Habershaw was deeply disapproving of their walks and claimed His Grace would catch his death in the night. Rebecca noted, of course, the termagant never expressed concern that she might catch her death.

"Where shall we go today?" Oliver asked as they stepped outside. Her hands were wrapped around his arm as she guided him toward the small pond, frozen over with a thin glazing of ice that would likely melt in the next day's sun, but still pretty.

"The moon is lovely tonight. There's a halo surrounding it," Rebecca said, looking up to the starlit sky.

"I cannot see it," Oliver said with a frown. "I wonder if the spectacles will help."

"I imagine they will. Mrs. Habershaw seems to think I am not ready to go to London, but if all we do is visit the jeweler and a tailor, I don't see why we cannot go. Certainly, I will not be put into a position to embarrass you."

Oliver looked down at her and smiled before leaning to kiss her cheek. "We shall leave on Saturday."

Rebecca couldn't help herself—she gave a small jump, like a little girl who'd just been promised a treat. "Saturday? Oh, I cannot wait, Oliver."

He laughed and pulled her into his arms. "I have already procured a hotel suite for us. I have a townhouse, but it's currently rented and I could hardly throw the poor family out. I don't expect to be in London long enough to rent a place; I'd like to be home for the holidays. Perhaps next year we can open the townhouse and stay there. It's a grand old place and my father loved it. I haven't been there since I was a boy, of course, but I remember a sweeping staircase and a chandelier with so many candles, my eyes hurt to look at it. I imagine it's gas lit now, though."

"It sounds lovely, but a hotel will suit for our brief visit. London shall be wonderful, don't you think?"

"No. To be honest, I dread it," he said, causing Rebecca to laugh and making him smile at his own curmudgeonliness. "You cannot know how difficult it is to traverse a city when you cannot see. I am unused to crowded streets, but I shan't ruin your visit by complaining overmuch." He kissed the tip of her nose, overwhelmed with the love he felt at that moment. Talking of going to London, looking forward to the holidays—these were things that had been beyond his imaginings not long ago. The thought they might have a baby by the Christmas after was nearly unmanning. Even now, Rebecca could be carrying his son. Or his daughter.

"Have you memorized Debrett's?" he asked, just to tease her.

"As a matter of fact…" She paused for greater effect "…no. I am helpless and a little bit rebellious. Mrs. Habershaw—"

"Means well," he said with mock sternness, and Rebecca pressed her lips together until he kissed her.

"How long do you think we'll be in the city?"

"No more than three weeks, though I hope to be there and gone in two. We'll both be fitted for a proper wardrobe and the clothing can be shipped home. I cannot imagine my spectacles will take longer than that. Mrs. Habershaw recommended we go to Hatton Garden for the spectacles and Bond Street for our clothing."

Rebecca looked down at her plain and serviceable gown. It would be nice to have the latest fashions, to actually look the part of a duchess. Perhaps if she wore the costume of a lady, she would find it easier to become one.

London in November could be mild, but that was not the case when they departed the train. It was overcast and raw, the sort of bone chilling, damp air that no amount of clothing could protect one from. Having only stayed in London a single night on her way to Horncliffe, Rebecca felt exactly like what she was—a country girl completely out of her element. All around her were masses of people, every one in a hurry to go somewhere. The air seemed oddly thick and carried with it the scents of horse, stagnant water, garbage, and smoke. It was so unlike what Rebecca was used to, she found it difficult to take in a full breath.

"Air is a bit pungent, wouldn't you say, Your Grace?" Oliver said next to her.

"I have never in my life experienced air that I could chew," she said, and he laughed.

They stood on the platform waiting for their servants to disembark and gather their luggage. Though their stay was set to be less than a month, it was necessary to bring Darlene, Oliver's new valet, and the underbutler, a Mr. Davis, two footmen and three maids. Of course Mrs. Habershaw brought her own maid, a dour, homely woman whom Rebecca had never seen smile. It was no wonder, given her employer. Mr. Starke had requested to stay behind and Mr. Winters readily agreed.

Mrs. Habershaw, who had complained incessantly the entire trip about the lack of accommodations, stood next to Mr. Winters a few yards away, glowering at the workers who were removing the luggage from the baggage car. Rebecca had been a bit dismayed to find both Mr. Winters and Mrs. Habershaw were accompanying them, but she had to admit it made sense that they did. Mrs. Habershaw knew London far better than any of them, and Mr. Winters had insisted he come along to supervise the servants.

"Neither of you have any experience with such matters," he'd said, and neither Oliver nor Rebecca could argue the point.

Though the day was overcast, Oliver squinted his eyes against the light and Rebecca gave his arm a squeeze of sympathy. "Your spectacles will surely make this sort of light more tolerable," she said, and he looked down and gave her a smile.

During the trip to London, Rebecca had gained a better understanding of what Oliver must endure—not only with his eyesight, but with the bold stares and finger-pointing. Thankfully, his eyesight was so poor, he was not acutely aware of the rudeness, but his hearing was excellent and more than one person commented on his appearance. Each time, he would stiffen and his cheeks would redden. Rebecca had become so used to him, she had turned blind to his unusual appearance. He was her husband, the man she loved, and nothing more. If there was any positive side to his albinism, it was that the beggars were wary of them and so kept their distance.

As they waited, a small boy, whose parents were distracted by the disembarkment, approached Oliver and, with a wide-eyed stare, tugged at his sleeve. Oliver looked down at the little boy, who showed only curiosity as he looked up at him.

"What happened?"

Oliver looked about for the child's parents before directing his attention back to the boy. "Do you mean why am I all white?"

The little fellow nodded, and Rebecca smiled.

"When I was very small, I wandered away from my parents at a train station very much like this one. There was a man there, quite odd looking, and he frightened me, and ever since, I've looked like this." Oliver sounded so serious, Rebecca nearly burst out laughing.

"Truly?"

"Truly," Oliver said solemnly.

"I'm not afraid of you," the boy said boldly.

Rebecca could see Oliver was suppressing a smile. "I believe your mother is about to become quite worried about you." He nodded to the boy's mother, who indeed, seemed a bit frantic. When she spied her son, she rushed over, admonishing him for wandering away.

"Thank y—" She stopped when she looked up at Oliver. "Oh. Th-thank you."

"I'm sure His Grace was once a small wandering boy," Rebecca said kindly.

"His Grace. Oh!" The woman dipped a curtsy. "I'm so sorry, Your Grace." As she pulled her son away, the little boy asked his mother what a grace was, and Rebecca imagined her explaining a duke's title.

"You handled that quite well, Your Grace," Rebecca said, smiling.

"I have noticed that children are merely curious rather than cruel. The adults, however, are another story entirely."

Rebecca was about to ask what he meant when Mr. Winters and Mrs. Habershaw came up to them to let them know a carriage had been arranged for them and another for the servants and luggage.

No one would ever know the terror Oliver felt at that moment, knowing people stared at him, knowing he could not see them, only hear the whispers. The little boy's tug on his sleeve had made his heart nearly jump from his chest, for he had not seen the child approach and, with all the noise around him, could not hear his footsteps as he neared. The only things that stopped him from going back into the safety of their train car was knowing he would not be able to find his way on his own and Rebecca's comforting and calm presence by his side. Her hand remained on his arm in silent support. When Mr. Winters and Mrs. Habershaw came up to them, Rebecca dropped her hand, but he could still feel her warmth.

The platform was crowded with people, some still waiting for luggage, others hoping to get on the train when it departed. It was noisy, porters yelling, carts of luggage rumbling past, children crying, and an old lady holding a small, skinny dog that would not stop barking at everyone who passed. It was in that chaos that Oliver realized he was alone. The small group had walked off without him, and he stood, like a statue, uncertain what he should do. Should he try to follow them? Remain where he was?

He was jostled and took a small step, suddenly feeling vertigo. Even with his walking stick, a necessity to discern the depth of steps, he felt uncertain and unsteady. His breathing became short, his vision even more dim as fear paralyzed him. How long had it been? One minute? Ten seconds? It felt like an eternity. A humiliating wash of fear left him shaking. What sort of man was he, who could not manage by himself in a train station, who became lost, like a child, when left alone?

"Your Grace?"

A woman's voice sounded softly next to him, and he turned, seeing the vague outline of a woman. He knew, because she wore a hat, the same hat worn by the little boy's mother.

"I-I seem to have lost my party," he said. "My eyesight is quite poor, you see." God, he tried to appear nonchalant, but he feared he sounded as terrified as he felt.

"There they are," she said. "Is that woman your..."

"The Duchess of Kendal. Yes."

"A duchess," the woman breathed. "Oh, my."

He could see an image rushing toward him and knew it was Rebecca, and his body immediately relaxed, to a remarkable degree.

"Oh, Oliver, I'm so sorry. I didn't realize you weren't next to me and then I turned around and you were nowhere to be seen." She clutched his arm and he smiled.

"I'm not a child; I would have found my way to you somehow," he said, forcing a light tone. He turned. "And this good lady and her husband would surely have helped me."

"Oh, yes, Yer Grace. Of course!"

"Thank you, madam." He dug into his pocket, withdrew a sovereign, and handed it to the woman.

"I couldn't, Yer Grace."

"I insist."

"Thank you, Your Grace."

When they were alone, Oliver let out a shaky breath. "I am glad you came back," he said with a small laugh.

"I know you will never admit it, but I am sure you were a bit out of sorts to be left alone, especially in such a place as this."

"I only cried a bit," he jested. "But it was edifying. I really would like for you never to leave my side in such a place. Perhaps when I have my spectacles it won't be quite so disconcerting." Terrifying was a much better word.

"I am sorry, Oliver. I forget, sometimes, just how poor your eyesight is since you get around Horncliffe so easily."

He brought her hand up and kissed it, through her kid glove. "I am sorry that you have married a man who must be treated like a child."

Rebecca laughed. "You're hardly a child, Oliver," she said, her tone teasing. "I shouldn't want to kiss a child right now the way I want to kiss you."

"Madam, if you persist, I will have to find the closest hotel and have my way with you, regardless of the conditions." He was bending his head to kiss his wife when he was interrupted by a harsh throat-clearing.

"Such public displays are highly unseemly." Mrs. Habershaw had caught up to them and was glaring at the pair as if they were miscreant children. Oliver reluctantly pulled back and dropped his wife's hand as well as any notion that he might kiss her in the midst of this bustling crowd. "If you insist on gazing upon your wife in such a fashion, people will come to the worst possible conclusion."

"That I am madly in love with my wife?" Oliver asked calmly.

"That your wife is unworthy of you, Your Grace. I am only looking out for her best interests."

Oliver sighed, recognizing there was some truth to what Mrs. Habershaw was saying. "Very well, Mrs. Habershaw, I will wait to ravish my wife until we are safely in the carriage."

The old lady gasped, outraged by his comment, which only gave Oliver a bit of satisfaction. The group continued on their way toward the waiting carriages, where Mr. Winters was directing the staff. "You mustn't antagonize her, Oliver," Rebecca whispered. "It only makes her angry."

"That was my intent," he said, and he felt her shake with silent laughter.

The cold streets of London were filled with traffic and pedestrians, all trying to reach their destinations as quickly as possible to get out of the cold. With all the rushing, traffic was nearly at a standstill and it took nearly an hour to arrive at the Brown's Hotel in the West End. It was not ideally situated, for it was located quite far from the shops where the two intended to make their purchases, but Mrs. Habershaw had insisted it was the only establishment worthy of a duke. When they stopped in front of the hotel, Oliver pulled back the velvet curtains, squinting his eyes against the light. In front of him was a large, white structure that seemed to stretch nearly an entire city block.

His eyes stung from the light as a footman opened the door and dropped the steps. "Welcome to Brown's, Your Graces," he said, stepping back. Rebecca exited first, murmuring her thanks to the footman, and no doubt winning a frown from Mrs. Habershaw, who insisted Rebecca stop acknowledging servants in such a manner. Oliver saw no harm in being polite and thought it rather endearing of his wife. Putting his walking stick out in front of him, Oliver was able to gauge how steep the steps of the carriage were and stepped down without incident. Still, he was grateful when Rebecca instantly came to his side and wrapped her hand around his arm. It had been years since Oliver had been outside of Horncliffe grounds, and he knew it would take some practice to remember all the possible obstacles he might encounter. Something as small as a single step down, no matter how shallow, could end disastrously, with him careening forward as if he was falling from a cliff.

They entered the grand hotel, their heels clicking on the gleaming marble floor. "Oh, a lovely thick carpet," Rebecca said, and he smoothly stepped up slightly, giving Rebecca a grateful squeeze. "I do believe the hotel manager is heading our way," she warned.

"Your Grace," a man intoned. "Welcome to Brown's Hotel. I am Jonathan Humstead, manager of this fine establishment. I do hope your stay will be satisfactory. Please do not hesitate to let me know if anything is not to your standards."

A lovely speech. Oliver hoped Mr. Winters appreciated it.

"I am the Duke of Kendal, and this is my duchess," Oliver said with good humor to the manager, who was warmly addressing Mr. Winters.

"Oh, my deepest apologies, Your Grace. I was under the impression you were a much older man," the manager said smoothly, bowing sharply. "The lift will take you to the fifth floor and your suite of rooms, Your Grace." The manager snapped his fingers and a uniformed bellboy stepped forward to lead the way.

"Have you ever been on a lift?" Oliver asked Rebecca.

"No." She looked longingly at the curving staircase, then dubiously at the cage they were to squeeze into. "Will we all fit?"

"Another adventure, Rebecca."

She looked up at him, smiling, and it really was the most difficult thing not to kiss her. Only Mrs. Habershaw's presence prevented him, so when the lady turned her back to them for a moment, he took the chance to kissed his wife's upturned lips. "You are a daring fellow, aren't you?" Rebecca asked playfully.

The four of them, plus the lift operator, squeezed inside the cage, which shuddered and swayed a bit before lurching upward. Rebecca clutched his arm almost painfully, while Oliver marveled at the mechanics of it. The lift was the first ever hydraulic apparatus installed in London, and though it had been in place for more than two decades, it was still a novelty to him and his wife.

"I'll have to have one of these installed at Horncliffe, don't you think, Your Grace?"

"I prefer to exercise," Rebecca said, letting out a small sound when the elevator jerked to a halt, far above the hard marble floor of the lobby.

"That was jolly fun," Oliver said, earning a frown from Mrs. Habershaw.

The entire floor was theirs. Once a series of townhomes, the rooms were joined by narrow, wood-lined hallways that dipped and curved and contained small steps between the now-connected buildings. It rather reminded Oliver of Horncliffe's hidden passages, but where he was comfortable traversing those hallways, this was a bit of a challenge. He needed both his walking stick and a reassuring grasp on Rebecca's arm.

"Your rooms, Your Grace," the bellboy said solemnly, opening the door to a painfully bright, expansive room. Given how narrow and dark the hallway was, Oliver was surprised to find the room so large. A sitting room with a fire cheerfully burning in the grate adjoined a large bedroom with a massive bed that rivaled the one back home. "Her Grace's rooms—"

"Are here," Oliver said firmly. Piled off to one side was the luggage, waiting to be unpacked by the servants. That meant the room would soon be invaded by his valet and Rebecca's maid. "Mr. Winters, you may tell the servants to settle in. They may come and unpack in an hour. No, two. And please take care of this gentleman."

"Yes, Your Grace," Winters said, and Oliver could tell he was displeased. He didn't care. He wanted to make love to his wife as he'd been unable to do during their travels.

When they were alone, Oliver prepared himself to seduce his wife, but the door had hardly clicked closed when she was in his arms, her lips pressed against his.

"I thought we would never be alone," she said, tugging at his cravat. Oliver laughed, so filled with joy he could hardly contain it inside his body. All his life, he'd wondered what it would be like to feel loved, to be the one cherished person in someone's life, and now he knew. It was intoxicating and far beyond what he'd imagined.

In a matter of minutes, they were naked on the massive bed, entangled with each other and the sheets, madly trying to please one another. Her hand grasped his manhood, her thumb teasing the sensitive tip, and he let out a low moan of pure pleasure. And when he felt her hot mouth taking him deep, he arched his back, thrusting mindlessly, on the very edge of release.

"You have decided to kill me," he managed to say, and he heard her giggle. "Come here, wife, before this ends far sooner than I intend."

Rebecca moved up his body, leaving a path of kisses, creating an exquisite friction on his exposed skin. When the apex of her thighs met his erection, she straightened, and looking down at him like a seductress, impaled herself, closing her eyes and letting out a sound of satisfaction. She swallowed, then opened her eyes to gaze down at him as his hands found her taut hips and slowly eased her up, guiding her, creating an unimaginable need inside him. Gritting his teeth, he tried to think of something other than her hot tightness around him, her muscles contracting, squeezing him. He hardly recognized his harsh breathing or the sounds coming from deep within him. When he lifted his hands to caress her breasts, to lightly pull on her hard nipples, she hissed in a breath and let out a small keening sound as she quickened her pace. And when he touched her slick center, erect and sensitive beneath his thumb, the rhythm increased, her flat stomach tensing, and he knew she was close. Together they rose and together they crashed down on wave after wave of release, until she collapsed on top of him, still pulsing around his member.

It was quiet but for their breaths and beating hearts. She draped herself atop him, all loose limbs and satisfied woman, a smile on her face that matched his own.

"I do not believe we should go so long without one another again," he said, chuckling. Rebecca nuzzled her lips against his neck and nodded. At that moment, Oliver wondered how it was possible his heart could remain in his chest, for it felt overlarge. He loved her so much his heart ached from it. "I am the most fortunate of men."

"I have always thought so."

Morrison's Fine Jewelry and Gifts was a tiny store tucked between two much larger establishments on a busy thoroughfare that was congested with carriages and pedestrians. Its proprietor, a diminutive man with a nose that would have been better suited to a man twice his size, reluctantly withdrew his gaze from whatever he'd been working on to greet his customers. His eyes widened, as so many people's did when they saw Oliver, but instead of looking wary, the man smiled as if he were seeing an old friend. "Your Grace," he said, his voice stunningly low for a man so small. Indeed, when he jumped from the stool he'd been sitting on, he was a full head shorter than Rebecca.

Oliver looked at her, silently wondering how the man knew who he was, and she gave her head a subtle shake.

"When last I saw you, Your Grace, you were with your father. You had the most remarkable eyes I had ever seen. He stopped by, inquiring about a pair of spectacles." He dashed to a large cabinet, opened the door and rummaged about for a time before producing an object with a flourish. "These. Your father never came back for them and I hadn't thought to ask for an address, else I would have certainly sent them to you. I thought perhaps he had changed his mind."

Mr. Morrison stepped to a glass counter and placed a small pair of odd spectacles atop it. Rebecca and Oliver bent and peered at them.

"I fear they won't fit you now, Your Grace, but be assured I can create another adult-sized pair for you."

Rebecca picked them up, marveling at the design and intricacy of the glasses. The rims were round and made of a thin metal surrounding an extraordinarily thick bit of glass. The truly marvelous thing was that two more lenses, made of dark-tinted glass, could be arranged to cover the clear lenses. It was very much like a hinged door that gently snapped in place, covering the clear lenses with the tinted. And when they were not needed, one could merely fold them back where they snapped against the stems.

Oliver took them from Rebecca's hand and held the pair close to his face, his eyes taking in the design. "I am sorry, I do not recall being here. I was quite young, you see, and my father died shortly after that visit. I'm sure he intended to return." Despite the fact the glasses were far too small for his face, Oliver put them on. His beautiful eyes were magnified to a rather comical extent, but when he turned and looked at Rebecca, she could see his eyes had filled with tears.

"My God, man, these are miraculous."

Mr. Morrison beamed a toothy smile. "I was rather proud of this pair. Now, your eyesight may have changed over the years. I'll no doubt have to make some adjustments. I see that the movement in your eyes has decreased since you were a lad."

"Yes, I believe it has," Oliver said, pulling the spectacles off. "How long will it take you to create another pair?"

Mr. Morrison propped a hand beneath his chin in thought. "No more than a week. The lenses must be special ordered to my precise specifications, but I happen to know just the man to create them for you. He's the same gentleman who creates most of the lenses for Britain's lighthouses. I'm certain a job this small will be a treat for him." The shopkeeper stared at Oliver with an almost paternal look. "You know, you've caused quite a stir. How long have you been in London?"

"Only two days." Oliver gave him a sheepish grin. "I do tend to cause a stir wherever I go."

"The Ghost Duke and all that. A ridiculous moniker but one that is proving to increase interest in your visit."

"The Ghost Duke?" Rebecca asked, wondering how the name had followed them to London. "Where did you hear that?" She had not read the gossip columns since leaving St. Ives and her friends. The five of them would pore over the scandal sheets often, trying to determine whom the writer was referring to. They would spend hours discussing the gossip, all the while pretending to be knitting for one charity or another. At least, the other girls had. Rebecca had knitted and sold her creations for a bit of extra pin money to hold the family over when her father had been gone overlong.

"In *The Tattler.*" He reached beneath the counter and brought out the scandal sheet. "'The Ghost Duke has all of London abuzz," he read, "having lived a life of seclusion for nearly twenty years. His duchess is unknown among the higher circles and speculation about who she is and where she comes from is rampant. Will the pair attend Lady G's ball?'" Mr. Morrison looked up, a questioning look on his face. "Will you?"

Rebecca looked at Oliver, who seemed as flummoxed as she felt. "I don't believe we have been invited. Was that piece in today's edition?"

"Indeed it was. Lady G is most certainly Lady Greenwich, who will most certainly send you an invitation now that this has run. It will be quite the coup to be the first in the ton to have His Grace attend an entertainment. I shall make certain your spectacles are completed by then."

Oliver shook his head and frowned. "I have no intention of attending Lady Greenwich's ball or any other ball for that matter. Such events are tedious and difficult for me."

"They *were* difficult for you," Rebecca said, picking up the glasses. "I believe it will be far better if you can see."

"Or worse. I am not immune to the stares, Your Grace, and if I can see those around me better, it could very well be disconcerting," Oliver said, his voice gone cold.

Rebecca had been aware of the stares but had not realized Oliver was. How awful for him to feel like such an oddity whenever he went out. While most were simply curious, others had appeared almost hostile. She'd said nothing, not wanting to upset Oliver.

"I do believe once the novelty wears thin, they will simply see a man. Or rather, a duke," Mr. Morrison said kindly. "I recall as a boy gray squirrels were a rare sighting in London. Every time someone saw one, people would gather and exclaim. But as their numbers increased, people simply accepted their existence. The novelty was gone."

Oliver smiled. "Thank you, Mr. Morrison. You are kind."

The older man's face reddened, and the tip of his overlarge nose nearly glowed. "It is not kindness, but only the truth. Now, let us determine the strength of your lenses, shall we? If you do attend the ball, you will want to look your best. And see your best." He chuckled at his own humor.

For the next hour, Mr. Morrison carefully held lenses up to Oliver while he attempted to read letters on a chart placed ten feet away. Without the lenses, Oliver could not discern a single letter, not even the largest one, and Rebecca felt her eyes prick with tears, for she could see each line clearly. Her husband was blind. She'd known this, of course, but for some reason, seeing his frustration at being unable to even recognize there was a chart with letters struck her hard.

Slowly, Mr. Morrison tested his eyes and each time, Oliver's grim expression grew more relaxed. Finally, Mr. Morrison pronounced them finished. "Even with the spectacles, you will not be able to see as well as most people, Your Grace. But I am convinced your eyesight will be vastly improved and allow you to navigate this world a bit more comfortably."

"It is quite exciting," Oliver said. "I have become rather isolated over the years and was not aware anything could be done."

"I do hope you do not plan to become a social butterfly. I like our isolated life," Rebecca said. She said the words lightly but she couldn't stop the trepidation that filled her at the thought of attending balls and suppers and all the other things the aristocracy did to fill their time. Oliver insisted he did not care that her diction marked her as a commoner, but he had not faced the scrutiny of the ton. One of her dearest friends, Harriet Anderson, had obtained all the polish that Rebecca had not, but her dealings with the ton were still fraught with censor and distrust. Harriet's background was even more common than Rebecca's, yet she had married an earl. Harriet's mother, however, had prepared her daughters well, despite their low birth, for both girls looked and sounded as if they were born into the aristocracy they were now a part of. How would Rebecca fare when she not only looked like a commoner, but also sounded like one?

"If we are invited to the ball, do you think we should decline?" she asked.

"Oh, you cannot do that," Mr. Morrison exclaimed, as if he had particular interest in whether they went or not.

"And why can we not?" Oliver asked, his tone slightly amused.

"You have a chance to erase every rumor that has ever been spoken about you in a single night. One appearance could change your life," Mr.

Morrison said. "Everyone of importance will be at the ball, Your Grace. If you are invited and do not attend, why, it would only increase the rumors surrounding you."

Rebecca felt slightly queasy, for what the jeweler said rang true. "He is right, Your Grace," she said. "If we are invited to the ball, we shall attend and you shall show everyone that you are a great man worthy of your title." *I just pray the invitation does not come.*

The next day, a thick envelope with expensive stationery arrived at the Brown Hotel for the Duke and Duchess of Kendal. The only person in their group who did not seem distressed was, oddly enough, Mr. Winters. Mrs. Habershaw looked as though she might faint.

"You must go," she said, then closed her eyes. "She will humiliate you the moment she opens her mouth."

"Mrs. Habershaw, I have been patient with your assessment of Her Grace's readiness for society but that is about to end. You will cease your criticisms and from this moment on, only provide constructive suggestions and praise."

The older woman's face flushed scarlet, but Rebecca could not tell whether it was rage or shame that caused the blush. "Of course, Your Grace." The words, said tightly, did little to assuage Oliver's worries.

"Entering society will be difficult for both of us. Perhaps it has escaped your notice," he said, "but I have not been to a social event for nearly a decade. While my diction might pass muster with you, my social skills are rusty at best. We shall muddle through, she and I, and I do wish you would keep your mouth closed unless you are saying something pleasant."

Rebecca wanted to shout hurrah, but felt at that moment a bit of dignity might serve her better after her husband's wonderful defense. For her part, Mrs. Habershaw pressed her mouth together, looking as if she was eating something unpleasant. "Your Grace, you brought me to Horncliffe for a reason and I have done my best to fulfill my obligation. I fear I have done all I can to assist Her Grace. Perhaps another can succeed where I have failed." The lady looked completely affronted.

"I was a rather difficult student," Rebecca said, not wanting Oliver to become estranged from one of his few remaining relatives. As caustic as the woman was, Rebecca had to believe she was doing her best. "I shall make every endeavor, Mrs. Habershaw, not to bring embarrassment or shame to His Grace. I dare say, I shall be so nervous I will not be able to speak at all, never mind carry on a conversation."

"Perhaps she can claim laryngitis," Mr. Winters said, displaying a rare bit of humor. Rebecca gave him a quelling look, but Oliver chuckled.

"Between my appearance and Rebecca's lack of polish, we shall be a curiosity," Oliver said with what sounded like forced cheer. "I wonder if it is a mistake all around to attend. Our formal clothes may not even be ready in time. I can hardly wear anything in my current wardrobe and Her Grace is in a similar situation."

"I'm to see the seamstress today," Rebecca said. "I shall make certain she is aware of the date of the ball." In spite of her trepidation, the thought of attending a ball and wearing a gown she would never have dreamed of owning was a bit of a thrill. She looked down at the invitation. Nine days. She had nine days to improve her diction and lose every bit of St. Ives that clung to her.

"Mrs. Habershaw, I would like to work on my diction, but I pray you exhibit a bit more patience with me and know that I am trying my best."

Mrs. Habershaw looked at her with what Rebecca hoped was a bit of admiration. It was difficult to tell whether she felt any emotion other than disappointment. "Very well. We shall meet each morning at ten for a lesson. That should give you enough time to study other matters."

In truth, Rebecca had not taken her lessons all that seriously so far, but with the ball looming and a deadline set, she found herself inspired to improve.

"My tongue is tired."

Oliver chuckled. "I really do not believe all this diction practice is necessary. What will people do, run in terror from you when one of your vowels is too broad? I can tell you now, that they will be so distracted by my appearance, you will hardly register."

She frowned adorably. "I am not certain whether you just insulted me or yourself. Probably both."

The two were on their way to pick up his spectacles. Already, they had stopped by the tailor to have a final fitting of his formal wear; the clothes were to be delivered by the evening. Rebecca was expecting a ball gown and other garments to be delivered as well, a highly anticipated event. Though he knew little about women's fashion and could hardly see well enough to tell whether someone was fashionable or not, he knew enough to recognize that Rebecca's existing dresses were serviceable rather than stylish. The day prior, dozens of boxes had arrived from the milliner and Rebecca had happily spent two hours trying on all of the hats, the more outrageous, the larger her smile. Each required a different hair style, Darlene insisted, though that would wait until Rebecca wore the hats in public.

His wife was a bundle of nerves and he only knew one way to calm her, so he pushed himself off his seat and squeezed his larger frame next to her, making her giggle.

"What are you doing, Your Grace?" she asked with mock outrage.

"I am ravaging my wife," he said.

"Are you? I hadn't notic—" She sighed into his mouth, the loveliest sound he'd ever heard, and her hands immediately went to his neck to hold him close. It was like that between them. They could hardly keep their hands off one another. With one glance, she could have him hard and looking for the closest place where he could enter her sweet body.

Last evening, he and she, along with Mr. Winters and Mrs. Habershaw, had dined at the famous Café Royal. Rebecca sat across from him, which seemed entirely too far away. During the second course, when a tray full of grapes was served, Rebecca put one into her mouth. Slowly. He could tell she was unaware of how erotic that motion was—at first. When she saw his gaze, she withdrew the grape and, with excruciating slowness, sucked it back into her mouth. Never had Oliver been so grateful for a table cloth. The room might have exploded around him and he would not have been able to tear his eyes away.

"Your Grace," he said, his voice sounding oddly strained to his own ears.

"Yes, Your Grace?" the little imp replied innocently.

He smiled, his body tense and aching, his groin heavy with need. "If you persist, our departure from this restaurant will be delayed." He raised one eyebrow.

"Perhaps we should ask for the check?" she suggested, smiling.

Mr. Winters and Mrs. Habershaw looked between the two as if they were speaking a foreign language.

"Are you feeling unwell?" Mr. Winters asked.

"I'm uncertain if I can stand. Perhaps something we ate," he said, but he could hardly get the words out, he was laughing so hard, which only served to confuse the older pair even more. He took a long drink of wine. "Yes, we should ask for the check. I jest. I am perfectly well."

Until they were ready to leave, he kept his eyes off his wife and his thoughts as far away from her lovely mouth as possible, lest he be forced to remain seated and unexposed. If he stood, it would have been impossible to hide his desire.

The moment they'd reached their rooms, they were on one another, like two starving people, undressing each other with frantic haste. Oliver wondered if this was unusual, if this passion between them was something odd, a cause for concern. She only had to look at him a certain way, and he was ready to throw up her skirts and enter her. Could that be at all normal? Of course, he had no one to ask, no older brother, no chums, and he could hardly ask Mr. Winters. As far as Oliver knew, the man had never been with a woman and certainly had never shown a bit of interest.

Oliver simply could not get enough of Rebecca, and not just her body—though that was exceptionally lovely. Her voice, her laugh, her scent all combined into a strange recipe that filled him with constant arousal. If they were not careful, and they were not always so, others would notice how consumed they were with each other. Rare was the aristocratic marriage that was founded in love. Mrs. Habershaw was correct in her estimation that they would appear unseemly if they were not better at concealing their thoughts. Still, it was great fun to give Rebecca one look and see her cheeks flush and know without a doubt that she was as aroused as he.

"I do believe we are abnormal," Oliver said after they'd finished one particularly vigorous round of lovemaking. She lay atop him, her silky hair tumbling down one side, the softest of smiles on her lips. She was close enough so he could see every detail of her face; the freckles that covered the bridge of her nose, her smooth skin, her full pink lips. My God, he was besotted. "Kiss please," he said.

Rebecca had lifted her head and pressed her mouth against his as she let out a low sound. That sound alone could make his cock stand at attention, and even though they'd just finished, it stirred a bit, making Rebecca laugh.

"Insatiable," she'd said, clearly delighted.

Now, sitting next to her in the carriage, he found himself growing uncomfortably aroused just thinking about the previous evening. He *was* insatiable. It could not be normal.

"When we return…"

She smiled. "Yes?"

Her eyelids lowered and she leaned forward to kiss his cheek. "Your Grace, we must depart this carriage quite soon. You'd best get your thoughts in order."

"How can I with you sitting here, all warm and lovely and smelling like a summer day."

"Waxing poetic now?"

He laughed. "Always. I feel bewitched."   ·

The carriage came to a halt and he couldn't stop the sharp feeling of anticipation at the prospect of donning his glasses. He prayed he was not disappointed; he'd told himself a dozen times at least the improvement would be minimal at best. Still, he couldn't help but hope the spectacles would help to make him feel a bit more confident on their outings. It was demeaning to be forced to clutch Rebecca whenever they went anywhere that was not familiar.

This time when they entered the jeweler's shop, a customer stood at the counter, a woman, judging by the dim outline he could see. "Ah, Your Grace," said Mr. Morrison with a beaming smile. "One moment please."

Upon hearing the title, the woman at the counter turned, and Oliver was close enough to see her eyes widen. He felt the familiar blush burning his cheeks as he registered her shock.

"Your Grace," the woman said, as if delighted to see him. "I am Lady Forrester. My husband was Lord Forrester, God rest his soul. I had heard you are in town. I remember your father with great fondness. He and my husband were classmates at Oxford."

"Were they? It is a pleasure to meet someone who knew my father. He was a great man," Oliver said, feeling a rush of warmth toward this woman. Perhaps her reaction was not due to his appearance but her happiness to be meeting him.

"Indeed he was. And this is?"

"My apologies, my lady. Please let me introduce my wife, Rebecca Sterling, Duchess of Kendal."

Beside him, he felt Rebecca stiffen, and he knew she was likely beyond nervous to greet this woman. It would be the thing to do, but he knew she was quite self-conscious about her Cornish accent.

"It is a pleasure, Lady Forrester," Rebecca said with excruciating care, and Oliver's heart wrenched at bit to hear her. He squeezed her arm to silently tell her bravo; only the most learned linguistic expert would have detected an accent.

Lady Forrester was a tall, slim woman with pale, intelligent eyes and brilliantly white hair carefully coiffed beneath a black hat that had some sort of feather decorating it. Oliver felt her assessment, uncertain whether she was looking at him with fondness or curiosity.

"You must forgive me, Your Grace. I realize this is short notice, but I am holding a small dinner party this evening. No more than ten guests. It would be wonderful if you could join us. At eight?"

"Dinner…" he repeated stupidly.

"Yes. If you have other plans…"

"No, Lady Forrester. I would be honored to attend," he said with far more confidence than he felt. A normal man would have either come up with an excuse quickly or graciously accepted, and Oliver was determined not to embarrass himself or Rebecca. Forcing himself to do things that frightened him to tears was the only way he would be able to become part of society. He was a duke, one whose name had been disparaged for years. Perhaps it was not too late to make amends, to become the man he knew his father had meant him to be.

While they'd been chatting, Mr. Morrison had gone to retrieve his glasses and had laid them on the counter with a flourish. "Your Grace."

Oliver stared at the spectacles for a moment before reaching out and placing them on his face.

"Oh, they're lovely," Rebecca said, forgetting her diction in her excitement. Oliver clearly heard her accent and he hoped that if Lady Forrester had taken notice, it would not matter.

The first thing he looked at was Rebecca's face, her eyes lit, her smile bright and hopeful. "Well?"

He felt tears pricking his eyes and had to swallow hard. Mr. Morrison came around the counter and began fiddling with the spectacles a bit. "Your Grace, go to the window and look out," he said, after putting the clever darker lenses over the clear ones. Oliver walked to the window, amazed that he could make his way on his own. Everything was not entirely clear, but his sight was so much better with the spectacles on, it was unmanning. He stood there, looking outside, watching pedestrians and carriages go past, seeing details he had never seen before in his life. "Bloody hell," he muttered, pushing a finger up between the lens and his cheeks so that he could brush away a ridiculous tear.

"It's miraculous," he said. The dark-tinted lens made it far more comfortable to look outside at the bright, sunlit street. These spectacles, he realized, were going to alter his life in ways he could not now imagine.

"I think you look dashing," Rebecca said, and he turned to look at her, stunned by how clear her lovely face was to him. He could see her light freckles, curling eyelashes, brilliant blue eyes. Yes, he'd seen those features before, but he'd been so close, he hadn't been able to her face clearly as a whole. There she was, his beautiful duchess, far lovelier than he'd known.

"Mr. Morrison, thank you."

"It was my pleasure, Your Grace. I always wondered how you got on, and now I see that it has been a struggle for you."

Lady Forrester stepped toward the spot where Oliver stood with Rebecca, her gaze curiously sweeping over his wife before returning to him. "I shall see you this evening, then, Your Grace?" She handed him a card with her address.

"Indeed, yes," Oliver said, unable to stop the smile from forming on his face.

"Wonderful. Mr. Morrison, I shall return to pick up the brooch on Friday?"

"Yes, my lady."

After Lady Forrester departed, Oliver could not stop his joy from spilling over. He picked Rebecca up and spun her about, glad that she laughed and hung on tightly. Behind him, Mr. Morrison chuckled as well.

"I apologize for my unseemly behavior," Oliver said, "but I do not believe I have ever been this happy in my life." He grinned foolishly. "I can see you, Mr. Morrison. I can tell you are smiling. Your tie is green and..." He looked about. "That sign above your shelf." He squinted his eyes, for he could barely make out the lettering. "All sales final."

"Yes, indeed," Mr. Morrison said, beaming.

"You can read that?" Rebecca said, grabbing his arm. "Oh, Oliver, that is wonderful."

"I have a feeling my new life, the life I have been meant to live, begins tonight."

Chapter 10

Rebecca did her best to hide her terror at the thought of dining with such lofty people. Mrs. Habershaw was nearly as horrified by the news as she was.

"She's not ready," she said when Oliver announced the pair would be dining out. "She can hardly speak a sentence without reverting to her former speech. This is disastrous."

Oliver just smiled, for it seemed nothing this day could dampen his mood. "Her Grace is perfectly capable of attending a dinner," he said, giving Rebecca a quick kiss on her cheek, which only made Mrs. Habershaw moan.

"You cannot kiss your wife in front of others this evening." She turned to Mr. Winters, who looked on with amusement. Evil amusement, Rebecca thought darkly. She had no doubt that Mr. Winters was hoping she would fail.

"And I should not do this, either?" Oliver swept her up into his arms and kissed her until she nearly forgot where she was. The devil.

Rebecca gave Mrs. Habershaw a quick apologetic look; the poor woman seemed on the verge of fainting.

"Mr. Winters," the older woman said, obviously attempting to appeal to the man.

"His Grace is teasing you, Mrs. Habershaw. He is quite aware of etiquette and well versed in social norms. He, at least, is more than ready to dine with such notables."

Rebecca did her best not to scowl at the implied insult. Though she had wracked her brain trying to remember what title Lady Forrester held, her panicking mind could not recall her rank. As a duchess, Rebecca realized that, other than the queen herself, she outranked nearly everyone who might be at the dinner party. And that was why she felt like such a fraud.

She wondered if she would ever feel like a duchess; perhaps in her dotage she might be able to fool people.

"Rebecca's diction is much improved," Oliver said loyally, and Rebecca gave him a grateful smile that was only slightly tinged with the nervousness she felt. Embarrassing Oliver was the very last thing she wished to do. She only hoped that whomever she was seated next to found the person opposite enthralling. Perhaps if she limited her answers to yes and no or, better yet, she could simply nod? Rebecca swallowed down the lump of fear that was growing in her throat. This evening could be disastrous.

"At least she looks the part," Mrs. Habershaw said in a most begrudging manner.

Indeed, Darlene had outdone herself with Rebecca's hair, upon which sat a lovely little tiara that Darlene and Mrs. Habershaw insisted was entirely appropriate for dining with the dowager countess. Yes, Lady Forrester was a countess, as Mrs. Habershaw informed her, which meant the rest of the guests would likely be of the same ilk. To think Rebecca had been nervous to attend St. Ives' little John Knill ball, which compared to anything held in London was merely a provincial, country dance. What on earth had Oliver been thinking to marry her sight unseen?

Still, she adored him. Loved him. She would do what she could to make him proud. Perhaps she *could* claim laryngitis.

"Her Grace shall be the loveliest lady there tonight," Oliver said, his eyes behind his spectacles darkening with appreciation. Though Rebecca had not known Oliver long, this was the happiest she had ever seen him. This evening, this entire visit to London, meant far more to him than she'd realized. Living in isolation, fearing to be seen, shunning society—it had all worn at him. Now, though, he was becoming more confident, more like a duke.

That thought made Rebecca frown slightly, an expression that previously would have gone unnoticed by Oliver. Now, though, he saw it and moved to her side. "What is wrong?"

"You're becoming entirely too duk-ish, Oliver, and I'm not certain I like it."

"I am a duke, after all."

"Yes. But before we came to London, it wasn't quite so apparent."

Oliver just laughed, then took up her hand and pressed it to his lips, ignoring Mrs. Habershaw's throat-clearing. "I shall endeavor to not be too duk-ish tonight," he said gallantly, which made Rebecca laugh.

"You should be going. Traffic this time of night can be difficult," Mrs. Habershaw said. "And remember the topics I mentioned that are allowed. Nothing political or controversial. Nothing about animals or illness or—"

"Yes, I remember, Mrs. Habershaw. I shall endeavor to talk only of the weather."

Rebecca took a bracing breath and laid her hand on the crook of Oliver's arm, realizing he hardly needed her guidance anymore. It was still difficult for him to sense the depth of steps, but he walked with far more confidence toward their door.

"These spectacles..." he said, shaking his head. "I still cannot believe it. And I have you to thank, my love."

The ride to the Earl of Hampton's London residence was far too short for Rebecca's liking. She secretly prayed for a wheel to come loose or for the driver to lose his way and drive to Horncliffe instead. But, no, they arrived on time, with only a short queue of carriages to wait for before they could disembark. Oliver had no difficulty departing the carriage, for he had spent some time practicing doing so earlier that afternoon, something that made Rebecca realize how very important it was that he not appear in any way handicapped by his condition.

"Your Grace," he said, grinning and offering his arm.

"Your Grace," she said, smiling up at him impishly.

"Do not look so charming, else I will have to drag you back into that carriage and—" He stopped, realizing the footman was close enough to overhear. Rebecca realized that the servant had not reacted to Oliver's appearance, and she wondered if everyone had been forewarned. Though she was used to his pale skin and shockingly white hair, she did understand why seeing Oliver for the first time might be a bit jarring. As distracted as she was by her own trepidation, she couldn't help but feel grateful for Lady Forrester's thoughtfulness. Whatever had happened to Oliver when he was a youth to make him so reticent about going into public would not be revisited this evening, she thought.

Rebecca did her best not to gawk at the beautiful, massive house with its brilliant crystal chandeliers that lit up the grand entrance. In the center of the vast entry hall was a large statue of a shepherdess with three charming little sheep surrounding her. Though Rebecca knew little about sculpture, it seemed clear it was the work of a master, and she had to stop herself from hurrying over to examine it more closely.

Lady Forrester was there to greet them, along with her son, the Earl of Hampton, a robust-looking man with a full head of dark wavy hair. Next to the earl was his wife, a tiny woman who exuded privilege and class. Her blond hair was perfection, her smile confident yet restrained. Rebecca made a note to observe her in hopes of learning a thing or two about how to act properly. Rebecca had to stop herself from curtsying, something that was so ingrained, it nearly hurt to simply bow her head slightly in greeting.

"We are so glad you were able to come this evening," Lady Forrester said warmly. "My other guests are quite anxious to meet you both."

Rebecca couldn't help but wonder why. Was it Oliver's rank or was there some darker purpose; was it possible the dowager countess simply wanted to put the latest oddity on display? If this was all some sort of mean trick, Rebecca knew she would lose her lady-like demeanor in a second and let everyone attending know just what she thought of them. With those thoughts swirling about her head, they entered the room, Rebecca on edge, waiting for the slightest look, the vaguest comment that gave insult. Instead, they were met warmly by all.

Because she so feared speaking, Rebecca kept her greetings to low murmurs, allowing Oliver to take the lead, which he did with rather amazing aplomb. She had never seen this side of her husband, the man who was charming and outgoing, who entertained and spoke intelligently on a wide range of topics. She looked at him, wondering who this man was. Had she met him, she would have immediately considered herself far below his notice. It was almost as if she were standing beside a stranger—until he looked at her and smiled.

"Ah, there you are," she said softly, and he smiled apologetically.

"I was raised to be a duke, my love," he said near her ear. "I do believe this is going well so far."

Indeed, the entire evening went far beyond Rebecca's expectations. The guests—a baron and his wife, an admiral and his daughter, a member of the House of Commons and his wife, as well as the adult children of the house and their spouses—were nothing but kindness. No, it was more than that. It was as if they were all blind to the fact that Oliver was albino, as if they had known him for all their lives and simply accepted him for what he was. Oliver sat on the opposite side of the table adjacent to the earl, with the countess to his right and the dowager countess to his left. Rebecca had been placed between the admiral and the baron, who thankfully shared a love of breeding hunting dogs. They chatted over her nearly the entire evening, not expecting her to join in, for which Rebecca was grateful. Once in a while, one of them would remember she was there and say, "Don't you agree, Your Grace," to which Rebecca would nod. The evening thus far could not have been better.

As the evening progressed, she could sense Oliver relaxing and beginning to truly enjoy himself. The guests seemed to find him witty, and more than once Rebecca would tilt her head in an effort to hear what it was Oliver was saying that was so amusing. From time to time, he would look her way and give her a smile, but the guests kept his attention, leaving Rebecca to her thoughts.

Everything seemed normal, festive, and relaxed, but Rebecca couldn't help but feel slightly ignored. It was what she wanted, of course, but still, she was no more important than the chair she was sitting upon for all the interest she garnered. As each course progressed, Rebecca became more aware of one particular guest who seemed to be in thrall with her husband.

"I saw that miniature," the admiral's daughter said—Penelope was her name. She was a lovely girl with blue eyes and blond ringlets that bounced whenever she nodded or giggled. She seemed to giggle quite a lot and mostly at whatever Oliver uttered. "It was the loveliest thing I've ever seen."

"Thank you, Miss Martins," Oliver said, smiling at the girl, who blushed prettily. Rebecca found herself fighting not to roll her eyes. Clearly the girl was flirting with Oliver, as if perfectly oblivious to the fact that his wife was seated not three chairs from her.

"I remember wishing I could shrink down and explore the halls," she said. "Have you made others?"

"A few. I fear it was all that has occupied my time."

"I would love to see them some time," Penelope gushed, and Rebecca found herself bristling. "You could give me a little tour of your tiny creations."

"We would love to have you and your father visit Horncliffe someday," Rebecca said, so astonished by the girl's forwardness, she forgot to be quite as careful with her diction as she would like.

Penelope leaned over slightly, as if surprised to find Oliver's wife at the table. Had the girl not known was there? "Thank you, Your Grace," she said politely, if not slightly coolly. Then she tilted her head. "Do I detect a bit of Cornwall in your speech, madam? I only ask because my maid has a similar accent. It is so charming."

Rebecca could feel her face heat. "You have an excellent ear for accents," Rebecca said smoothly and with as much care as she could. "My family is, indeed, from Cornwall."

"The end of the Earth," the girl's father said, letting out a laugh. "However did the two of you meet?"

Rebecca shot Oliver a panicked look, one which she prayed he would be able to see. Why hadn't they come up with a story about how they'd met? They could hardly admit that they hadn't met at all before marrying, that they had married by proxy.

"My distant cousin introduced us," Oliver said smoothly, and Rebecca nearly sagged in relief. "I took one look and knew she had to be my duchess."

"How romantic," Lady Forrester said.

"Indeed it was. I know it's not the thing to admit, but I adore my wife." The married women at the table seemed to glare at their husbands. "We all adore our wives," the earl said quickly, and the other married men hastened to nod in agreement.

Miss Martin smiled politely but her cheeks were slightly flushed, as if she knew that the duke had been reminding her that he was not only a married man, but one who was in love with his wife. In that moment, Rebecca felt nearly overwhelmed with love for Oliver. Somehow he knew she'd been annoyed by Miss Martin, and likely heard her slight slip into her Cornish dialect. She couldn't wait until they were alone again so that she could let him know how very much she adored her husband.

After dinner, the men went into the study for their brandy and cigars and the women went to the parlor. This was the moment Rebecca had been dreading most of the evening. She was the newcomer here, and she had no doubt that people would be curious about her. She imagined Mrs. Habershaw standing next to her, ready to pinch her hard if she strayed from her rigid path of decorum. Already she'd allowed her temper to get the better of her and nearly revealed her common origins. She was under no illusion that she would escape unkind gossip should anyone find out the true story behind her marriage to the Duke of Kendal. Just the thought that her secret would be discovered made her slightly ill. Imagine someone learning that not only was she far below Oliver's station, but that she had practically been sold to the duke in exchange for the forgiveness of her father's gambling debts.

No matter how many times she told herself there was no way anyone in the room could possibly know her past, it still loomed large as she stepped sedately into the countess's lovely parlor with the rest of the women. The parlor was a long, narrow room, with rich gold drapes pulled back by black silk cords. The furniture was mahogany with silk coverings, the rugs beneath her feet thick and luxurious, all done in gold, blue, and black. Horncliffe's rooms, while spotless, lacked the warmth and charm of this room, and Rebecca made a mental note to discuss changing the décor with Oliver.

This mingling with the women was fraught with danger. No one here was her ally and it would take only a single question to unmask her. Panic was beginning to grow in her chest and she could feel an uncomfortable warmth spread in her body, making her perspire rather unbecomingly. Ladies do not perspire, Mrs. Habershaw had told her more than once. Well, this lady did and this lady was—to a horrifying degree.

"Are you quite all right, Your Grace?" Lady Forrester asked kindly.

"A bit warm," Rebecca managed before taking a seat, remembering to do so slowly and with grace. Mrs. Habershaw would be proud. She sat picturing a board strapped to her spine, an image Mrs. Habershaw said would assist her in maintaining good posture.

Miss Martins took the seat next to her, much to Rebecca's dismay. She certainly hoped the girl didn't intend to strike up a conversation with her. Her hopes were dashed when Miss Martins turned toward her. "I do not recall seeing you during last season," she said. "I'm sure I would have remembered."

"I did not attend the Season," Rebecca said. Short sentences. Keep calm.

"Last year was my first Season."

Rebecca smiled and nodded.

"I do adore all the parties and balls, though my father finds them wearying." She fiddled with her gloves for a moment, and Rebecca had a feeling Miss Martins was itching to ask her something. "The duke is… unusual, no?"

"Strikingly so."

The girl frowned a bit. "But a duke." She looked up shyly. "However did you—" She snapped her mouth closed, realizing she was being a bit crass, no doubt. "Everyone is curious, you see. My friends were terribly jealous that I got to meet him this evening."

"Oh?"

"He's all anyone can talk about. A mystery. And so exotic." She leaned forward. "It's said he hasn't been to London since he was a child, has lived the life of a recluse. Yet here he is, in Lady Forrester's home, and here I am in the very same house. It's quite exciting." She clasped her hands together as if she could hardly contain her excitement. What on earth was going on with this girl? They had only been in London a few days—how could word have spread so quickly?

"Exciting?"

"He is the Ghost Duke!" she said, as if that explained everything. Seeing Rebecca's expression of dismay, Miss Martins looked immediately chastened. "I do apologize, but it is what people call him. That lovely pale skin and white hair. Marvelous, isn't it?"

"Yes, my husband is quite handsome," Rebecca said, emphasizing the word husband. This girl was going on as if Oliver were some famous opera singer or a star cricket player.

"Yes," she said, somewhat subdued. "You say you were introduced to him by his cousin?"

"A distant cousin, yes." This was true, so Rebecca felt no twinge about lying.

"But if he was a recluse, how did you meet?"

Rebecca felt her heart pick up a beat. "I first met his cousin, an older gentleman who acted as His Grace's guardian since his father's death when he was a boy. Mr. Winters thought we would suit and so introduced us."

"Mr. Winters was in Cornwall?"

Rebecca smiled tightly. "Yes."

"How...fortuitous for you."

"Very." The girl might look like a china doll, but she was clearly intelligent and rabidly curious—a combination that was more than a little disturbing.

"And he brought you back with him?" She tilted her head and smiled.

"Your Grace, you must sit in our box tomorrow evening." Rebecca wanted to kiss the baroness for interrupting their conversation. "Vivaldi's *Argippo* is performing and we have two extra seats."

"That sounds wonderful, my lady, but I shall have to ask His Grace first. I am afraid I do not know if he has plans."

"Of course. We would be honored to have you attend with us."

When the lady left, leaving Rebecca slightly perplexed about their sudden popularity, Miss Martins leaned toward her and whispered, "Your husband is in high demand and the baroness knows it. I predict you'll have far more invitations than you can possibly accept. People are curious, Your Grace. They want to see His Grace. And you, of course," she added hastily.

A furrow appeared between Rebecca's brows. "I shouldn't like for people to put His Grace on display like some sort of pet," she said, feeling slightly ill at the thought. Was this what was happening?

Miss Martins looked horrified at the idea. "Oh, no, Your Grace. That is not it at all. It is only that his father was well-known in the ton and when he died, it seemed as if His Grace disappeared. Some even wondered if he were still alive. To have him here, in London, back where he belongs, is causing a bit of excitement. Yes, his appearance is unusual, but he is the Duke of Kendal! It is one of the most prestigious titles in all of England. And he is here in this house. I sat next to him and had a lovely conversation. You cannot know how jealous all my friends will be. The Duke of Kendal."

To say Rebecca was taken aback by the starry-eyed Miss Martins would have been a vast understatement. Her husband, apparently, was gaining celebrity.

By the time the men had settled in with their brandy and cigars Oliver, who could not stomach cigars and politely declined, was having a wonderful time. His life had been so constricted, he'd never had the pleasure of male companionship, and he found he was quite enjoying himself. Just listening to the others, who had experienced far more of life than he had, was fascinating. The admiral, of course, regaled the men with stories of adventure and heroism, and was such a good story teller, one could almost close one's eyes and taste the sea spray. Never in his life had Oliver been with such a diverse group of peers and he found himself feeling quite at home. No one stared at him, made him feel less of a man. No one whispered behind his back or treated him as if he were some sort of imbecile who could not understand the King's English. This experience was so far removed from his one disastrous foray into society, it was quite heartening.

The only time any of the men noted his appearance was one of Lady Forrester's sons, Michael Henley, who found his spectacles fascinating.

"Clever design," he said, when Oliver handed them over for his inspection.

"People with my condition tend to have poor eyesight and are excessively sensitive to light."

Mr. Henley gave him a look. "My wife said you are the most dashing member of the peerage." He handed back the spectacles. "If I were you, I'd count myself lucky that I found a bride without having to attend London's marriage mart. I have a feeling if you had arrived looking for a wife, the mamas would be on you faster than a starving flea on a dog."

Oliver laughed as he put his spectacles back on. Each time he did, he was surprised anew at how well he could see with them. "I am a lucky man, indeed, Mr. Henley."

"How did you go about that?" Baron Ashly asked, turning toward the pair. "I still have two daughters I need to marry off and the thought of spending two seasons putting them on display is enough to produce nightmares. Not only the expense, but the tears and hysterics."

"I was lucky enough to be introduced to Her Grace by my distant cousin. I was immediately besotted," Oliver said sheepishly.

"Do me a favor, will you?" Michael said. "Don't let on to all our wives how much you love Her Grace. We shall never hear the end of it." He spoke in a falsetto, "If the Duke of Kendal can publicly declare his love, why can't you? Why can't you be more like the duke?"

"My apologies," Oliver said, chuckling. "I shall endeavor to scowl at Her Grace whenever we are in public."

"A few of us are going to be at Whites tomorrow night," Michael said. "I know your father was a member and I've no doubt you would be welcome. Why not join us?"

A wave of happiness hit Oliver with unexpected force. Here he was, in a room full of strangers, men he should have known his entire life, men who had accepted him without question. He could not have created a better outcome of their trip. It was as surprising as it was welcome.

"I should like that. Thank you." He paused. "What is White's and where is it?"

Silence followed; then the baron and Michael burst out laughing. "By God, Your Grace, you have been out of London far too long. Whites is an exclusive men's club, one that only those of the highest rank are allowed to join. Your father and I used to play faro for hours when we were young, before…"

"Before he married my mother."

Lord Ashly cleared his throat. "Yes. Indeed, yes. To be able to meet his son is a privilege that I'm sure you cannot fully appreciate."

"Perhaps some day you and I can sit and you can tell me all about my father's youth. I was so young when he died, I have very few memories."

"I would be honored, Your Grace."

Once the brandy and cigars were finished, the men rejoined the ladies, and Oliver went directly to Rebecca's side. It struck him hard that not a week ago, he would have been unable to find her in a crowd of women. But there she was, looking beautiful, if not a bit overwhelmed by her surroundings. He had to remind himself that she was unused to such gatherings. Though he had never participated in society, it seemed this was all second nature to him; years of polish had well prepared him for such evenings and any shyness he'd initially felt was long gone. By god, he was enjoying himself immensely. It was almost as if he'd been missing something without even knowing it, and now felt as if he'd come home.

"You look pleased," Rebecca said when he joined her.

"I am," he said softly. "Everyone has been incredibly welcoming, a far cry from the last time I socialized. I've been invited to White's tomorrow evening. We don't have any plans, do we?"

"The baroness did ask us to attend the opera, but I could tell her you have plans."

"No, love, we'll go to the opera and then I shall be a man about town, shall I? I've no doubt we'll be receiving invitations to other events."

"Everyone is curious about the Duke of Kendal, it seems."

"I had no idea my father was so well-liked. It seemed that when I was a boy, he was always about, but he must have traveled to London frequently. I've lived my entire life without realizing what I've been missing out on."

"I am so glad you are happy, Oliver."

He thought he sensed a bit of hesitation in his wife. "And you? Are you happy?"

"More terrified than anything," she said, laughing.

"I daresay, if I can do this, you can. You are lovely and I, despite the warm welcome here this evening, am a bit of a curiosity. I know they still refer to me as the Ghost Duke."

"True. But you were born into this world. I feel as if I'm a fraud, that any minute now, someone will discover I'm a common girl from a common family. I think they already suspect it."

Oliver tilted his head to better see her expression. "You are perfect to me, you know. I particularly adore it when you call me your 'usband."

Rebecca narrowed her eyes in mock anger. "I haven't dropped an h in at least three weeks," she said. "Mrs. Habershaw raps my knuckles whenever I do."

Oliver lowered his gaze to her lips. "Would it be too shocking if I kissed you right now?"

"It would be entirely too shocking. Dukes are not supposed to love their wives, did you not know that?"

He moved closer until he could breathe in her perfume, and said softly into her ear, "Dukes are also not supposed to constantly picture their wives unclothed even when they are wearing such a pretty frock." He laughed aloud when her saw her cheeks turning pink and couldn't help but think of her other pink places. Breathing in, he stepped back before his body reacted to his wayward thoughts. "I cannot wait to get back to the hotel."

"I agree. I am reading a book that is ever so fascinating. It's about the flora and fauna of Wales."

"That does sound wonderful, but I have something else in mind."

Giving him an innocent look, she said, "I cannot imagine what. You know how I adore reading about the flora and fauna of Wales. Would you deny me my pleasure?"

"Never," he said meaningfully, and won himself another blush.

"I thought I told you to stop looking at your wife as if you adore the ground she walks on," Michael said loudly, slapping Oliver on the back. "Makes the rest of us look bad."

"My apologies, Henley. I am newly wed and still infatuated with my wife. I am certain in a week or so I shall grow bored and look at her far less frequently."

Rebecca pressed her lips together and smiled, looking so adorable, he couldn't help but find himself staring at her again and smiling.

"Good God, I give up," Michael said, throwing up his hands in mock despair. "Are you certain you can tear yourself away from your bride long enough to attend Whites? There's an entire city we'd all like to share with you, Your Grace."

"I am looking forward to discovering my father's London with great anticipation."

Rebecca sat on one of the hotel's pretty but uncomfortable chairs, the type that look soft and cushioned but actually hurt one's derrière. The upholstery was pink and cream striped, the wood dark and highly polished, and Rebecca was sick of looking at it. This was the third night she'd spent alone in their suite while Oliver went out and "discovered London." Apparently, her husband was making up for all those years lacking male companionship. He'd discovered a fencing club and spent his afternoons sparring with new friends, the sort he would have made in school had he attended university. At night, he was lured to various men's clubs, where he relished the banter and camaraderie of his peers. He returned to their bed, smelling of cigars and whisky, too exhausted to do more than pull her close and kiss her neck.

He was ecstatic, and Rebecca was simply bored. Yes, the invitations poured in, but they were addressed to both of them. She could hardly attend a supper party or concert without Oliver. And so while he enjoyed all that London had to offer, she sat in her room, sitting on an uncomfortable chair, fuming.

"You're angry with me," Oliver said, looking in the mirror and adjusting his cravat. "I promise, we shall go somewhere this afternoon. Perhaps the Royal Academy. I think Mr. Henley mentioned some sort of exhibit there. Or was it Sir Wendell?"

"I don't know. I wasn't there," she said, frowning when he didn't acknowledge her acerbic tone.

"And tonight is the opera. Though I cannot say I am looking forward to it. Last time I could hardly see a thing."

Rebecca had been bored silly during the opera they'd attended with Baron and Baroness Ashly and she'd been dreading going this evening. "I adore the opera," she said, just to be contrary.

"Do you? Then we shall go every night this week. A different opera house each evening."

She picked a piece of lint from her sleeve, pouting. "Perhaps we could go home soon?" Hope bloomed in her chest. Already, with the ball this Friday, they were staying longer in London than first anticipated. Spending so much time alone—Mrs. Habershaw was visiting her sister, who lived just outside of Mayfair—Rebecca found herself missing her St. Ives friends terribly. She'd written them yesterday to tell them about all her wonderful adventures, but in truth, she longed for St. Ives' cool, fresh breezes and the scent of the sea. Though winter had not hit London yet, the air seemed dense and dirty. It didn't help that but for one day, it had been overcast and drizzling. But unlike the refreshing mist of St. Ives, Rebecca found London fog raw and miserable.

"Of course we'll return before the holiday," Oliver said cheerfully. "I'm having such a smashing time right now, I rather dread going back to Horncliffe. It seems so dreary now that I've experienced a bit of the city." He came over and kissed her cheek. "I promise, you'll have fun this afternoon. I know I've been neglecting you…"

Rebecca instantly felt guilty. Poor Oliver had never had much fun at all in his lonely existence, and here she was feeling sorry for herself. "You go have your fun, Oliver. Goodness knows you deserve a bit of gaiety in your life. I shall be content to stay here. Perhaps I can go out shopping while you are gone. I'm sure Darlene would love to accompany me. I don't want you to worry about me."

"Was I worried?" he asked, clearly jesting.

"I truly thought you might expire from worry. I know you can hardly enjoy yourself at all knowing I am here alone."

"I shall endeavor to have some fun," Oliver said, then kissed her again. His expression turned serious. "Are you certain, love? I would hate to think you unhappy whilst I run around London."

"I want you to enjoy yourself, Oliver. Truly. I was feeling a bit melancholy because I do miss my friends back home and I suppose I am a bit jealous of your popularity. It's just that I don't have anything in common with the women I've met so far."

"That shall change after the ball. Everyone will adore you."

The night of the ball was bitter cold and a light snow fell on the city, unusual for November. The flakes, glittering in the light of the gas lamps, looked magical to Rebecca, who marveled at how cold it was, how beautiful.

"Oh, it's snowing! I've never seen the snow. It's like little fairies floating to earth," Rebecca said.

"The snow is like fairies?"

"You see, the moon is shining and the snowflakes are glittering, like fairy wings." Oliver chuckled at her fancy. "Do you think it will snow a lot?" she asked, and Oliver smiled indulgently. Snow was a common event for someone from the north. "Enough to build a man of snow?"

"A snowman, you mean? If it does, we shall venture out of doors tomorrow and build one."

"Your Grace, we only have two hours before you must leave," Darlene reminded her as she bustled around the room, taking out all she would need for the ball. The gown was a lovely deep red with cream lace in the latest style—or so the seamstress had boasted. It was by far the prettiest and richest dress Rebecca had ever worn. Her shoulders were exposed and cunning little lace sleeves left her arms mostly bare. A series of oversized draping bows cascaded down the back of the gown making her just as alluring coming as going—that was what Oliver said at any rate. Unused to having quite so much flesh exposed, Rebecca worried that the dress was too risqué, but Darlene tutted and reassured her the style was quite acceptable, particularly for a married woman.

"It's a dress worthy of a duchess," Darlene said, lifting the heavy silk gown and laying it on the settee. "And how lovely your ermine stole will look, Your Grace. Truly, you will be the envy of every lady present."

Mrs. Habershaw had returned from visiting her sister in time to drill into Rebecca the rules of attending a ton ball, and Rebecca's head whirled with the information. "She is not prepared for such an event," she'd warned earlier that day, but Oliver waved away her concerns.

"Rebecca will be the belle of the ball," he said grandly, making her laugh and Mrs. Habershaw scowl.

"Can a married woman be the belle of the ball?" she asked.

"No."

"Yes."

Mrs. Habershaw and her husband answered in unison and Rebecca couldn't help but laugh again.

"I shall endeavor to remember all your fine teachings, Mrs. Habershaw. I believe I am ready."

Despite her reassurances, Mrs. Habershaw wrung her hands together in worry. "They can be so cruel," she said softly, an odd pain running quickly across her face as she darted a look to Mr. Winters.

"They wouldn't dare," Oliver said. "I have come to learn in these last days that the Kendal title commands great respect. My father was well liked and that regard has thankfully been transferred to me. I have powerful allies in the ton, Mrs. Habershaw. No one will dare insult my wife."

Rebecca gazed at her husband with surprise. She'd never heard him speak so authoritatively, and she couldn't help but feel a bit of pride in him. He was acting more like the duke he was every day.

His words, however, seemed to do little to reassure Mrs. Habershaw. "I do wish I was able to attend with you." Rebecca found herself moved by the older woman's real concern. While it did nothing to put her mind at ease, it was a bit of a surprise coming from a woman she'd thought didn't care a whit about her.

"That is not possible," Mr. Winters had said, sounding irritated with the older woman. Rebecca looked from one to the other, wondering if they'd had some sort of tiff. Usually the pair seemed as cozy as two peas in a pod.

Now with the ball just two hours away, Rebecca's confidence wavered. Even with a beautiful gown and her hair intricately coiffed, she was still just a common girl from St. Ives underneath. If only one of her friends was in attendance to shield her, she would feel so much better. But every woman at the ball would be a stranger and from a world that was far from her own experience.

Which would mean she would be thrust into society with Oliver as her only ally.

Chapter 11

Rebecca gazed at her reflection in the mirror, entirely too pleased with the image that looked back at her. Her knowledge of fashion was limited at best, as she'd never had the sort of money that would allow the purchase of even a single gown like the one she was now wearing. And her hair, piled on her head in an intricate style that had taken Darlene more than an hour, perfected the image of what a duchess should look like. Glowing on her head was a tiara, larger and more glittery than the simple one she'd worn to dinner. Rebecca Caine wearing a diamond-encrusted tiara and going to a London ball. It seemed like a dream—and one she was gaining enthusiasm for.

She looked…like a duchess.

Oliver came in and stopped suddenly, as if he'd walked into a wall. "By God, you are lovely," he said, coming up behind her. Rebecca could feel herself flush with pleasure. This night that she had dreaded for so long just might be the most wonderful night of her life. She'd worked so hard in the last two weeks, even gaining praise from Mrs. Habershaw, who had returned from her visit in time to drill her on decorum, proper topics of conversation, and a rejoinder to always, always remember her diction. Though she still insisted Rebecca was not prepared well enough, her thin praise gave Rebecca more confidence to face the ton. Above all, if something did go awry, Mrs. Habershaw reminded her she must never show emotion, neither anger nor hurt. Rebecca found that advice slightly unsettling. After all, what could happen at a ball to make her angry?

"I am actually looking forward to this evening," she said, looking at Oliver in the mirror.

"I have something for you," he said, suddenly sounding a bit shy, and Rebecca turned to him. "We do have family jewels locked up in Horncliffe. I didn't think to bring them as I hadn't expected that we would be attending a ball. So I visited Mr. Morrison and purchased this."

He handed her a large velvet box. "Oh." Rebecca felt her eyes prick. And when she opened the box to reveal a stunning necklace of rubies and diamonds, she gasped and very nearly dropped it. "Oh, Oliver. It's lovely. It's the most beautiful necklace I have ever seen."

"Allow me," he said, taking up the necklace and moving around her so he could fasten the clasp. "Mr. Morrison assured me these are of the highest quality gems. It's quite heavy."

Her hand fluttered to her neck to touch the necklace. The rubies matched her deep red ball gown perfectly, and she was touched that Oliver had taken the time to inquire about the dress.

"Look at you, Your Grace. You look like a princess, you do," Darlene said, her own eyes looking a bit misty.

"Oh, Oliver, thank you." She twirled around and gave her husband a quick kiss on the cheek. "Tonight is going to be the best of nights."

It took Rebecca only a handful of minutes upon entering Lady Greenwich's mansion in St. James Square, to realize that something was slightly off. Though not experienced in society, she soon sensed that those in attendance were staring at her. At first, still floating on a cloud of happiness, she assumed they were looking at her lovely gown, her stunning jewels. But as the night went on, she because of aware of whispers, titters of laughter, sly glances, that seemed to be directed her way. At first, Rebecca assumed it was mere curiosity. She was, after all, someone unknown to them and someone who had married the Ghost Duke. Any malevolent intention must be her imagination.

Oliver stood by her side, greeting a few fellows who stopped by for a handshake or a hearty backslap. No one, not a single person, acknowledged her. While it was clear Oliver was well liked and highly sought after, after the third couple came up to him and struck up a conversation without even a glance in her direction, it became clear something was afoot.

Remembering Mrs. Habershaw's instructions that she must never show emotion of any kind, she continued to stand by Oliver's side and smile as Oliver engaged in animated conversation. Seeing how relaxed and happy Oliver was made Rebecca momentarily forget her own discomfort. It was as if Oliver had been part of society all along. He was charming and funny and attentive, full of a confidence that had been missing not two weeks ago. Rebecca wished she could exude the same confidence and polish, but in reality, her insides were all ajumble and she found herself growing more and more terrified that she would do something to ruin their evening.

Why was no one talking to her?

Mr. Henley spied them from across the room and came over to give each a greeting, something that Rebecca vastly appreciated. Perhaps it was her imagination. After all, she had said nothing to anyone, why would she assume anyone should speak to her?

"You must see my stables," he said, clearly proud of his horse stock. "Once you see them, I daresay you'll want to start your own stable. Never met a man with so few horses. Perhaps I'll even sell one or two of my own."

"For an exorbitant fee, I'm sure," Oliver joked.

"Of course," Henley said, laughing. "Listen, I hear there's a lovely billiard room here somewhere. Heberts is already there. Why don't you join us?"

"Well..." Oliver said, looking down at Rebecca.

It was clear he was itching to go, so Rebecca smiled and said, "I shall be fine whilst you play your game. But do not be gone too long."

"Never," Oliver said fervently, making Henley roll his eyes.

"I thought we told you not to act so besotted," he said, drawing Oliver away.

Rebecca watched the two men leave, and laughed, pleased that Oliver had found such a good friend.

Left alone in a sea of strangers, Rebecca felt increasingly uneasy, and she realized just how much she had come to rely on Oliver. No one came forward to introduce themselves, and Rebecca hardly had the courage to walk up to a nearby group of women and insert herself into their group. With a smile plastered on her face, chin perfectly parallel to the floor, back straight and steps small, Rebecca made her way to the refreshment table, keenly aware that she was drawing attention to herself. The ballroom was quite a crush, and maneuvering from one side of the room to the other was nearly impossible, but she could hardly remain where she was, standing alone in the center. It appeared the orchestra was about to begin playing, so she tried to hurry her steps. A small group of debutantes, dressed in pastels and surrounded by an air of privilege, blocked her direct path to the table. Rebecca waited patiently for a small space to open up so she could squeeze through and fetch something to eat, even though she had quite lost her appetite. Her stomach felt odd and tense and the worst was not knowing why or even if she were imagining things.

Finally able to navigate past the small group, Rebecca offered one girl a smile. The young lady quickly turned her head. Had she just been given a…cut? Feeling a flush of humiliation, Rebecca continued on her way, that smile still lingering despite her discomfort.

"Harlot."

She stopped and slowly turned. The group of young women stood still as statues, as if surprised she would have the audacity to turn and confront them. Clearly, that horrible word was meant for her.

"I beg your pardon, but do you know to whom you are speaking?" There, she sounded like a duchess. Almost.

"I am sorry, but no one said a word to you." This from a girl with dark brown ringlets. Her eyes were cold, her mouth set. Rebecca told herself she should simply carry on and continue to the refreshment table, but she could not. That word, the venom behind it, had clearly been directed at her.

"I am the Duchess of Kendal," she said, trying in vain to keep her voice level, to sound calm when her instinct was to leap on the girl with the smug face and tear the hair out of her lovely head.

"Are you…quite certain of that?" one of the girls asked with stunning smugness.

"As I married the Duke of Kendal, I would say I am quite certain, yes. Who are you?" Though Rebecca's heart hammered in her chest and she could feel her face flushing, she was proud that her voice remained level, her expression bland.

"Lady Suzanne Dawson. And you are no duchess."

One of the girls in the group gasped. "Suzanne!"

Rebecca smiled tightly. "As I said, I am married to the Duke of Kendal, so I do believe that makes me the Duchess of Kendal."

"If you say so," the first girl said, as if Rebecca had just told her she was the Queen of England.

Shaking her head slightly, Rebecca continued on, feeling the hated prick of tears behind her eyes and baffled by the strange exchange. The girl seemed so hostile toward her, a person she'd never met before. Why had they come to this stupid, stupid ball? It was clear to her that someone had started an ugly rumor about her. For what reason, she could not fathom. She had half a mind to return to the group of girls and demand to know why they had said such a horrid thing to her. *Do not cause a scene. Do not show that temper of yours,* Mrs. Habershaw had warned her. It was almost as if she'd known something would happen this evening.

Rebecca stared blindly at the offerings on the table, small pastries that looked entirely unappetizing. Swirling around, she looked around the vast room for Oliver, but he was nowhere in sight. She wanted to leave, go back to their hotel and pretend none of this had happened. Imagine, calling a duchess of harlot. Why? Why would they say such a thing?

Swallowing down a growing lump in her throat, Rebecca made her way to the ballroom's entrance, feeling stares directed her way, seeing men and women lean toward one another and whisper. What were they saying? Had someone somehow found out how Oliver had married his bride? Mrs. Habershaw had warned her the ton could be cruel to those who did not belong. And Rebecca did not.

She approached a footman who stood at attention outside the ballroom and asked where the ladies' retiring room was. He directed her down a hall, where Rebecca found herself blessedly alone. Instead of going into the room, she instead sat in a chair in a small alcove beyond the room, quite hidden from whoever was in the hall. Though she knew Mrs. Habershaw would be disappointed in her, Rebecca planned to stay exactly where she was until Oliver came to find her. The urge to flee the house was strong, but hidden in that little space, Rebecca felt safe. As she sat there, she began to feel a bit foolish. Perhaps she had been so nervous about the ball, she'd imagined everything. Perhaps whoever had said the word harlot hadn't been referring to her. How awful if she had made the wrong conclusion. Still, cowardly as it was, she had no intention of returning to the ball, and tucked her skirts even closer to her just to make certain they could not be seen by anyone passing in the hall.

It wasn't until she'd calmed herself that she heard the voice of the same girl who had spoken to her earlier and realized her hiding spot was ideal for eavesdropping. Mrs. Habershaw would be horrified by such behavior, but Rebecca didn't care.

"What if they are wrong, Suzanne? You may have made a dangerous enemy. Really, you do need to be a bit less awful." Though the words sounded as if Suzanne's friend was chastising her, they were said with such glee, Rebecca had the feeling the girl was only having a bit of fun.

"Is calling a duchess a harlot so wrong?" Suzanne retorted. Rebecca's blood nearly boiled. So, the slur had been directed to her. She balled her fist and prayed for the strength to remain still and silent. The other girls giggled. "She's a nobody. My maid has more blue blood in her than that pretender does."

"That is true. Since she's your half sister." More laughter.

"Don't be cross, Mary. There is a reason the classes are separated. If we allow them to mingle with us, it will taint our bloodlines."

"Now you sound like your mother," a soft voice said. "I believe that sort of thinking is a bit antiquated, do you not? The House of Commons is filled with commoners, and they are far more powerful than the House of Lords now. Does it really matter who sired her?"

"Cecelia, will you hush? You will never find a husband if you insist on discussing politics. Suzanne is right. We cannot allow such a scandalous woman to walk among us as if she belongs. Calling herself a duchess. Really."

"Should we not also shun the duke? Is he not just as culpable for bringing her here?"

"Honestly, Cecelia, you sound like one of those awful suffrage women. Such an entirely unattractive group of women has never before existed in England."

The three voices became muffled as they entered the ladies' retiring room. Suzanne had called her a "pretender." That must mean that somehow someone had discovered how Oliver and she had married. Her stomach tightened uncomfortably. How could they have found out so quickly? Had Oliver perhaps told one of his new chums and the fellow had repeated the story? Rebecca knew how things could be twisted about in the retelling. For all she knew, everyone now thought she'd been rescued from the gutters, secretly married to the duke. She could understand a bit of snobbery, and had been prepared for it, but to call her a scandalous woman seemed a bit far fetched. Did the ton really think her marriage scandalous because her parents were not of the aristocracy? And why on Earth had that woman called her a harlot?

Rebecca remained where she was, stiffening when she heard the voices again as the women left the retiring room. This time, they had moved on to another victim, apparently. "She really should do something with that hair. It looks as if it's made of sheep's wool."

"My mother says she should shave it off and wear a wig..."

Once Rebecca was certain the girls were gone, she stood and went in search of Oliver, doing her best to show a calm façade when inside, her nerves were frayed.

Oliver had followed his friend down the hall that led to the billiard room, looking forward to mingling with the men whom he had gotten to know in the past weeks. But when Henley had finally stopped, Oliver had found himself in a study.

"Please, come in, Kendal," Henley said as he closed the door, the noise from the ballroom instantly muted. "I need to speak to you."

Curious, Oliver walked into the room, an unsettled feeling hitting him. Henley was rarely a serious bloke, and Oliver sensed something was wrong. "What is on your mind, Henley?"

"Do you mind?" Henley asked as he turned up one of the sconces. He beat a hand softly against his thigh, his expression solemn, and Oliver's anxiety grew. "This is difficult," he said finally.

"Should I sit down?"

Henley gave him a small grin. "Perhaps. There is a rumor going around, a vicious one, about you and your wife."

Oliver grew still. "Go on."

"People are saying Her Grace is in actuality your mistress, that you are not married and you have been parading a soiled dove as your duchess. On a lark."

Oliver stared at Henley a beat, then burst out laughing. "You must be joking."

Henley remained solemn. "I am not. The thing with rumors is that they are quite difficult to dispel once they take hold. And this has certainly taken hold."

Now that he thought of it, he had sensed something strange about the way people had looked at the two of them when they'd entered. He was used to being heartily welcomed, but those who greeted him when they'd arrived had seemed a bit subdued. "Who would start such a rumor? What could possibly be the motive behind such a thing?" Oliver ran his hand through his hair, the scope of the problem beginning to hit him. It was not amusing in the slightest that someone would not only disparage him, but say such awful things about Rebecca.

"I have no idea, but the rumor has been running like a wild fire."

His white brows snapped together. "I fear I am not well-schooled in how to address this sort of thing. Simply denying it will do nothing." He let out a puff of air. "Shall I have to produce our wedding license? Good God, what is wrong with people? And just when I was beginning to feel a part of society. This is rather disastrous, isn't it?"

Henley gave his friend a helpless look. "I have never encountered such a sordid rumor in my experience, and certainly not one directed against someone of your status. But if is it a lie, it can easily be proven false."

"If?" Oliver asked, irritated with his friend—until a terrible thought struck him. If Oliver could have grown paler at that moment, he would have, for he felt the blood drain from his face. "My God."

"What is it, Kendal?" Henley asked, stepping forward, clearly concerned.

Oliver gave his friend a steady look. "What I am about to tell you must never leave this room. Swear it."

"I swear," Henley said.

"Rebecca and I were married by proxy. My former guardian, Mr. Winters, was there in my stead. I was reluctant to travel at the time, a bit of a recluse. I saw a portrait of her and instructed Winters to marry her."

"Marriage by proxy is unusual, but it is perfectly legal," Henley pointed out.

Oliver was silent for a long moment. "I've never actually seen the marriage certificate."

Henley inhaled sharply. "Are you saying there is a possibility you are not married?"

Oliver felt like hitting something, preferably Winters's face. A rage was building inside him, one that was nearly blinding. With a sharp nod, he acknowledged that there was a possibility he was an unmarried man. The thought that Winters would do something so nefarious made him nearly sick.

"Bloody hell, Kendal."

"Mr. Winters made it clear from the beginning that he did not approve of my marrying Rebecca." The betrayal he felt at the possibility that Mr. Winters was behind these rumors nearly drove him to his knees. The man, for all his flaws, had been like a father to him. Certainly, he had been misguided in his attempts to protect Oliver from harm, but would he go as far as to stage a false wedding? To deliver a girl to him who had been duped into thinking she was marrying a duke? It was all too possible. "I have to leave. I have to find Her Grace and remove her from this place." He closed his eyes briefly. "I am sure she has not received a welcome here. By God, if anyone has hurt her, I shall wring their necks, lady or no."

Henley laid a steadying hand on his shoulder and Oliver resisted the urge to knock it off. The urge to strike something was nearly overwhelming. "Settle down. When you leave this room, you must act as if nothing has happened. Do not glare at anyone, do not say a word. It will only fuel the rumors and completely destroy whatever standing you have in the ton. Look bored. Look anything but what your expression is now saying."

"I am not certain I can do that."

"You *must*. I shall accompany you. Oliver," Henley said, and Oliver looked at his friend, "I shall be there for you no matter what. If this rumor is true, I know you were duped. You can make this right."

"Of course. I'll marry Rebecca in a traditional ceremony immediately."

Henley dropped his hand and sighed. "I am not certain that will do."

"What do you mean?"

"Your wife, if this is true, has been ruined beyond repair. She would be seen as a woman who has been living in sin with a man. No better than a whore." Henley put up a staying hand when Oliver let out a low growl. "As unfair as it is, the ton will never accept her after this. And if you marry her, I do not believe they would accept you, either."

"And you, Michael?"

"I have said I will stand by you. But you should be prepared that no one else will."

"If Winters knowingly did this thing, it will be a difficult thing not to kill him," Oliver said.

"Another poor idea. Come on, Kendal, let us find your wife and get her the hell out of here. Be calm, man. Are you ready?"

Oliver took a deep, shaky breath, and schooled his features.

"Your fists, Kendal. Unclenched might be better."

At that Oliver had looked down, slightly bemused, for he hadn't realized he'd been clenching his fists. Now, as he released them, his hands ached from the effort. Fencing had taught him to hold in his temper, and he sought that training. "I am ready."

"I see that you are."

Henley led him out of the study and toward the ballroom, where Oliver did his best to lazily scan the crowd for Rebecca. Even with his spectacles, it was extremely difficult to see across the room. Everything was a foggy blur. "Do you see her?"

"No," Henley said, then, "There. She is standing alone near the entrance. In a deep red gown, is she not?"

"Yes." Red. The color of a fallen woman, and Oliver wondered if Mrs. Habershaw had somehow conspired against Rebecca. Swallowing down the rage that threatened to erupt, Oliver began a slow stroll toward his wife, Henley by his side.

"Steady, Kendal," he said, sounding very much like a man trying to calm a nervous stallion.

As he made his way toward her, Oliver nodded politely to those he passed, for all the world looking like a man who had no care in the world. When he reached Rebecca, he knew instantly that she was aware something was terribly wrong.

"We must leave," she said calmly, and his heart ached for her. She was being so very brave.

"I agree. But first, we must dance." He leaned toward her ear so that no one nearby would be able to overhear his words. "There is a terrible rumor going about. We shall dispel it and act as naturally as possible. Then we shall leave."

Rebecca looked at him, her eyes wide, and he could tell she was trying very hard not to cry.

"Be brave, my love." He gave her a smile. "I shall explain everything when we are safely alone in the carriage."

As the orchestra began playing one of the more popular waltzes by Johann Strauss, Oliver bowed to Rebecca and held out his hand. He knew very well how to act the gentleman at a ball, even if this was his first such event. Rebecca placed her gloved hand in his and they calmly walked to the dancing area and began moving to the music.

"I am very proud of you, my love," Oliver said softly.

She gave him a tremulous smile. "Please do not be kind. It will only make this more difficult."

He grinned. "Very well. Shall I step on your toes, then?"

That produced a small laugh. "Then I can claim my tears are of physical pain," she said, and he found it exceedingly difficult not to draw her closer to him. But for this dance, they would maintain the utmost decorum.

When the music ended, Rebecca placed her hand in the crook of his arm and he led her from the floor. Both held their heads high, their expressions bland, even as they were aware they were the center of everyone's attention—whether discreet or not. They sought out their hosts, Lord and Lady Greenwich, who were gracious when they announced they were leaving the ball.

Outside, the temperature was frigid, their breaths making plumes in the air as they waited for a footman to lower the steps of their carriage. The horses stamped impatiently, no doubt wanting to get out of the cold and back into the relative warmth of their stable. Rebecca pulled her ermine wrap tighter around her, grateful for the warmth of the fur.

Once they were both inside the vehicle, Oliver immediately went to her side and pulled her to him. "That was an unmitigated disaster," he said against her ear. "Do you know what is being said about us?"

Rebecca shook her head, unable to talk past the lump in her throat.

"It is upsetting, but it is something that I am hopeful can be set to rights. Apparently, someone has started a rumor that we are not married, that you are my mistress only, and that I have been passing you off as my duchess on a lark."

Rebecca pulled back and stared at Oliver to judge whether he were joking with her. "You are serious."

"Yes. Mr. Henley is the one who told me."

"That explains those horrid women," she said, her sadness quickly giving way to anger. "One called me an unpleasant word and hinted I was not the duchess I claimed to be. Who would circulate such a terrible lie?" Oliver looked away, and something in his pensive expression set off alarms bells. "Oliver?"

"It may not be a lie."

Rebecca felt as if her blood froze in her veins. "What can you mean?"

"Mr. Winters. He was against our marrying. I would not be surprised if the proxy marriage was somehow illegitimate. Do you recall signing any documents?"

Rebecca thought back to that day. She had felt ill and lost, and probably more frightened than she had ever been. "I'm not certain. I was in such a state. Oh, Oliver, what if we are not married? It would mean I have been living with you without the benefit of marriage." She shook her head. "No wonder that woman called me a harlot."

"A harlot?" Oliver repeated angrily.

"It matters not now. If it is true, if we are not married, that is how society will see me. How everyone will see me. Could Mr. Winters have done such a terrible thing?"

Oliver placed a palm gently on either of her cheeks. "I pray not. But if he did, we will simply remarry."

Rebecca's eyes filled with tears. "If he did do this thing, Oliver, I cannot marry you. Do you realize how this scandal would stay with us? With our children?" She began crying in earnest. "How could he be so cruel? I cannot believe that even Mr. Winters could have done something so abominable."

Oliver sat back and was silent for a long moment. "Who do you think spread the rumor, my love?" he asked quietly, his tone telling her he suspected the same person as she.

Rebecca closed her eyes. "Winters."

"I can think of no other person. We will put this to rights. If we are not married now, we bloody hell will be soon and society be damned. I will not lose you, Rebecca."

Rebecca looked out the window at the gaslit streets, feeling as if her entire world had just crumbled beneath her. Oliver's standing in society had been greatly damaged, but she knew she had been completely ruined. Society would never welcome her back. To think she had worried everyone would find out she was a commoner, not worthy of a duke. How could Oliver possibly enjoy London again when she was ostracized, as she most assuredly would be? The man he'd become, outgoing and charming, full of life and friends, would disappear again if they were to marry. Wives would not allow their husbands to chum around with a man who'd married a commoner, a commoner who had shared his bed for weeks without a proper wedding. It would not matter that they had been tricked; who would believe such a thing? Their lives this night had been irrevocably changed. Rebecca was fairly certain that Oliver was unaware of the dire consequences of Winters' betrayal.

Oliver deserved to become the man he'd been born to be. To mingle with his peers, to make friends. To have children with a woman society did not consider a whore. Her heart breaking, she looked at Oliver and smiled, then leaned over to give him a lingering kiss. "I love you," she said. "I shall always love you."

"You will not do that, Rebecca," he said, giving her a little shake. "You will not say good-bye to me."

She pulled back, her cheeks flushing, for he seemed to have read her mind. "I said I love you, not good-bye."

"I am not a fool. If we are not married, we shall get married. Is that understood?" he asked, his expression fierce. And then his face tightened. "Unless you do not wish to remain married to me." His entire body had gone still, his expression taut, and even behind his glasses, Rebecca could see the pain in his eyes.

Perhaps a more noble woman would have told him she did not want to remain married. But she loved him, with every bit of her heart, and the thought of leaving him made her feel dead inside. Tears filled her eyes and she pressed her lips together before saying, "Of course I shall marry you." In that moment, she meant it, but she also knew a better woman would refuse.

With a groan, he pulled her against him, pressing his mouth against her neck. "Good, then."

"But you must promise to never resent me, never regret your decision."

"Never. You are my life, Rebecca. Without you, I shall again become that ghost living in a tower room."

The carriage stopped outside their hotel and swayed as the footman stepped down to lower the stairs. Rebecca was about to step down when she turned back to Oliver. "Do not murder Mr. Winters, though I am sure you would like to."

Oliver let out a bitter laugh. "I should have murdered him long ago, I think. I was so blind…"

"We do not know anything for certain yet, Oliver." But her intuition told her that Mr. Winters had been behind the rumor—and if the rumor were true, had coldly calculated to make certain they would not find happiness.

"He's gone, Your Grace, returned to Horncliffe Manor."

"Gone, what do you mean, gone?" Oliver demanded of the under butler.

"He received a telegram after you and Her Grace departed this evening. He did not say what the message contained, but informed me he must return to Horncliffe posthaste."

Oliver muttered a curse, and Rebecca laid a gentling hand on his arm and was shocked at the iron strength beneath her fingers. "How soon do you think we can have everything packed for a journey home, Davis?"

"A half day, Your Grace."

"Make it so."

The under butler bowed and left, no doubt to tell the other servants that they would be leaving for Horncliffe the following day.

"Oliver," Rebecca said when he'd departed, "I'm going to speak to Mrs. Habershaw about this. I have a feeling she may have been aware of what Mr. Winters planned and may even have been culpable."

He furrowed his brows, and it was clear that the thought had occurred to him too. Rebecca recalled the warning Mrs. Habershaw had given her about maintaining her composure no matter what. "I'm sure Mrs. Habershaw is abed," he said. "And I need you in my bed this night."

Rebecca grinned. "You always need me in your bed. But I shall not be able to sleep if I do not speak with her. I'll be back soon and then…"

"Come here," Oliver said, drawing her against him. He kissed her lightly, then rested his forehead against hers. "I adore you, you know."

"I know. I shall return shortly."

Rebecca made her way through a short maze of halls until she reached Mrs. Habershaw's suite of rooms. A light shone beneath the crack in the door, and Rebecca wondered if the older woman had been waiting for them to return. Perhaps she had predicted an early arrival. She knocked and waited for only a moment before the door opened.

"Good evening, Mrs. Habershaw. May I speak to you?"

Mrs. Habershaw, her eyes wide, took in the fact Rebecca still wore the ball gown, and nodded, backing into the room. Rebecca had never seen the woman look so ill at ease, almost meek in her demeanor. Rebecca followed her into a small sitting space with a cheery fire in the hearth and sat in a chair opposite the woman.

"You are aware what happened this evening?" Rebecca asked.

Mrs. Habershaw lifted her chin, ever proper, but then something flickered in her eyes and she looked away, toward the fire. "I can guess," she said softly. "And how did you fare?"

"Are you asking if I conducted myself as a duchess should? Then yes, I did," Rebecca said, anger flaring in her chest. "How could you, madam?"

To her shock, Mrs. Habershaw's eyes filled with tears. "I did not want anyone harmed, particularly His Grace. Such a lost little boy when his father died. And left in the care of that horrid man."

"You mean Winters, of course."

When Mrs. Habershaw looked at her, all evidence of tears was gone, and Rebecca wondered if she had imagined them. "Of course. Mr. Winters has information about my husband that I am desperate to keep a secret. I would do anything to protect his name, to protect my children."

"So he blackmailed you."

"Yes. For so long I lived in comfort, thinking that all was forgotten. I am of little consequence in the ton, so I had grown complacent. But when he contacted me about tutoring you in the ways of society, I suspected he had nefarious plans. I am sorry, Your Grace, but I truly had no alternative other than to do what he said."

"You called me Your Grace."

Mrs. Habershaw looked taken aback. "Of course I did. Why would I not?"

"Then the rumor you and Mr. Winters spread is not true." Rebecca nearly felt like crying in relief.

Mrs. Habershaw continued to look confused. "But it is true. You are a commoner, a nobody…" She gave Rebecca a long stare. "That is not the rumor you heard, is it?"

Rebecca shook her head. "No. That we could have survived. The rumor is that we were never married at all, that we have been living together, unwed. That His Grace has been showing off his mistress as his duchess as a jest."

Mrs. Habershaw turned pale. "My word. That is…despicable, even for Mr. Winters. I swear to you that I had no part in spreading such terrible lies. I never would…" She was so horrified, the woman could hardly speak. "That is far more devastating than anything I could have devised. Oh, my poor dear, you are truly ruined beyond repair."

"I know," Rebecca said bleakly. It was clear that Mrs. Habershaw was not aware of the manner Rebecca and Oliver had married or that they might not be married at all, but Rebecca did not want to enlighten the woman. At this moment, she had a bit of an ally, but if Mrs. Habershaw knew the truth, that might change. "We are returning to Horncliffe as soon as everything is packed and ready."

"Of course."

"And then I would like you to pack all of your belongings and leave."

The older woman's cheeks turned pink, and she seemed to lose a bit of her composure. "Yes, I think that is for the best."

How different was the journey back to Horncliffe as compared to the one to London. The newlyweds had been filled with excitement and nerves then, but now a depressing pall seemed to have shrouded even the servants.

Oliver stared out the window, taking in the bleak, bare trees that lined the road. What a fool he had been. He couldn't help but believe that all of this lay on his shoulders. If he had taken control of his life, of his title, as he should have, none of this would have happened. He was filled with self-loathing, yet at the same time, felt the loss of someone who had been his friend. Except, Winters never had been his friend, nor his father. He had been an evil presence, shading everyone's life at Horncliffe, instilling fear, and all the while, Oliver had turned a blind eye, so desperate was he to feel as if someone in the world cared for him. It hurt, and that it hurt was just as humiliating as the fact he had allowed it all to happen.

"I know you are blaming yourself." He jerked his head around to look at Rebecca, and his heart clenched painfully in his chest. How did he deserve such a lady as his wife? She looked unusually pale, her hair striking in the dim light, but dark smudges marred the delicate skin beneath her eyes, and it looked as if she carried the weight of the world on her shoulders.

He forced a smile. "I am the only one to blame. I allowed Mr. Winters to become the monster he became."

"I do not know a man or woman who would not have been scarred by the way you were raised. He created you, day after day, year after year, but now, Oliver, you are fighting to become a better man."

"I cannot help but think how disappointed my father would have been." He swallowed hard and returned his gaze out the window. It was far easier to look at the barren landscape than his beautiful wife, who insisted on seeing him as someone noble, someone to be admired. She sighed and shifted in her seat.

"What shall you do about Mr. Winters?"

He clenched his jaw. "I shall have him removed post haste and then I shall go about hiring a secretary and estate manager, someone who will know far more about caring for my properties than I do."

His wife was silent for a long moment. "He will try to convince you that what he did was for your own good."

"Yes, I am aware of how manipulative he can be." Oliver forced himself to look at Rebecca. "It will not work this time, Rebecca. I swear to you. He has gone too far."

Giving him a pensive look, she said, "I know it will not be easy. As angry as you are, Mr. Winters has been your guardian for years. Your friend."

"I thought of him as such, yes. But I was mistaken. Terribly so. Believe me, Rebecca, when he leaves Horncliffe, I shall feel only relief." He held out his hand to her. "Come here."

She came willingly, climbing onto his lap and settling her head against his shoulder. "You're so warm," she said, and he could feel her light breath against his neck. He moved one hand up and down her arm to take away the chill. No matter what happened, he would never let this woman go.

After several days' travel via rail and carriage, Horncliffe came into view. The house had become dear to her, with all its idiosyncrasies, and Rebecca was fiercely glad they were finally home. She was exhausted, but knew an emotional scene awaited them.

"Do you want me to stay with you when you speak to Mr. Winters?"

"No," Oliver said, his jaw tightening as it had so many times on their trip home. "I fear I shall say things to him that are not fit for your ears."

When they entered the manor, Mr. Starke was there to greet them. "It is good to have you home, Your Grace," he said, as he took both their coats and handed them off to a maid. "Your spectacles are quite impressive."

"It is good to be home, Mr. Starke. And these spectacles are more than impressive—they are miraculous." Oliver looked about him. "This is the first time I've seen what this entry actually looks like."

"I hope it is to your expectations, Your Grace."

Smiling, Oliver said, "Indeed it is. Mr. Starke, is Mr. Winters home?"

"He is. I believe he is in his rooms. Shall I fetch him?"

"No. I'll go to him. Thank you, Mr. Starke."

The butler left them alone, and as Oliver was about to head up the sweeping staircase that led to the private quarters, Rebecca touched his arm. "Do you know what you plan to say?"

"I do. I rehearsed in my head the entire way home. By this time tomorrow, Mr. Winters will no longer call Horncliffe home."

"I am glad, Oliver. Still, I do know this will be difficult."

"No, my love, it will not." He smiled grimly. "I'll see you in our room when I am done and I'll tell you all about it." He leaned in and pressed a kiss against her forehead.

"Do you think cook will mind if I raid the pantry? I must admit I'm a bit famished. I'll bring something for you as well if you'd like."

"The cook's brown bread with butter would be perfect, if she has a loaf."

"She always has a loaf of brown bread," Rebecca said on a laugh. He was about to head up the stairs when she threw herself into his arms and squeezed him tight. "Try not to be too violent."

"I promise not to murder him. That's the best I can do."

Rebecca sighed and let him go, watching worriedly as he walked up the stairs, his steps determined, his fists clenched.

A burning rage filled him at the thought of what the man had done, a man he had trusted. After Oliver rapped sharply on the door, Winters opened it, a bland smile on his face.

"Ah. You have returned early." Oliver pushed past him, forcing the older man to stumble back. "You seem upset. Did something happen?"

Oliver whirled around. "You know very well what happened. What I want to know is why."

Winters gave him a blank stare, and for just a moment, he thought perhaps he had been wrong about him. Lord knew he wanted to be wrong. Then something shifted in Winters' expression; his face grew hard, cynical. "I did what I had to do. I did what was necessary."

"You made me look like a fool and you insulted my wife. I will not stand for that."

"Your *wife*." Winters let out a small laugh. "Do you really believe I would allow you to marry such a creature?"

Oliver felt the blood drain from his face at this confirmation of his worst fear. "What are you saying?"

"You are such a fool to believe I would allow you to taint the family blood with a whore."

Oliver launched himself at Winters, grabbing him by his robe's lapels and slamming him hard against a wall, causing his head to snap back with a violent thump. Fear filled his eyes briefly before Winters gave him his characteristic look of boredom, and it took everything Oliver had not to strike the man. "So it's true. I am not married to Her Grace."

"Good God, no."

Later, Oliver would not recall raising his fist, but in a matter of seconds, Winters was on the floor, blood gushing from his nose. Oliver stood over him, his damn hand stinging, breathing harshly as he stared down at Winters. "I should kill you," he said. "I *want* to kill you."

Winters put his hand to his nose and gave his bloodied fingers a casual look. "You will not kill me and one day you will thank me. For God's sake, man, you picked her from a painting. She is a nobody from a family with no status. Why not marry one of the maids? Do you really wish to bring such a creature into society? To introduce her to the ton? I will hazard a guess that the ball was an unmitigated disaster. They no doubt saw her as the fraud she is. You might find her country accent charming, but I can assure you, Your Grace, no one else does. Tup her all you want. Make her your mistress, but I implore you, do not make her your wife."

"How could you?" Both men turned abruptly to see Rebecca standing in the entrance to Winters' room, and Oliver felt as if his heart stopped. She looked from Oliver to Winters, who was still on the floor, still bleeding. "You, sir, are the worst kind of scoundrel. I wish you to perdition." She looked at Oliver and his heart broke. He knew at that moment that she had hoped all of it was a terrible lie. "I wish I knew terrible words to throw at you." Tears filled her eyes and Oliver felt completely helpless.

"I have done what I thought I must," Winters said, rising from the floor to stand.

"But the vicar…"

"Even vicars can be bribed," Winters said, taking up a handkerchief and pressing it against his nose.

Her eyes filled with tears, her face contorted in pain. "Then he is right. I am a whore." The truth of what had been done to her seemed to hit her with force and Oliver would have done everything in his power to protect her if he could. But he felt just as helpless as before she'd wrought such changes in his life.

"No, Rebecca." He took a step toward her, but she moved back.

"I know I am not to blame. I know you are not to blame. But in the eyes of the ton, and to everyone in my village…I am ruined. Mrs. Habershaw said as much." She looked up to the ceiling and let out a bitter laugh. "I'm not a duchess. I'm a whore."

"You are *not*," Oliver said, and walked over to where she stood. "You are not."

"You can say that over and over, Oliver, but the truth of the matter is that I have had relations with a man I was not married to. Even now I could be carrying your child. An illegitimate child."

Oliver laid his hands on her shaking shoulders. "Rebecca, we shall simply get married in truth as we discussed. Please, my love, I know this is difficult, but we can make it right. We can."

She took a deep, shaking breath. "We'll discuss this in the morning with more level heads," she said, giving him a tremulous smile. Before leaving, she gave Winters—attempting to look dignified despite his blooded nose—a scathing look, one that he seemed to find amusing, and Oliver clenched his fist again.

When Rebecca was gone, Oliver said, "I want you gone tomorrow. Pack your things and never return."

"Don't be ridiculous, Your Grace," he said, tugging on his sleeves.

"If you do not leave of your own volition, I will have you escorted out."

"Very well," he said, mockingly. "We can settle our accounts tomorrow morning."

Oliver's brows snapped together. "Accounts?"

Giving him a level look, Winters said, "I have spent my life caring for you. Since the time you were six years old, I have sacrificed everything to keep you safe, to give you some sort of life. I managed your estates, handled all grievances, made all decisions. For years." This last ended on a shout. "I believe that deserves some compensation, do you not?"

As much as it galled Oliver to pay him, he knew denying Winters would only delay his parting. "Very well. I shall give you an income of one thousand pounds per year."

"Five."

Much to his humiliation, Oliver had no idea how much money he had or even if he could afford one thousand pounds, never mind five thousand. "Two. Or nothing."

Winters gave him a brief smile. "Very well. Good evening, Your Grace." He gave him a mocking bow, then turned away.

Oliver left the room, closing the door softly behind him, feeling utterly exhausted. He pulled his spectacles off and rubbed the bridge of his nose. He was glad Winters was going, but he had no idea what he was going to do to save Rebecca from the ton. The weight of the disaster he had created was very nearly crushing.

On his way back to his suite, he stopped by the portrait gallery and looked up at the image of his father. The painting was the only thing he had left of him, and he prayed it was an accurate depiction. As he stood there he realized that other than his pale skin and white hair, he looked exactly as his father had. "What have I done, Father?" he whispered, feeling closer to weeping than he had in a long time.

Before he returned to his wife—for he would continue to think of Rebecca as his wife—he gave the gallery a long look, pausing when he heard what sounded like a woman singing. His hearing was excellent, and he stilled, tilting his head to listen. Silence. With a small chuckle, he realized he'd just heard the famous ghost of Horncliffe Manor.

Shaking his head, he left the hall and headed to his rooms. Just picturing Rebecca lying in his bed waiting for him made him quicken his steps.

Exhausted, Rebecca had made her way back to her rooms, her feet feeling as if her shoes were filled with lead. How stupid she was, to have allowed Winters to trick her so. Hadn't her mother or father made certain the documents were correct and valid? They probably knew as much about proxy marriages as she did. And she could not believe Vicar Smythe would have done something so nefarious as knowingly conduct a ceremony he knew would not be legitimate. Then again, people often did terrible things in the name of money.

Now, her stomach rumbled loudly. Despite the events of the day, she still had an appetite, so she decided to head to the kitchen as she'd originally planned. Her fear that Oliver and Mr. Winters would get into a physical alteration had prompted her to follow her husband. She almost wished she hadn't. Mr. Winter's words, the derision in his voice, would stay with her for a long time.

Something sweet would make her feel better, certainly. In her house in St. Ives, she would often sneak into the pantry and grab a late-night snack, and she saw no reason not to head to the kitchen now. As she walked past the portrait gallery, a sound cause her to stop still.

"Hello?" she called, stepping into the long, dark room. She turned up the gaslight sconces and peered cautiously toward the spot where she'd thought she'd heard—

There. Again, a woman talking or laughing, so faint it was easy to dismiss, but she moved forward quietly and heard the distinctive sound of someone singing, a lilting, haunting tune that made the hair on her arms rise. When she reached the end of the room, where the paneled walls held no sconces, she stopped. Remembering the secret passages, Rebecca ran her fingers along the wood, searching for a secret opening, a latch or handle hidden in the thickly carved wood. Slowly, she moved, pressing here and there, growing more excited as the woman's voice became more clear. Suddenly, her hand felt the faintest breeze, a small bit of air seeping through a small crack in the wood. As she pressed her ear against the crack, her heart picked up a beat—the woman's voice was even more clear. Perhaps it was only a servant. Perhaps this secret passageway led to the servants' quarters.

Moving her fingers along the crack, she searched blindly for something that would open the hidden door. Up and around, tracing the edge of a door so small, she would have to duck to enter it. And then, quite by accident, her foot touched something on the floor, a trigger, and the door sprang open, a sharp blast of air hitting her face. Rebecca gasped. Even though she'd suspected the paneling concealed a hidden passage, she was still surprised to find one.

Cautiously, she opened the door further and peeked in. It was nothing but utter blackness and the smell of damp. When she pulled the door completely open, the dim light behind her glinted off a bit of glass—two oil lamps on a shallow wooden shelf. The singing, still faint, was a bit easier to hear now. If this was a ghost, she had a pleasant voice. Brushing her fingers along the shelf, Rebecca found a box of matches and quickly lit one. She lifted the lamp's shade and lit the wick, turning up the light so she could have a good look around. To her surprise, she found herself looking at a set of steep steps that wound around until they were out of sight, dropping down into the dark. The walls were lined with stone that glinted near the bottom with water. Behind her, the door began to shut, and Rebecca, her heart hammering at the thought of being trapped, wedged a match between the edge of the door and the wall to stop it from closing completely.

Hiking her skirts up in an unladylike fashion, Rebecca checked the level of oil in the lamp before holding it up high and beginning her descent, all the time moving toward the lilting voice that drew her.

As she made her way down the steps, she was aware of a chill that permeated the air. Her travel gown, even with its high neck and long sleeves, did little to keep the cold air out, and she found herself shivering, the light from the lamp dancing shakily on the stone walls. The steps spiraled downward seemingly endlessly, but as she made her way, the sound of the woman's voice kept her going.

Finally, her legs aching from the long descent, she reached a long passageway, its stone floor stretching beyond the reach of the lamplight. When the woman suddenly stopped singing and let out an eerie laugh, Rebecca stopped, her heart beating madly in her chest. This was no ghost, but a living person. Who could she be and why was she in what appeared to be Horncliffe Manor's dungeon? The thought occurred to Rebecca that she should probably turn back and fetch Oliver to explore with her, but a slice of light in the distance had her moving forward once again.

Walking as silently as possible, Rebecca made her way closer to the bit of light that sharply cut through the darkness of the passage. And then she found herself standing outside a thick wooden door, the only thing that separated her from the woman who now hummed softly as she moved around on the other side. A shadow passed over the light, and that was when Rebecca noticed a small opening at the bottom of the door, covered by a sliding bit of wood and iron. Next to the door was a large ring holding two skeleton keys, a big one that looked like something from another century and a much smaller one.

"Hello?" she called out. The humming immediately stopped. All was quiet but for the sound of dripping somewhere nearby. "Hello?" She repeated. "I heard your singing—"

In a flurry of movement, the woman rushed to the door, her feet and her body hitting the wood with a jarring sound. "Who's there?"

"Rebecca. My name is Rebecca."

"Oh, sweet Mary, you must release me. Please."

Release her? Was this woman being kept prisoner? Her gaze darted to the keys. If the woman were mad or some sort of criminal, should she be the one who let her out?

"What is your name?" Rebecca asked, her breath shallow as she stared at the rough wood of the ancient door.

"Molly. Molly Holly." A sob. "His Grace has been keeping me here for years."

Rebecca stared at the door as the woman's words penetrated her mind. Molly Holly, the little maid who had disappeared ten years ago—*ten years*—was on the other side of this door. How was this possible? It was unfathomable. Yet even though her heart rejected the notion that Oliver had kept this poor woman prisoner, she could not deny what her eyes and ears were telling her. With a shaking hand, the drew the ring over the hook that held it and grabbed the big key, putting it into the keyhole and giving it a hard turn. Weights tumbled and the door opened slowly. What met her eyes was so unexpected, Rebecca was momentarily disoriented.

Molly, wide gray eyes staring at her, backed into a small room, a thick chain dangling from her wrist. She had been tethered to the wall like some sort of animal. A thin mattress lay on the floor and a threadbare carpet covered the cold stone beneath her feet, but the room held little else except for a chamber pot, pitcher, two lamps, and an odd collection of cloth dolls. Dozens of the things sat propped on the bed and along the wall, their macabre stitched faces gazing at her. Molly herself was dressed in a clean, serviceable gown, her hair in a long braid that fell over one shoulder and down to her waist. She was a tiny thing, with blond hair and gray eyes that at the moment were filled with a mixture of fear and relief.

"I don't understand," Rebecca said, looking around and finally settling her gaze back on Molly.

"Shut the door," she whispered fearfully. "If he comes, you'll be done for."

"Who?" Rebecca asked, making sure the door would not lock her in before shutting it.

"The duke." Molly ducked her head but not before Rebecca noticed a faded bruise high on her cheek. "What year is it?"

Rebecca was loath to tell her. How would the poor woman react when she learned she had been held captive for ten years? "You've been here a long time, Miss Holly," Rebecca said in an attempt to lessen the blow.

"How long?" Her gray eyes were now filled with utter despair.

"It is eighteen seventy-nine."

The woman covered her face with her hands, letting out a low keening sound. "Ten years, it's been." She dropped her hands. "All this time... My mum must be beside herself. If she's still alive. He kept me here all that time because I saw him. A monster. Surely you know, if you live in this house that—" She stopped, her eyes scanning Rebecca, taking in the expensive and fashionable traveling dress she had yet to remove. "Who are you?" she asked suspiciously.

"As I said, I am Rebecca, Duchess of Kendal. His Grace's wife."

Molly backed up as is she'd just sprouted devil's horns on her head. "Oh, Lordy, please don't hurt me." Tears filled the woman's eyes.

"No one is going to hurt you, least of all the duke," Rebecca said, knowing that despite what she saw in front of her, Oliver could not have harmed this woman. It was beyond belief.

Molly looked at her as if she were daft. "I tell you, he kept me here a prisoner. Don't ya think I would have left right off if given the chance?" She held out her wrist, which was manacled to a long chain attached to a thick ring in the wall. It was positively medieval.

"The man I know would never do such a thing."

"His Grace is a monster," Molly said, looking about the room frantically, before she began grabbing up a few items that apparently meant something to her. "Do you think I'm the only one he done this to? There was another one." She jerked her head. "She was already locked up when I first was put here. He kept her in the next room over. She got sick and died. I listened to her moaning for days, and then it was silent."

It was impossible. Oliver could not be responsible for this woman's imprisonment, and yet...

"When was the last time you saw His Grace?"

Molly stopped collecting her dolls. "Ten years ago. I was new here and only sixteen. I was warned not to look at him, told I would turn to stone if I did, but I thought that was a bunch of nonsense. I was so stupid. When I saw him walking toward me, like some sort of ghost, I looked. It scared me good and right, it did. Those strange eyes staring like he could send me straight to the devil. I was scared and ran to the kitchen. That night, he come to my room in the attic, blindfolded me, and brought me here." She started to weep. "Ten years ago. Oh, Lord, my little sister is twenty-two." Her face crumpled for a moment before she regained control.

"You don't know what I've lived through. You cannot imagine what that monster… When he comes down, he makes me turn off all the lamps before he…"

Rebecca found herself holding her breath. "And when was he last down here?"

"Last night." She pulled out a watch. "I've been keeping track of time so I know when it's day or night. It helps for some reason, to get through the day."

Rebecca sagged against the wall, relief making her knees weak. Yes, she'd known in her heart that Oliver could never have kept this poor woman prisoner, but knowing for certain did ease her mind considerably. "We were not home last night," she said. "His Grace and I arrived from London just this evening." Then she slapped a hand in horror over her mouth. "Mr. Winters," she whispered.

Molly's eyes grew wide. "Mr. Winters? No. I would know…" Her voice trailed off. "It's been him all this time?" Her brows furrowed as she thought this through. "But he makes me call him His Grace. He gets angry when I don't." She dipped her head and absently rubbed at her manacled wrist before sinking down onto the bed. Rebecca rushed over to release her wrist from the manacle.

As Rebecca struggled to put the small key into the lock on the thick band of metal, Molly looked up at her. "Why would Mr. Winters make me call him Your Grace?" she asked softly.

"I have no idea. But I am certain of one thing. The duke and I were not here last evening. Perhaps it is not Mr. Winters. Perhaps it is someone else. It doesn't matter who. Not now. We must leave immediately. Leave everything here. Anything that's dear to you can be retrieved later."

Rebecca bit her lip as she jiggled the key in the lock, getting more and more frustrated when it wouldn't turn. Perhaps this was not the key to the manacle, after all.

"Lights out!"

Rebecca very nearly let out a scream at the loud order outside the cell door, but Molly's hand over her mouth stopped her. "Hide in the corner," she whispered, her eyes wide and filled with terror. "I'll turn out the lamps. He usually doesn't stay longer than he has to." She went about dousing the first lamp. "No matter what you hear, don't make a sound."

"What do you mean?"

Molly sprang to her feet. "Just a moment, Your Grace," she called.

"Where the hell are the keys?" he said, low and harsh, and Rebecca had to suppress a shiver. She could not be certain whom the voice belonged to, though in her panicked state, it did sound a bit like Mr. Winters.

Molly darted a terrified look to Rebecca, who stood in a far corner, the keys clutched in her hand.

"Y-you left them on the nail just inside the door, Your Grace." Molly jerked her head toward the nail and Rebecca tiptoed over to the door and placed the keys there as quietly as possible, given her hand was shaking uncontrollably.

Molly waited until Rebecca was safely in the farthest corner of the room before putting out the second lamp, plunging them into complete blackness. Rebecca, her entire body aching from the effort to stay still, to keep her breathing silent, stood with her back pressed into the cold stone, her eyes squeezed closed.

"Get on the bed," he said.

"N-not tonight, Your Grace. Please."

Rebecca's mouth dropped open as she realized what was about to happen. How could she stand there and allow it? But if she made her presence known, would she not be putting her own life in danger, or even Molly's? Never in her life had she been so conflicted, as she listened to the man slip his braces from his shoulders and unbutton his trousers.

"Please, Your Grace."

Rebecca started at the sound of flesh hitting flesh, followed by a cry of pain and soft weeping.

Soft scuffling, accompanied by a soft, pain-filled sound from Molly. "You filthy whore, open your mouth."

"Stop!" Rebecca blurted out. Stupid, stupid. But what was she to do?

"Oh, no," Molly said, a world of fear and despair in those two soft syllables. "What have you done?"

"Well, well. You have company this evening," the man said. "I do not recall issuing an invitation."

And that was when Rebecca definitely recognized the voice and a chill went up her spine. It was as she'd suspected. "Mr. Winters," she said.

"You will call me Your Grace," he shouted.

"Mr. Winters?" Molly asked uncertainly. Another slapping sound. "Your Grace!"

"You're mad," Rebecca said, her confusion overcoming her fear.

"I am the old duke's firstborn son. I am the rightful heir to the title."

"If that is true," Rebecca said as calmly as she could, "why are you not the duke?"

"Because my grandfather convinced my father that he would be foolish to marry my mother," he spat. "He used her and refused to marry her. And then my father was gracious enough to allow me to live in his house as a servant. Such a magnanimous thing for him to do, don't you agree?"

While he was speaking, Rebecca eased toward the door as silently as possible, hoping to make her escape and get help, both for her and for poor Molly. She felt along the wall, praying that her fingers would touch wood instead of cold stone. Once she reached the door, she would make a run for it. She must. But before she could find the door, a match flared, illuminating the room, illuminating her as she slid along the wall.

She stood still, as if the light had somehow paralyzed her.

"My mother," he said, as he calmly lit a lamp, "was the daughter of the third son of a baron." He chuckled. "She at least had some aristocratic blood running through her veins, but my grandfather thought her too far below my father socially and would not hear of a match. Can you imagine what he would think of you?"

He walked calmly over to her, his face devoid of expression, so Rebecca was shocked when he quickly grabbed her hair and yanked her hard, pushing her toward Molly.

"You're such a little fool." He let out a sigh as if the weight of the world were now on his shoulders. "What should I do with you?"

"You should let me go. Oliver will find me and then you shall be arrested and hang for what you have done."

He tsked. "Such fervor in your words. Do you really think that idiot you call a husband will be able to find you? I'll tell him you left when you discovered you were not married." He smiled. "You are, you know. Did you truly think your father such a dunce that he would not have been certain?" He looked at the ceiling and shook his head. "Does no one in this world have any intelligence at all?"

"Why would you spread such lies? Why would you tell Oliver such a thing if it were not true?"

He tilted his head as if commiserating with her confusion. "I had to make him see how wrong it was of him to have married you. You will taint the bloodline of our great title. You don't have a drop of blue blood running through your common veins. But I do."

Even as her mind told her how foolish it would be to challenge him, Rebecca could not stop her tongue. "It is not your title," she said. "And since I am married to His Grace, whether you like it or not, I outrank you. You will—"

He backhanded her, making her head snap back, and she crumpled onto the thin mattress, pain exploding in her jaw. She tasted blood, her teeth having cut the inside of her cheek at the blow. Never in her life had anyone, ever, committed a violent act on her person. When Winters took a step toward her, she cringed and scooted away from him.

"Stop, Your Grace," Molly said. "She don't know nothing. Let her go. You can keep me if you like. I won't make any trouble."

Winters stood over the two women, his control, momentarily lost, back. Tugging at his sleeves with a small frown, he said, "I cannot to do anything at the moment. My brother will no doubt soon discover his wife is missing and go looking for her." He smiled grimly. "He cannot find you. No one knows about this dungeon but me."

"I found it," Rebecca said, holding a hand to her throbbing jaw.

His brows furrowed briefly, as if that troubling thought had not occurred to him. "Then I shall have to make certain Oliver does not find it, shan't I?" He moved toward the door and stopped. "It may be some time before I'm able to return. As a matter of fact, Oliver demanded that I leave Horncliffe. If he insists, I daresay I won't return. I do hope you are not hungry."

With that, he grabbed the lantern Rebecca had used to find her way there, opened the door to their cell, and departed, pushing the heavy door closed behind him and locking them in.

Chapter 12

Tears filled Rebecca's eyes but she dashed them away. Even though her jaw hurt terribly, she refused to allow herself to slip into despair. She dared not think that the woman sitting next to her quietly weeping had been in this room for ten years. Surely, Oliver would find her soon. But what if he did have Winters removed from Horncliffe? How long could they last without food? She wished Oliver had heeded her concerns about Mr. Winters, though in her wildest imaginings she would not have thought even he capable of such villainy. Now, she must rely on keeping her wits and pray Oliver would find them.

Despite her determination, she could not help but think Molly had felt very much the way she did now—full of hope that someone would hear her cries. But all they would hear would be the ghost of Horncliffe.

"I could hear you."

Molly looked up with a look of utter hopelessness. "What do you mean?"

"For years, people have heard you, but they thought it was a ghost. Your ghost. Mr. Winters had a statue of a maid erected in the garden to frighten the rest of the staff. They actually believed the duke had turned you to stone. The statue was proof of it."

Molly thought on this a bit. "But that don't make sense. How could I be a ghost if I was a statue?"

Despite their situation, Rebecca laughed. "I don't know. All I know is that whatever noise we make, it needs to be decidedly unghostlike. And it needs to be loud."

"It's hopeless. I screamed my throat raw for days and no one came. I know my mum and dad must have looked for me, must have demanded to know where I was." Molly worried at the band on her wrist, then let out a small gasp. "Your Grace, look."

Rebecca looked down to see the small lock that held the manacle on Molly's wrist had sprung free. Apparently, the key had worked, after all. With shaking hands, Molly quickly took off the lock and opened the manacle, letting out a sound of pure joy. "Oh," she said, looking at her poor, chafed wrist. She rubbed it softly, and looked at Rebecca with a smile. "I'm free."

"Not yet," Rebecca said, taking the heavy chain in her hand. "But I think I've found something that we can use to wake this house up."

When Oliver entered his room, he stopped in confusion. Where was his wife? He'd expected to find her in bed waiting for him, her hair neatly plaited, with a welcoming smile on her face. It had been a long and wearing day and he wanted nothing more than to pull her against him and fall to sleep.

Then he recalled her mentioning sneaking down to the kitchen to gather something to eat. He'd thought she'd meant to bring the food back to their room, but perhaps she'd stayed in the kitchen and eaten her fill there. He had half a mind to join her, but he found he was too tired to bother.

Instead, he undressed, taking care to neatly fold his clothes—his new valet had been horrified by the way he'd been treating his clothing—and climbed into bed to wait for his wife. He was bone-tired and wished this entire day had never happened. Another man might have reached oblivion by drinking; Oliver had always found solace in sleep. He fell into a deep slumber within minutes of his head resting on his pillow, knowing he would awaken when Rebecca climbed abed.

Oliver woke with a start, sensing something was wrong. He reached beside him and was slightly disturbed to find the bed empty next to him. "Rebecca?"

Silence met him. Could she have returned to her own rooms? Without bothering to put on a robe, Oliver strode to their connecting door and walked in without knocking. The moon shone brightly, illuminating her bed. Her empty bed. Still, Oliver walked up to it to be certain. How strange.

"Rebecca?"

His cat rubbed against his shins, purring loudly, and he absently bent to give the tabby a pet. "Where is our duchess?" he asked.

Going back to his own rooms, he raised the gaslight just enough to see a clock that sat on his wardrobe, and his blood ran cold. It was just past three in the morning. Something had to have happened.

His heart racing, Oliver quickly donned his spectacles, then threw open his door and began running toward the kitchen. Had she cut herself? Choked? Fallen down the stairs? His bare feet slapped on the cold marble floor as he ran toward the kitchen, silently praying that he would find her safe. Perhaps she'd eaten and fallen asleep at the table?

But when he reached the kitchen, he found it empty with no signs that anyone had been there. Turning up the gaslight, he looked in the large basin where the dishes were washed. Knowing Rebecca, she would have put her dishes there. It was empty. Furrowing his brow, he left the kitchen, a nagging worry beginning to hit him. It was the middle of the night; where could she be?

While Horncliffe was a large and rambling home, all those who resided there did so in the west wing. This was where the tower was, the bedrooms, the portrait gallery and library. He doubted Rebecca would have wandered to the other wing, so he confined his search to those rooms he thought he might find her. Perhaps she had gone into the library for a book and fallen asleep on a settee? While it seemed unlikely, he simply had no other explanation. Surely she was there. He smiled, picturing her curled up before the fire, an opened book by her side as she slept.

But when he reached the room, it was dark; no fire was lit in the grate, and the chill would have certainly made Rebecca retreat. Still, he raised the gaslight just enough so that he could see beyond the shadows and frowned when he realized that the library, too, was empty. Could she have gone to the tower room? For what purpose?

Real fear began growing, like some virulent disease spreading through his body. She'd been so upset earlier, but surely she would realize that he would make everything right again. She had promised him, after all.

Oliver ran to the tower, taking the curving stairs two at a time, shouting her name as he went, only to find his room precisely as he'd left it. His heart hammering madly in his chest, fear clogging his throat, he went via the passageway back to his rooms, crazily thinking he might find her lost within the dark and narrow halls.

"Rebecca!"

Only silence answered his call. When he made it back to his room, he looked again, in his suite and in hers, hoping that while he'd been off searching for her, she had returned. But she had not.

"Mr. Winters," Oliver shouted, as he left his room and headed for the other man's suite. "Mr. Winters!"

Upstairs, he could hear the sound of servants opening their doors to see what the commotion was. Mr. Starke appeared wearing a nightcap and gown, his eyes bleary from sleep. "Your Grace, whatever is the matter?"

"The duchess is missing," he said. Those words, said aloud, made his heart feel as if it had turned to a block of ice.

"Certainly not," Mr. Starke said, though the look of concern on his face was anything but comforting.

"What is wrong? What has happened?" Winters called from down the hall.

"Rebecca is not in her rooms, nor in mine. She went down to the kitchens earlier to find a bite to eat, but she was not there either. I've searched this entire wing."

Darlene came out into the hall, her brown hair in a long braid down her back. "Surely she's in her room, Your Grace," she said, pushing by the others in the hall.

"I fell asleep. She was going to the kitchen to fetch something to eat, but it appears she did not. That was four hours ago. Four hours." He felt like screaming and would have if he thought it would have made Rebecca appear.

"Your Grace. A word." Darlene stood in the hall, her expression unreadable, and Oliver's blood turned to ice. He followed the maid into his wife's room, dread filling him.

When they were inside, Darlene looked back to be certain no one had followed. "Her dresses are gone. The ones she brought with her. At least some of them. And her bag is gone too, Your Grace."

The implication was clear. Rebecca had left in the middle of the night without saying good-bye, without allowing him to...

"No. She would not do that. Rebecca would never leave me without at the very least telling me she was doing so."

Darlene looked at him with a mixture of pity and concern. "Yes, Your Grace." She pressed her lips together. "But the dresses..."

Oliver shook his head in denial. He would not believe Rebecca would do such a thing; it was unimaginable. Then again, she had been terribly upset to learn their worst fears had come true. Did she think that leaving him would be for the best? That he would somehow be grateful for it?

"Oh, God." The words tore through his throat, and tears filled Darlene's eyes.

"I'm so sorry, Your Grace." She worried her hands together, clearly at a loss what to do or say. She left him there, alone. He glanced around the room, fighting the despair that threatened to paralyze him. How could Rebecca have left him? It seemed inconceivable. And yet, her dresses were gone. She was gone.

He sat down heavily on her bed and stared unseeingly at the cold grate. Soft footsteps drew his attention; Mr. Winters stood at the door, his expression one of sorrow, and Oliver fought the urge to launch himself at the man and put his hands around his throat.

"You may not think so now, Your Grace, but it is for the—"

Oliver stood abruptly. "Don't you dare say it is for the best. Don't you dare. Get out of my sight. You make me sick. This changes nothing. You are to leave at first light."

"You're upset."

"You are correct, sir. I am murderously upset." He took a step toward Winters and the man's eyes widened.

"You found her in a painting," he said, stretching his arms out to either side, as if that explained all.

Oliver looked at the ceiling and squeezed his eyes shut. "It matters not how I found her. It matters only that I did and that I love her." He dropped his head and looked at the older man, not bothering to hide the raw despair in his eyes. "Do you not understand that, Philip?"

Winters stiffened. "I do apologize, Your Grace, but I do not. If you mean to bring her back, I would suggest leaving at first light. She cannot have gotten far. The stage to the rail station does not leave until ten. You'll have time to stop her should you choose to."

"Of course I choose to," Oliver spat. "And if you believe I can wait until the morning to fetch her, you are mistaken." He strode through the door and into the hall, where a small group of servants still huddled, discussing the excitement of the night. "Mr. Starke, order me a carriage immediately."

"Yes, sir."

Oliver returned to his rooms and hastily dressed. When he found Rebecca—and he would find her—after he hugged and kissed her breathless, he just might shake her for causing him so much worry.

"No one will hear this time of night. They're all four stories above us," Molly said wearily as she lay on the mattress.

Rebecca, short of breath and exhausted from banging the chain against the stone, sagged in defeat. Truthfully, the chain wasn't making all that much noise each time she smashed it against the wall. She had to admit that no one, especially in the middle of the night, would hear the noise she was making.

"You're right." Rebecca willed away the tears that threatened. "I don't know what else to do."

"Survive. As I have done all this time."

Shaking her head, Rebecca sat down on the mattress next to the other woman. "We shan't survive if Mr. Winters is told to leave. Who will bring you food and water? Who will take your chamber pot?"

Molly shrugged indifferently.

Then a thought occurred to her. "Molly, were there ever long stretches when no one came to bring you food?"

"That's one thing I could count on. Every day just after nine in the morning, a tray appears in that little slot." She motioned to the small sliding door that was part of the larger door.

The impact of her words silenced Rebecca, horrified her, actually. If someone had been bringing Molly food, another person in this house was aware that she had been kept here prisoner for years. Knew and had done nothing. How many people in this house were complicit in her imprisonment?

"You don't know who? A man or woman?"

"A man. At times he'll cough, but he never says a word. And he never comes in."

"If Mr. Winters is forced to leave, perhaps whoever is bringing food will let us out? At the very least, we can plead with him."

Molly laughed, an ugly sound. "Don't you think I've tried? Don't you think I've cried and begged and sworn I wouldn't tell a soul just as long as they let me go? They're monsters, the two of them. I didn't realize it wasn't His Grace—" She frowned. "Mr. Winters who was bringing me the food at first, but I figured it out. I figured a man like that wouldn't lower himself to bring me food."

Rebecca laid a hand on the other woman's wrist. "I am so sorry this happened to you. And I want you to have faith that we will escape. My husband will find us. I know he will."

Her words did not appear to give the other woman hope. "For a long time, I've known I will die here, that no one in my family will ever know what happened to me. I can't have hope now." She looked up, her eyes beseeching. "Don't give me hope. It crushes me, it makes this more unbearable."

Rebecca pushed back so that she could lean against the wall. As tired as she was, she couldn't bring herself to lie down. "What time is it?" she asked.

Molly pulled out her watch and glanced down at it. "Half past three. You've been here four hours." She giggled and put her watch away. "I remember counting hours. Then days; then I just stopped counting." She let out a sigh. "I'm tired, Your Grace. I'd like to put out the lamp and go to sleep. I don't like it when I run out of oil."

Rebecca wanted to argue but stopped herself. If they did run out of oil before they were found, they would be in utter darkness, something

Rebecca hoped not to experience. "Very well. It doesn't make much sense to try to get anyone's attention now. They are all abed and too far away to hear us at any rate."

Molly got up and doused the lamp before returning to the mattress. "Here, I'll make room." Rebecca could feel Molly moving over to accommodate her. "Thank you. Good night."

She lay next to the maid, stiff and frightened, her eyes open and staring at the blackness of the room. After a minute, she felt a hand on her wrist; Molly gave her arm a gentle squeeze. "I know it's horrible for you to be here. I know that. But I'm glad you're here." A pause. "I don't mean to sound as if I'm *glad* you're here—"

Rebecca smiled slightly. "I understand."

Next to her, Molly sighed, sounding almost content, then turned on her side, facing away from Rebecca. In a few minutes, her breathing became even, and Rebecca sensed she'd fallen asleep. Rebecca lay there, straining to hear a sound from above. All she heard, though, was water dripping somewhere nearby. How far under the house was she? Those stairs had seemed to spiral endlessly.

Tomorrow, she could call for Oliver. She would call, over and over and over until she couldn't call any more. No ghost would call out his given name. Surely, he would hear her. Or someone else would. Suddenly, her body heated with a new fear. What if Mr. Winters harmed Oliver? The man was obviously unhinged, calling himself the true duke. What if he decided he must eliminate Oliver so that he could become duke in truth—at least his own warped truth?

As she lay there, she wondered what Oliver would think when he discovered her missing.

Her eyes drifted closed, and as much as Rebecca wanted to stay awake, sleep overcame her.

Oliver strode to the stables, ready to rouse his driver and find out where he'd taken his wife. "Mr. Stevens," he called, his eyes adjusting to the dark room. A horse nickered and stomped its hoof, annoyed with the disruption. His driver emerged from his quarters in the back of the stables, pulling on his braces and carrying his boots in his hand.

"Yes, Your Grace?"

"Where did you bring Her Grace this evening?"

The man gave him a confused look. "I didn't bring Her Grace anywhere. Haven't left the stables."

Could she be afoot? That made no sense when it would have been a simple thing to order a carriage. "Are any horses missing?" he asked, knowing how ridiculous it would have been for Rebecca to have saddled her own horse. Then he recalled that she didn't ride.

"No, Your Grace. All the cattle are here and well." The man scratched his head, his brow furrowing. "Is something wrong, Your Grace?"

"The duchess is missing," he forced himself to say. "I assumed she went to town."

"Ah, bit of a lover's quarrel then, Your Grace?" the man asked good-naturedly.

"Perhaps." He looked about the large stable absently. "Thank you, Mr. Stevens."

Oliver turned to go, and his driver called out, "If I see or hear anything, I'll be sure to report it."

Oliver waved his hand, acknowledging the man, but continued on, his head whirling with dark thoughts. It was frigid out, the ground covered with a light dusting of snow. He searched the grounds and found not a single footprint; had Rebecca left that evening, surely he would have seen signs of her departure in the snow. It had stopped snowing soon after they'd arrived. He tried to quell the panic that was growing in his chest, but it was becoming more and more difficult to come up with a logical explanation for her disappearance.

Unless something horrible had happened to her. He tried to shake the thought away, but he could think of no other explanation. She'd been upset. Perhaps she'd wanted to be alone and found a room where she could think things through and could at this very moment be injured, dying…

With a bracing breath, he pulled upon the door to find the grand entry filled with servants, all looking worried and no doubt wanting to hear news, any news. "She has not left," he said. "The duchess is somewhere within these walls. I would like every room thoroughly searched, including the root cellar. I fear she may be in trouble, perhaps unconscious, for certainly she would have responded to my calls if she could have." God, those words were difficult to say. Raw fear closed his throat momentarily, and he swallowed forcibly. If she had fallen, hit her head…

"Even the west wing, Your Grace?"

"Every room. I realize you would all rather be in bed and I greatly appreciate your help."

"We'd do anything to help Her Grace," one footman said, and the others nodded.

"Very well. Let's find our duchess, shall we?"

With that, the servants dispersed. Oliver headed directly to his rooms, then stopped cold, as a terrible thought occurred to him. He had not searched Rebecca's bathing chamber when he'd gone into her rooms. What if she had taken a bath to soothe her nerves? What if she had slipped on the slick tile and fallen? With a growing, sickening dread, he made his way to the door that connected their suites and headed for the bathing room, stopping just outside the door.

"Rebecca?"

Silence. He pushed open the door, a wave of relief nearly felling him when he found the room empty. "Thank God."

Collecting himself quickly, he headed for the secret passage, intending to search every inch before expanding his search. Though he couldn't imagine why Rebecca would go into the passage, she had once before and might have done so again. Perhaps she'd heard something in the walls; his bloody cat was always getting trapped in the passageway and meowing piteously to be let back in.

Just as he opened the passage, the cat appeared and dashed past him into the darkness. Despite the gravity of the situation, Oliver couldn't help but smile at the wily little beast. Oliver knew the passages well and was used to navigating them in the dark, but this time he brought a lantern with him. If she was in the passage, he didn't want to miss her.

"It's morning."

Rebecca slowly opened her eyes, then groaned as she realized where she was. It hadn't been a nightmare; it had been real.

"How can you tell?" Rebecca asked, turning around to look at her cell mate.

"I always wake up just before seven." Molly dangled her watch in front of Rebecca's bleary eyes. "The first thing I do is light my lamp. Like a sunrise."

Rebecca gave her a weak smile. "Good morning." But it was not a good morning. It was an awful morning and Rebecca found her eyes pricking with tears.

"I won't mind if you cry. I cried a lot over the years."

"It's only that I thought His Grace would have found us by now. I'm sure he's realized I'm missing and begun a search. If he hasn't found us, then he doesn't know this place exists. I thought he knew about all the secret passages in the house."

Molly furrowed her brow. "There are other passages?"

"Every room has a passage." Rebecca sat up and her stomach growled loudly. It had been nearly a full day since she'd eaten anything.

"Food usually arrives before eight. I wonder if he'll bring more, if he even knows there's someone else down here with me."

It was unlikely Mr. Winters would have told anyone what had happened. Molly got up and retrieved some bits of cloth from the corner. "I'm making another doll," she said with a shrug. "It helps pass the time."

Rebecca sat next to her as the woman worked, slowly pulling stitch after stitch into what looked like a tiny pair of pantaloons. While she worked, Rebecca counted the dolls—thirty in all, and even smaller ones sitting on those. The dolls had children, it seemed. "You don't have any men dolls," she said. "How could the ladies have babies if there are no men?"

Molly looked up from her work, then burst out laughing, as if that were the most amusing thing she had ever heard. Rebecca had meant to be funny, so she joined in. "I haven't laughed that hard in years." Then she sobered. "Ten years." Putting her sewing to the side, she said, "I had a man, you know. Peter Stevens. He worked in the stable, caring for the horses, and was the gentlest man I had ever met. I was so sweet on him."

"Was he sweet on you, too?"

She smiled. "Yes. Though he only tried to kiss me once. It was right before..." She frowned, and looked at Rebecca. "Do you know if he still works for the duke?"

"Mr. Stevens is now stable master. And as far as I know, he has never married."

"Oh." Molly worried a piece of cloth in her hand. "I'm sure he's not waiting for me. I'm sure he thinks I'm long dead."

"I don't know, but I am certain he will be pleased when the duke finds us and lets us out."

Molly shook her head. "You shouldn't talk like that. No one is coming. Not even your duke can find us here. You know, sometimes I thought I was so far down into the earth, I was close to the very devil." She looked at her watch. "Half past eight. No food today."

Rebecca felt like crying. "Have you gone many days without food?"

"A few." Molly picked up the sewing again. "Those are the worst days of all because I wonder if I'll ever eat again, if I've been forgotten or if the man who brings me food has died. And then I think, maybe that would be a good thing. Death. It would end this."

Rebecca grabbed her arm. "I know you don't want me to say this, but we're getting out, Molly," she said fiercely. "We are. I promise you." When Molly's eyes filled with tears, Rebecca gave her a little shake. "None of that. We're getting out and we're getting out now."

Rebecca slid off the mattress and got to her feet, walking over to the door with determined steps. When she reached it, she pressed her mouth close to the edge of the door, to a place where more sound might escape. And then she began calling, over and over, for Oliver.

"Mr. Winters has gone, Your Grace," Mr. Starke said.

Oliver looked up from the table where his breakfast sat uneaten. How could he eat when his wife was missing? All night, he and the servants had scoured every inch of the house, to no avail. It was almost as if she had disappeared into thin air. Just after dawn, Oliver had ordered one of the footmen to go into town to make inquiries there, but the man had returned in an hour with nothing to report.

Oliver wasn't surprised; the lack of tracks in the snow told him that no one had left the house that night.

He hardly registered any reaction to the news that the man who had caused so much ill over the years was gone. "Thank you, Mr. Starke."

He'd dismissed the butler, but the older man continued to stand in the doorway as if he had something further to say. With a sigh of impatience, Oliver said, "Is there something more, Mr. Starke?"

"Indeed there—" He stopped, and the expression on his face made Oliver realize he was about to learn something unpleasant.

"Out with it," he demanded, bracing himself to hear the worst. Someone had found her.

"Mr. Winters was an evil man," he said finally, surprising Oliver.

"Some might find him so," Oliver said. Despite all that he had done, Oliver believed the man's motives were good even if his means were twisted.

"No, Your Grace, he is evil. There can be no question. And I have been his accessory."

Oliver gave the older man an assessing look. The poor fellow looked as if he were on the verge of tears. "Do come in and take a seat," he said, indicating the chair adjacent to his.

"Oh, no, sir, I couldn't…"

"I insist." The butler lifted his chin and carefully sat down as if he planned to leap to his feet at any moment. "Please, tell me what is on your mind."

"Very well." Starke closed his eyes briefly, his hand moving nervously across the linen tablecloth in front of him. "Do you recall a maid, Molly Holly?"

Oliver could feel his face heat. He very much remembered the maid who'd seen him and then become so hysterical she'd had to be dismissed. "I do. She was dismissed more than ten years ago, I believe."

Starke swallowed heavily. "She's still here, in this house."

"I'm not certain I follow."

"Mr. Winters has been keeping her in the dungeon. Another woman who came to visit was also kept there for a time, but she died of a fever." Oliver suddenly found it difficult to breathe. "You are not jesting."

"No, Your Grace. I wish I were. He... He made me bring her food every day. And remove her chamber pot. I wanted to refuse. I wanted to leave. But without a reference, I never would have found employment. I had just started here and had little experience. I felt I was lucky to have found such a position. He threatened to fire me, Your Grace, and spread word that I was a thief. I wanted to free her, I did. But I thought, she's being fed. She's not being harmed."

"My God, she's the ghost, is she not? The woman's voice we've all heard. I thought it came from the servants' quarters all this time." Oliver stood abruptly, startling the older man. "We must go immediately and free her."

"Your Grace," Mr. Starke said, staying him. "I fear he's done something to the duchess. He made no secret that he held her in contempt."

"If he has, he will die."

His words seemed to shake Mr. Starke, but the butler nodded in agreement. "I will show you the way."

"The portrait gallery, I've no doubt."

"Yes, Your Grace. A secret door."

They began walking to the gallery, Oliver's footsteps quick on the marble floor. "I thought I knew all the secret passages. I understood the way to the lower levels had been blocked off years ago, before my father's time even."

As soon as they turned the corner into the gallery, Oliver stopped, holding out his arm to halt Mr. Starke. And then he grinned. "It appears my duchess has been locked in the dungeon as well, Mr. Starke." Indeed, they could hear a woman calling "Oliver" quite clearly. Mr. Starke hurried to the back of the gallery and stepped on a clever trigger in the floor, which caused a door to pop open just far enough so it could be prised open with one's fingertips.

Oliver was about to run down the steps, when Mr. Starke stopped him. "One of the lamps. It's missing," he whispered.

Oliver turned to look at the older man, who was pointing to a small shelf at the top of the stairs. "If a lamp is missing, that means Mr. Winters is down there."

Oliver tensed, realizing that Rebecca's calls had abruptly stopped. He stepped back cautiously, quietly. "I am going to fetch my rapier. Should Mr. Winters return before I do, keep him here."

Moving as silently and quickly as possible, Oliver ran out of the gallery and down the hall to where he and Winters had spent so many hours fencing. He grabbed his rapier, making sure to take the safety tip off before running back to the gallery, where Mr. Starke nervously waited.

"Now we can proceed." He gave Mr. Starke an assessing look. "You don't have to come with me, if you'd rather not."

"I shall, Your Grace. It will be a pleasure to assist you in any way I can." With that, Mr. Starke took up the remaining lantern and lit it, exposing a steep, winding stairway that disappeared into the darkness beyond the light of the lantern.

Rebecca had given up shouting for the time being. Now she and Molly sat on the bed, chatting about their childhoods. In another life, Rebecca might have been Molly's friend, but she knew when they escaped—and they would escape—it would be difficult for them to talk this way. Rebecca had insisted Molly call her by her name, and the woman reluctantly agreed to it.

"My mum was carrying a babe when I disappeared," she said wistfully. "I wonder what she had? I've a brother or a sister that I've never met, who is near ten years old. Seems so strange to think on it." Suddenly, she tensed, and whispered, "Someone's coming."

When they heard the jingle of the keys, both looked at each other worriedly. Only Mr. Winters would use the keys. "I'd hoped he would be gone," Rebecca whispered. "Maybe we can bash him on the head with the chamber pot. Now that we're both free…" Her eyes widened. "Put the cuff back on."

Molly hurriedly placed the cuff attached to the chain back on her wrist, grimacing as she did, but was careful to leave the lock open.

Just as she completed the task, the door swung open, revealing Mr. Winters, lantern in hand. Rebecca immediately stood and Molly followed; sitting seemed to put them at a disadvantage. "Good morning, ladies," he said pleasantly, making a shiver run up Rebecca's spine. "I've decided to clean up some loose ends before I take my leave. Kidnapping is a hanging offense, you see, and I should like to avoid the gallows. Can't take the chance that someone will find either of you. Really, Your Grace, all that shouting. It was positively shrill."

Rebecca stared at him in disbelief. "Whoever has been bringing Molly food knows of your crime."

"He will never betray me." He clicked his tongue. "Fear is the best motivator. Fear of death. Fear of starvation. Fear of being destitute. Starke is my accomplice. Why ever would he implicate himself? He may be a sheep, but he is not a complete idiot."

"Mr. Starke," Rebecca said, unable to comprehend how such a kind, gentle man could possibly have been Mr. Winters' accomplice.

Winters smiled blandly. "You may be correct, though, Your Grace," he said mockingly. "Perhaps Mr. Starke is another loose end that must be eliminated." He reached down to his boot and withdrew a vicious-looking knife, the metal gleaming in the lamplight. "I'll make it quick," he said calmly, twisting the knife slowly in his hand as he examined the blade.

"Murder is a hanging offense as well," Rebecca said, staring at the knife, her blood running cold.

"Yes, but who will know I am the murderer?" He frowned and tapped an index finger against his mouth as if deep in thought. "Let's see, who should be first?"

Rebecca's eyes darted to the chamber pot, which both women had used that morning. It was the only object in the room heavy enough to do damage, but it would be impossible for her to reach before she was stopped. Oh, God, she was going to die.

"The duchess is first," Winters said conversationally. "You don't have to watch if you don't wish, Molly. I fear it won't be pleasant."

"There's no need to kill us, Mr. Winters," Rebecca said, her voice trembling. "I swear, we won't tell a soul you did this thing. You'll swear, too, won't you, Molly?"

"Yes. I swear," she said quickly, her eyes filling with tears. "I just want to go home and see my mum."

"I just want to go home and see my mum," Winters mimicked cruelly. "I am not a stupid man. Now, duchess, come here and kneel before me. I will make this as quick and as painless as possible."

"You're insane," Rebecca said, backing up a step, her heels touching the mattress.

In one quick movement, Winters grabbed her by the hair and pulled ruthlessly, shoving her to the ground in front of him, pulling her head back and exposing her neck.

"Our Father, who art in Heaven—"

"Shut up," he screamed, jerking her head.

Tears streamed down her face. This was it, she was going to die at the hands of this madman. She would never see Oliver again, never hold their baby. Never see the sunset over the sea. Rebecca closed her eyes and prayed silently as she felt the cold steel against her neck, just under her left ear.

Molly let out a feral scream, and suddenly, Rebecca was free. It seemed impossible. She stood and whipped around to find Molly standing behind Mr. Winters, the chain around the man's neck. He slashed out with the knife, cutting Molly's arm, and she dropped the chain, crying out in pain. Rebecca lunged for the chamber pot, lifted the heavy vessel, and swung at Mr. Winter's head with all her might, the impact jarring her arm. Urine splashed out, covering him as he staggered from the force of the blow. With a strength she hadn't known she possessed, Rebecca swung again, slamming the chamber pot across his face, leaving a large gash on his cheek. The knife flew from his hand and Molly pounced on it, holding her injured arm close to her body.

Mr. Winters was on the floor on all fours, panting, swaying, blood dripping onto the floor, when Molly plunged the knife into his back. He collapsed onto the cold stone, and Molly stabbed him—again and again—chanting, "Die, die, die," over and over as she sobbed. The sound of the knife entering his flesh was sickening, and eventually she wore herself out and slumped back to sit on the ground, leaning against the wall, her eyes glazed.

Panting, Rebecca looked from Molly to Mr. Winters' inert body. "I think you've killed him," she said. Molly looked up, the realization of what she'd done hitting her; it showed in her eyes—the horror, the fear. "I'm glad, Molly. He deserved to die."

The maid nodded shakily. "He did at that."

A noise from the hall had both women coming alert, and Molly stood, clutching the bloody knife, ready to take on whoever might be approaching.

"Rebecca, it is I, Oliver."

Rebecca began sobbing as she went to the door, pulling it open with force, and throwing herself into Oliver's embrace. She wrapped her arms around him tightly, burying her head against his chest as she sobbed.

The relief Oliver felt was profound. Rebecca was alive and safe and in his arms, where he'd feared she would never be again. He held her tight, wishing he could have protected her from whatever had happened here.

"Are you hurt?" he asked. She shook her head, her head still buried against his chest. Oliver looked over her shoulder to see another woman, her eyes slightly wild, standing in the middle of a small, rough room, a bloody knife in her hand. "Molly?"

"Yes, Your Grace." She had the presence of mind to dip a quick curtsy. "I'm so sorry, Your Grace. But he was going to kill us, he was." Her eyes darted to the left and Oliver followed her gaze to find Mr. Winters face down on the floor, a large pool of dark crimson surrounding his body. It was clear the man was dead.

Oliver gently pushed Rebecca away, wanting proof that she was well, and gasped when he saw her neck was covered with blood.

"My God, Rebecca, you are injured." Rebecca lifted her hand to her neck, her eyes widening in surprise.

"I didn't know. Mr. Winters, oh God… He was going to cut my throat. He held the knife to my neck and was about to…"

"I killed him," Molly said, her chin lifting slightly, as if she were preparing herself for censure.

"I am grateful," Oliver said, horrified by what he was learning. He had known Mr. Winters was a strict taskmaster, but he never would have believed his guardian was capable of such a heinous act. He couldn't help but think he was to blame for all of this. If he had taken his rightful place, if he hadn't hidden away in the tower room all these years, certainly he would have known something was terribly wrong with his house, with the man he'd thought of for years as a father. "And I am more sorry than I can say that this happened to you, Molly. I swear, I will make it up to you as much as I can. You will never want for anything again."

Oliver turned to Mr. Starke, who'd been standing behind him silently. "Get the footmen to bring the body up to the green parlor and have someone fetch the constable."

Molly turned pale. "The constable," she said, her voice a squeak.

"Only to report Mr. Winters' crime. You will not be harmed in any way. You have my word. Mr. Winters will have to be examined, will need to be buried. We certainly cannot say Mr. Winters stabbed himself in the back, can we?" The woman still looked wary. "I give you my word, Molly."

"Yes, Your Grace."

"Oliver, Molly saved my life." Rebecca's hand trailed along the thin cut on her neck. "If not for her, I would be…" Rebecca withdrew from his arms and ran over to the other woman, embracing her. The two women clung to one another for a long moment before Rebecca turned back to him. "I think Molly should go home before she talks to anyone. Let's get her freshened up first, then call the carriage 'round to bring her. The constable can go to her."

"Of course, my love."

Chapter 13

Nearly a month had passed since Winters' funeral. Rebecca had not gone, but Oliver had attended, just to be certain he was buried and gone. His memories of Mr. Winters were not all bad. The two had shared many meals together and hours fencing or playing chess in the evenings. To think that all this time, he'd had a half brother. He wondered if it would have made a difference in their relationship had he known that Winters was his father's bastard.

"The post, sir." Mr. Davis, promoted to Horncliffe's butler, stood by his side holding a small bundle in his hand. Oliver had reluctantly given Mr. Starke a tepid letter of recommendation and the man was now working for a far less prestigious family in Coventry. A banker, as far as Oliver knew. Mr. Davis ran his house efficiently and fairly, and it was obvious the other servants admired the man.

"Anything of interest?" Rebecca asked.

They were taking tea together, something they'd begun to do, a homey routine that he had never experienced before and quite liked. Oliver flipped through the correspondence, putting most of the items aside for later. He was finding being a duke was far more work—and far more interesting—than he would have thought. It came as a surprise to him that he enjoyed managing his estate, working with his staff, making certain all was running properly and that his tenants were happy and healthy. He had vague recollections of his father holing up in the study for long hours, and as a boy wondering what could possibly engage him for so long. Now he knew.

A post from St. Ives parish caught his eye and he gave Rebecca a quick look.

"What is it?"

He took his spectacles off and held the letter close to his eyes so he could examine the envelop more closely. Taking a bracing breath, he said, "I took the liberty of writing to St. Ives parish to inquire about the ceremony. I know Mr. Winters confessed the marriage was legitimate, but I wanted to be certain. If we were duped, we shall be married posthaste. And if we were not, if we are truly married, I want to open up our London townhouse and throw a wedding reception."

"I fear no one will come. Even if it is true, everyone now knows I don't have a drop of noble blood."

"I am a duke, Rebecca. Dukes throw balls and the ton attends."

She gave him a skeptical look. He, himself, wasn't sure of the reception they would receive if he did throw a ball. It didn't matter at any rate. He would be content living out his days in Horncliffe, sharing every day with his wife. And children, should they be so blessed.

He broke the seal and withdrew two sheets of thick paper, a letter... and a certificate of marriage. He was careful to keep his face blank when he looked up. Rebecca sat there, frozen, seemingly holding her breath.

"Do you love me?" he asked.

"Oh, no."

"Do you love me?" he repeated.

"You know I do."

"Then you shall be happy to know you are stuck with me for the rest of your life." He grinned, unable to keep his features solemn a second longer.

Rebecca's face lit up. "We're married?"

"It appears so."

They both stood and ran into each other's arms, hugging and laughing like two children who'd just learned they would be getting a pony.

Rebecca pulled back, her brow furrowed. "Why on earth would Mr. Winters have lied?"

"I have no idea and I do not care." He kissed her softly, then again, more thoroughly. "All I know is that we are married and soon the world will know. I do believe you have your first ball to plan, Your Grace."

"Oh, dear."

Oliver laughed and pulled her close. "When I was waiting for your arrival, I never dreamed I would have this."

"This?"

"This...feeling. Love, I suppose. It's difficult for me to express what I feel for I have never felt it before."

Rebecca kissed his cheek softly. "I think it's called happiness, Oliver."

"Yes," he said, gazing down at her beloved face. "I am happy." He smiled and shook his head.

"Do you have any room for more happiness?" Rebecca asked with grin.

He scowled. "I am not certain. I'm quite full up."

"I am carrying your baby."

Oliver took a step back, stumbling a bit in his shock, and Rebecca laughed. "A baby?" He was overjoyed and frightened near to death. What if the babe came out looking like him?

"You look terrified," she said, clearly stifling a laugh.

"I *am* terrified. I am to be a father. You are to be a mother."

"That is how it works." She gave him a gentle smile and placed one hand on his cheek. "It will be fine, Oliver."

Tears welled up in his eyes, and Rebecca looked at him worriedly. "What's this?" she asked, brushing her thumb beneath one eye.

He swallowed heavily, overcome with joy. "I do believe that's my happiness overflowing."

Epilogue

"Blast it all, how long do babies take?"

If Rebecca screamed one more time, he was going to storm into their room and accost the physician.

"The first can take days." Eliza, Rebecca's best friend, had immediately come to Horncliffe when she received the letter from her friend announcing she was to have a baby. Oliver found himself enjoying her company and glad to see Rebecca having a jolly time with her. "My sister took two days."

"And everything was well?"

"Yes, thank God."

Her words were not comforting it the least.

Eliza, her long, curly dark hair bundled haphazardly on her head, had not been what Oliver expected. She was the granddaughter of a viscount, well bred and exceedingly aware of propriety, and yet she had a bit of a devil-may-care attitude about her that kept Rebecca laughing for hours. Oliver had listened, a smile on his face, as Eliza had recounted the girls' many adventures in St. Ives—adventures that might have been landed Eliza in Scotland, living with an aging spinster aunt if her mother had ever discovered them.

"That would have been the end of me," she'd said dramatically.

Both had stayed with Rebecca during the early phases of delivery, but the midwife had shooed them out when the time grew closer for her to push the baby into this world.

"I don't know how much more I can bear. To hear her—" He froze when the distinctive sounds of a baby crying reached him. "The baby."

The two ran down the hall and skidded to a halt outside the room, just as the midwife slid through the door, a smile on her face. "Your Grace, you have a daughter."

"A daughter," he said, awe in his voice. "A little girl." He collected himself and asked, "May I see my wife and daughter now?"

The woman peeked back into the room, then widened the door to allow them access. His eyes went immediately to his wife, who looked lovely even with her hair damp from her exertion and circles under her eyes. To him she had never looked more beautiful. She lay on the bed, propped up by pillows, and smiled gently at him.

"I'd like to call her Claire, after my mother, if that's all right with you," she said, then looked down at the little bundle in her arms.

"Claire," he said softly, and stepped to the side of the bed. He was a father. To a little girl. He was afraid to look at her, so he kissed Rebecca on the forehead, closing his eyes and thanking God that she was well.

"Oliver," Rebecca said, laughter in her voice. "You can look at her, you know."

Oliver couldn't bring himself to drag his gaze away from his wife, who was smiling gently at him. "She's beautiful."

He furrowed his brows, still unwilling to look. "Is she…"

"She has red hair. Just like me. And a stubborn little chin, just like you."

He sat down at the edge of the bed, his legs suddenly unable to hold him up, and finally looked at the red-faced baby tucked against his wife. Her hair was red. Bright and beautiful. "I feared—"

"I know you did. But she is beautiful. And if she had been born like you, she would have been just as beautiful. And we would have loved her just the same. Maybe even more."

Oliver, his eyes welling with tears, held out his index finger to touch his daughter's little fist, and she immediately grasped it and held on with surprising strength for one so small. "She likes me," he said with a light chuckle.

"Of course she does."

He shook his head in disbelief. "I do believe I will be unable to allow any man to court her."

This caused Rebecca to laugh out loud. "Unless she finds someone like her father."

"That would be me," Oliver said. He'd thought he'd found joy before, but realized nothing could compare to this, to seeing his wife hold their child, to listening to the sweet little sounds his daughter made. To knowing they had created something so beautiful. It was world-altering.

"I've never been part of a family before. I hope I do it right."

"You were never a husband before and you did that right."

"I want to..." He had to stop, for unaccustomed emotions were raging inside him. "I want to be the sort of father she'll be proud of."

"Oh, Oliver, you will be. You already are. You are not the man I met when I first arrived at Horncliffe Manor. You are the man your father would have wanted you to become."

Her words affected him profoundly. "With you by my side, and my little Claire, I do believe I could be."

He leaned down and kissed the top of his daughter's head, her soft, soft hair, feeling a sense of such fierce protectiveness, it was stunning. This moment would stay with him forever—the moment he realized he was worthy of such happiness and worthy of finding love.

Don't miss any of the Brides of St. Ives!

She's one groom away from true love . . .

THE BAD LUCK BRIDE

Jane Goodger

"Goodger writes romances that touch readers' hearts and bring a smile to their day."
--*RT Book Reviews*

Welcome to St. Ives, the charming seaside town where even a down-on-her luck bride might find her way back to love . . .

As if being left at the altar for the *third* time isn't bad enough, Lady Alice Hubbard has now been dubbed "The Bad Luck Bride" by the London newspapers. Defeated, she returns to her family's estate in St. Ives, resolved to a future as a doting spinster. After all, a lady with her record of marital mishaps knows better than to dream of happily-ever-after. But then Alice never expects to see Henderson Southwell again. Her beloved brother's best friend disappeared from her life soon after her brother's death. Until now…

Alice is just as achingly beautiful as Henderson remembers. And just as forbidden. For the notorious ladies' man made one last promise to Alice's brother before he died—and that was *never* to pursue her. But one glimpse of Alice's sorrow and Henderson feels a powerful urge to put the light back in her lovely eyes, one lingering kiss at a time. Even if it means falling in love with the one woman he can never call his bride . . .

Love can't hide for long . . .

THE EARL MOST LIKELY

Jane Goodger

"An unforgettable read."
–RT Book Reviews, **4 Stars**

The picturesque seaside town of St. Ives is home to all manner of treasures . . .

It's not every day a young woman is offered ten thousand pounds for a few months' work—especially the plain, shy daughter of a tin mine owner. The only thing special about Harriet Anderson is her extraordinary memory for even the smallest, most obscure detail. So when she's asked by a gentleman to help restore his once magnificent ancestral home, she simply can't refuse, no matter how scandalous the position. The money will mean freedom from her callous parents, and a life of independence. Harriet doesn't imagine dreaming of anything more . . .

Augustus Lawton, Lord Berkley, cares about only one thing: restoring his beloved Costille House to its former, historically correct, glory. His late wife had taken great vindictive delight in transforming the old castle into a modern Victorian nightmare. Harriet's remarkable memory will be invaluable in repairing it—and in helping him solve his wife's murder. Yet as they work together, Augustus finds that besides her uncanny gift, Harriet possesses other priceless qualities. And as the castle's beauty is gradually revealed, he can't help noticing, so is hers . . .

Love is a treasure . . .

DIAMOND IN THE ROUGH

Jane Goodger

"Fun, delightfully romantic—and sexy."
—Sally MacKenzie on *The Spinster Bride*

In the charming seaside town of St. Ives, a buried secret could bring an unlikely pair together for a lifetime . . .

Clara Anderson's mother has one mission: to marry off her daughter to a titled gentleman. Unfortunately, though the Andersons have come up in the world, Clara is still the granddaughter of a pig farmer, which means no self-respecting aristocrat will marry her. That's just fine with Clara, who's grown to disdain the upper classes. So when she meets an attractive man even more common than she is, she decides it's time to forge her own path . . .

. . . Except that handsome, rugged Nathaniel Emory, Baron Alford, is no more a commoner than Clara is a blue-blood. He's appeared on the scene for one reason only: to save his family's estate from ruin by finding the exceedingly valuable blue diamond his grandfather buried in the Andersons' garden fifty years ago. To do that, he must pretend to be a gardener. He didn't count on the most beautiful girl he's ever seen getting in his way. But Clara has made no secret of her dislike for aristocrats. Which means that once she uncovers his ruse, he's certain she'll never see him again . . .

About the Author

Jane Goodger lives in Rhode Island with her husband and three children. Jane, a former journalist, has written numerous historical romances. When she isn't writing, she's reading, walking, playing with her kids, or anything else completely unrelated to cleaning a house. You can visit her website at www.janegoodger.com.

CPSIA information can be obtained
at www.ICGtesting.com
Printed in the USA
LVHW110147100719
623646LV00001B/21/P